Praise for Jonathan

'Britain's answer to John Grisham . . . a tense, topical, convincing novel'

Daily Telegraph

'His story gives the reader a true feeling of living through the hazards and uncertainties of a criminal trial . . . not only entertaining but painfully convincing'

John Mortimer in the *Mail on Sunday*

'Emotionally searing'

Observer

'Davies' elegant unfussy prose displays warmth, humanity and humour as he takes us through the life of a modern barrister'

Express on Sunday

'Impeccable behind-the-scenes knowledge . . . a fine read . . . always entertaining'

Yorkshire Post

Also by Jonathan Davies
and available from Coronet Books

Given in Evidence
Undisclosed Material

About the author

Jonathan Davies is a defence lawyer and a judge. He is married to a doctor and they live with their children in south London. *On Appeal* is his third novel.

On Appeal

Jonathan Davies

CORONET BOOKS
Hodder and Stoughton

First published in Great Britain in 1998
by Hodder and Stoughton
A division of Hodder Headline PLC

Coronet paperback edition 1999

10 9 8 7 6 5 4 3 2 1

ISBN 0-340-70769-0

Typeset by Hewer Text Ltd, Edinburgh
Printed and bound in Great Britain by
Mackays of Chatham PLC, Chatham, Kent

Hodder and Stoughton
A division of Hodder Headline PLC
338 Euston Road
London NW1 3BH

Betty Williams
UCH 1936

Prologue

Scott couldn't find the damn radio station, and, where there were any, the street numbers seemed to be all mixed up.

He had been in a temper all week. At first he had thought it was going to be good living on his own again. He could do what he liked, get up, go to bed, not talk all the time, whatever. But it didn't seem to be working out like that, and he found himself in a bad mood, snapping at people and getting angry with things. It was a bit like the old days before he'd met her.

He walked back down the street from the top again. There was an estate agent, a funeral parlour, a sort of bookshop, a shop selling bricks, and a small coffee shop, but no radio station. Then he saw an arrow pointing down an alley to a door marked Zap Radio. A girl carrying a clipboard held the door open for a moment and then dashed off down the passage, back the way she had come. He followed her in and sat in what was obviously a waiting room. He listened to the loudspeaker on the wall. After a few minutes he discovered it was playing everywhere, even in the lavatory.

The woman who had met him at the door came back and introduced herself. 'Hallo, I'm Pansy. I'm sorry I left you, we're having a bit of a crisis today.' She twisted the heavy beads she was wearing in her fingers. 'One of Simon's guests didn't turn up and we've got a hole in the programme.'

'Simon?' Scott said.

'Simon Smallchild. That's him now.' She pointed at the loudspeaker, where the voice was laughing at people who read the *Guardian*. Scott remembered Smallchild's name. His stock-in-trade was insulting his guests.

'He seems to be managing quite well on his own,' Scott said. He was amused to see Pansy screw her face up. But the expression was momentary and she covered up immediately. 'Oh yes,' she said.

'I suppose he's what you would call very professional,' Scott said, giving her a way out.

'Oh yes. He is that.'

'Is that a compliment?' said Scott.

She laughed. It hadn't taken long to extract her real opinion.

'It depends how you say it. Still, can't stand here. Come and meet your presenter.'

She took Scott down the passage past a series of doors. One had a light on above it. 'That's the studio in use now. We're in this one here.'

Scott went in.

He had never been in a broadcasting studio before. It was a large room with a built-up table set in the middle. On one side of the table there was a chair placed before a console covered in switches, dials and lights, with a microphone sticking out in the centre.

Pansy showed Scott to a chair on the other side in front of another microphone cantilevering out towards his seat. Opposite him, the wall had a glass panel cut into it, and through it Scott could see what must be the control room. On the far side of that he could see into another studio. In it there was a figure bent over, speaking into a microphone. That must be Smallchild.

'Can we do a voice level test? Say something into that,' Pansy pushed the microphone down towards Scott. 'Gary,' she said, looking at the control room, 'voice test, please. Go on, Jeremy.'

He said, 'My name is Jeremy Scott.'

'A bit closer, with more enthusiasm. Cheer up,' she said.

Scott pulled the microphone towards him and said, 'I am a criminal lawyer. Normally I defend people charged with rape and things like that.' A man at the control panel behind the glass, presumably Gary, looked up at him, surprised.

Scott was feeling completely indifferent. He didn't care one way or the other whether they liked him. What he'd really like to do was go back to Amsterdam to talk to Catherine. But he couldn't do that, it would be the worst thing to do. He just had to wait and hope she'd come back.

'If you keep fairly still when you talk it will be better,' Pansy said.

'When are we on?' The strangeness of the experience was beginning to take the edge off his bad temper.

'Any minute now.' Pansy turned and gestured at the people who were watching them from behind the glass panel. She went round to the other side of the console and flipped a switch. 'Where is he?' she said into the microphone. They made gestures of 'Don't know', palms outward and shoulders raised, and returned to talking animatedly between themselves.

Pansy put on some headphones and said, 'It's only four minutes to go now. Hasn't he phoned?'

There was obviously a reply, but Scott couldn't hear it. He could only see the man behind the screen clutching a microphone and talking into it hard.

What was the man saying? Scott became aware of a tinny trickle of noise coming out of one of the headphones on the desk in front of him. He picked it up, put it to his ear and heard an angry voice. 'This is the second time he's arrived late this month. What shall we do? First a no-show with Simon's guest and now this. What a morning.'

'We'll have to ask Smallchild to fill in for him.'

'Oh God. Again. He'll charge us. But who've we got for him to talk to?'

'Jeremy Scott. He just did that voice level. Look, he's sitting behind me.' Scott noticed Pansy gesture towards him with her shoulder. He lowered the headphones beneath the console so the people in the control room could not see he was listening to what was being said.

'Who's he?'

'He's that lawyer, the one who was photographed kissing his client in the street. Don't you remember? Nicky recommended him.'

Scott glanced up and saw the producer looking at him. Nicky? Was Nicky here?

'We can't put him in there with Smallchild.' The voice rose in dismay. 'The man's been broadcasting on his own, no guests, for an hour. He's worked himself into a fury. He'll eat him alive.'

'So what?' said Pansy. 'Good radio.'

There was a pause.

'I told you, he's a lawyer. He's trained to look after himself.'

'I suppose you're right. Well, OK, then. Get the cuttings sheets over.'

Scott put the headphones down as Pansy appeared from the other side of the console.

'There may have to be a change of plan,' she said. 'If you could wait a moment.' She left the room carrying a manila

4

file and then reappeared in the studio at the far side of the control panel.

So that's why they'd asked him. It was nothing to do with the law, or at least only marginally. And now he was going to be interviewed by Simon Smallchild, a man whose only way of communicating with people was by insulting them, a man perpetually trapped in some wild autistic frenzy.

Well, Scott knew judges like that. Old Tom Meadowsweet, for example. Being rude was an everyday activity for him. He couldn't help it, it popped out, completely uncontrolled. Scott had had plenty of practice in dealing with rudeness. Did it matter? No one listened to the radio anyway.

Scott watched while Gary, the director, went through the pantomime of persuading the man at the microphone to carry on, occasionally turning round and looking at Scott. He did so, Scott noticed, with the look that the owner of a dog might have while giving instructions that it be put down.

Eventually Pansy led him through to the other studio.

The moment he walked in the door, he could feel the energy radiating from the other side of the table. The man was talking very fast. 'And you're going to have to put up with me for another hour. Luckily there's lots of things yet to be said, things I have to get off my chest. And where better to do it than the Simon Sm*aaaa*llchild programme?' He made a baying noise as he spoke his own name.

'I also have a guest coming in. A lawyer, apparently. What? I hear you say. A lawyer? S. Smallchild Esquire harbouring a lawyer on his programme? Well, ladies and gentlemen all, O listeners, O my Sm*aaaa*llchildren, he's not my guest. I didn't invite him. Would I heck? He was invited by that man, whose name I cannot even remember, who has not turned up to do his show, which he's paid to do, which he is not doing, which is why I am here, and which is why you're gonna have to put up with me for a little bit longer. What an amateur.'

Smallchild lifted his eyes and looked at Scott across the desk. While the sound came out of his mouth there wasn't a flicker in his expression, as though the words had nothing to do with him. He went on, 'Well. "Make do and mend." As my old granny used to say. "If you make do too much, you'll soon find yourself mending. So, throw it away and get a new one." And I agree. And here *is* the new one from the 'the Arctic Nightgowns.'

He pressed a switch, listened for a moment, perhaps to check that the right record had come on, took his headphones off and started snarling at Pansy.

'The moment that shit arrives I'm out of here. You understand? Right, where's that stuff?'

He snatched the manila file from the table. Scott could see newspaper cuttings and some photographs.

'So, Jeremy Scott, is it?' Smallchild looked up. Rarely had Scott seen such a look of concentrated nastiness. It made even Tom Meadowsweet seem normal. The man's face was long and heavy, his nose thick and pockmarked with little swellings. The nearest thing Scott had ever seen to that nose was Edward Lear's drawing of the Dong. His eyes were watery. Scott recognised the look of an alcoholic. He saw all this very clearly, the tension of the moment sharpening his reactions. He suddenly knew he wasn't going to take any shit at all from this nasty little man.

'You're a lawyer? You want me to ask you questions about the law?'

'No,' said Scott, 'I don't *want* anything. I'm only here because I was invited. Ask me what you like.'

Smallchild looked at him. 'We'll see,' he said. He put the headphones on and continued listening to the music. Scott sat looking at the top of the man's head as he bent over the desk opposite. His scalp was flecked with dandruff.

The record stopped and Smallchild's watery eyes flicked

back to him. 'Here we are, ladies and gentlemen, and of course Smallchildren, for another hour of the Simon Smallchild programme, and I now have here in the studio with me a Mr Jeremy Scott. A lawyer. I don't know why he's here, you don't know why he's here, all I know is that he was caught kissing a client in the street. I have the photograph here. A lissome young lady, I should say, well qualified to be one of Smallchild's scrumchies.

'Well then, Scott – that's how you chaps address each other, isn't it, by your last names? – well then, Scott, what do you say to that, then?'

'Grateful client,' said Scott. 'Legal aid. What can I say?'

'Legal aid?' Smallchild spat at him. 'Legal aid?' It was obvious Scott had mentioned one of his pet hates. 'She was being paid for by the state. Ladies and gentlemen, here we are in the presence of a man who sits right beside the fountain of money we spew out for legal aid. No doubt occasionally dipping his bucket in it.'

He spoke directly to Scott again. 'Of course, if she'd been paying you privately, she'd have got something better?'

'I don't see how much better she could have got,' said Scott. 'After all, she was acquitted. I suppose I could have worn white gloves while doing it, if you think that would have been classier.' Smallchild took a breath to speak but Scott went on. 'But since you dislike legal aid so much I would have thought you'd approve of people getting a second-rate service on it – as a disincentive from using it again.'

'You got her off? Probably in the teeth of the evidence. Another guilty party getting off through some technicality?'

Scott took his time and then said, 'As your friendly neighbourhood lawyer, I'd better remind you of the dangers of libel. She was acquitted. By talking about technicalities you're implying she was wrongly acquitted.'

'But that's what you do? You're a smart defence lawyer. You get people off?'

'That too, yes.'

'What do you mean, "that too"?'

'Well, no one calls me a smart lawyer in that tone of voice when I prosecute. It's odd, that. People like you are only upset when lawyers defend. I can tell you it takes more skill to convict an innocent man than it does to get a guilty man acquitted. You'd probably be pleased to know that, or maybe not. Perhaps you'd prefer it the other way round.'

'You admit it goes wrong, then?'

'Why shouldn't I?'

'How do you bring yourself to defend someone you know is guilty?'

'No problem, because you don't know he's guilty till the jury say he is. Your question is the same as asking a man betting on a horse why he always backs losers. He doesn't know he has till it happens.'

'Don't come that on me. Of course you know.'

'But what help is knowing? If people refused to defend anyone they thought was guilty, then anyone who had a lawyer to defend him would automatically be acquitted.'

'Why so?'

'Because the jury would say just what you're saying. The lawyer obviously knows the answer, and he says he's innocent.'

Smallchild looked at him across the table. Scott noticed that his eyes were swimming slightly more than before.

'We have a call,' he said.

Scott picked up the earphones and put them on. A slightly beery voice started speaking.

'Alf here, Simon. Alf from Welling. I'm a regular caller.'

'Hallo, Alf, what have you got to add?'

'Well, I wanted to tell you what happened in that cold

snap recently. Cold? You tell me. Look, I was out washing down the yard where we keep the dogs, lots of water, and I was wearing my wellington boots and standing there with the hosepipe, and suddenly there I was, stuck in the middle of the yard. Frozen. I'd become frozen, my feet had frozen to the ground. My wife had to come out with a pole to pull me in. Even then the boots stayed stuck where they were. What do you think of that, then?'

Smallchild looked at Scott bleakly and said, 'Well, it takes all sorts, Alf. Here's another call, Betty from West Ham.'

'I'd like to ask your Mr Scott, who calls himself a la-di-da lawyer, if he defends people who are guilty, where's the right in that? People who are guilty don't deserve a trial. It's too good for the likes of them.'

Scott tried to speak, 'Well, Mrs Betty . . .', but he discovered this wasn't a conversation. She carried on. 'Mind you, my William, he was fined the other day and he'd done nothing wrong. So if you ask me the whole thing is all topsy-turvy.'

'Thank you, Betty,' said Smallchild. 'There you are, Mr Scott, that's what my listeners think of you.'

'Fair enough,' said Scott. 'People don't like lawyers. That's OK by me. People don't like dentists much either. It all depends on the experiences you have with them. That's why they like nurses. Everybody has good experiences with nurses.'

'You're not going to defend yourself, then?'

'Against what?'

'Against my allegations.'

'You haven't made any.'

'OK . . . You're all crooks, then. How about that?'

'I've heard you say that before and always wondered what you meant. What do you mean?'

'Look at the fees you make.'

'Do you mean me? I don't suppose you've a clue how much I earn.'

'Another call. Ernie from Archway.'

Ernie from Archway came on the phone. He was breathing deeply. 'Ernie here. Hallo, Simon.'

'Get on with it, Ernie,' Smallchild said.

'Well, what I want to know is, all these foreigners. They come here and get legal aid.' He stopped and there was silence.

'Is that a question?' Scott said. That was a mistake. Smallchild was on him immediately. 'You know exactly what Ernie is asking. All these people who come here get legal aid. Why should they?'

'What do you want to do, have trials without a defence? It would be twice as expensive since it would take twice as long. If you refuse to pay for lawyers, presumably you'd refuse to pay for interpreters as well. So we'd have to conduct the case in Swahili or whatever. Put me in there and I save the system time and money.'

Smallchild was taken aback by the flow of words.

'Anyway, Simon' – Scott was determined not to let him go – 'I asked you a question. Don't you remember? I don't suppose you've a clue what I earn, do you? Let me guess what you earn, though. Last year, about three hundred thousand pounds, wasn't it?'

Smallchild boggled at him. 'What do you mean? That's nonsense. How do you know?'

'Well, if it's nonsense, how much was it, then? You're always banging on about lawyers and what they earn. You haven't got a clue what I earn. About the same as a police sergeant, as it happens.' Well, Galbraith didn't, he must be earning about what ten police sergeants earned, but Scott wasn't going to say that out loud. 'And you earning all that money yourself – for gabbling on the radio . . .' Scott nearly said 'gabbling rubbish', but stopped himself. He mustn't overdo it, that would immediately give this repellent man the advantage. Instead he said, 'What good does that do anyone?'

Scott looked up at the glass panel. There was a line of people staring into the studio from the control room. They looked astonished.

'Now for a bit of music.' Smallchild hit a button. Without lifting his eyes, he shouted at the control room. 'Who the fuck does this guy think he is?'

Scott didn't bother to listen to the reply – he was watching the consternation he had caused behind the glass panel. The producer was beginning to go through his repertoire of facial expressions.

Scott leant forward and said into the microphone, 'He can't take it, can he? He can dish it out to Ernie from Archway but he can't take it, can he?'

He had begun to get the hang of how the studio worked, and now he had the headphones carrying the conversation to and from the control room. Someone was saying, 'If we throw him out, Simon, it'll be all over the papers.'

'Quite right,' Scott interrupted. 'I'll telephone the papers the second I leave. Especially after what Pansy said about my being eaten alive by this monster.'

The music was winding down.

'Well, Mr Scott, if you want to play hardball, then we'll play hardball,' Smallchild said, looking at him with his whisky eyes, and he switched the main microphone on.

'That was our number five by Wailing Wall and at the moment we have Mr Jeremy Scott, a lawyer with attitude, in the studio . . .'

Scott cut in, '. . . and Simon's just been trying to have me thrown out. So, listeners, if there's a sudden silence then you'll know what's happening. Simon Smallchild, the man who can dish it out but can't take it.' It seemed reasonable to repeat the remark. The audience hadn't heard it. 'Now, Mr Smallchild, you were going to tell me how much you earn so we can compare figures.'

'No I was not.'

'Hang on. You started it. You said, "Look at the fees you make." I assume you know what fees I make.'

'I didn't mean you personally.'

'Yes you did. You said "You're all crooks" to my face. What do you know about me? How do you know I'm a crook? I'm not going to say anything like that about you, since all I know about you is what you look like. That I do know. I can see, for instance, that you're nervous. There's a bead of sweat just about to drop from your forehead.'

Smallchild brushed distractedly at his eyebrow.

'And now you've wiped it away. I know you're not prepared to tell me what you earn. I know you've got lots of prejudices because you boast about them, but I can't know if you're a crook, can I? So how can you know whether I'm a crook?'

There was a buzz on the earphones and a voice said, 'Mary from Fulham.'

Smallchild said, 'Mary from Fulham.'

'Hallo, Simon, dear,' said a fluting voice. 'You shouldn't let that horrid man push you around. He's just being a bully.'

'Ooh, Mary,' said Scott. Now he was beginning to enjoy himself. 'I bet that's the first time you've ever had to say that. Normally it's the other way round. But then I argue with people for a living. I've been doing it for years. Mr Smallstrap here is only a beginner. How long have you been doing this, Simon?'

If there was one thing more infuriating than having someone get your name wrong, then Scott hadn't discovered it yet. Smallchild began to show signs of extreme anger.

Scott went on, 'But you talk to her, Simon, she thinks I'm bullying you. Do you think I'm bullying you? No, Mary. We're old chums, in fact.'

Smallchild said nothing. 'Go on, Simon, speak to her,' said Scott.

There was a voice in their earphones again.

'Next caller,' said Smallchild.

Scott saw Smallchild flick a switch and look at him. 'Do you know, I don't like you,' he said.

'Good Lord, is the microphone on?' said Scott. Smallchild looked at him. 'Why don't you say that on air so we can discuss it?' Scott continued. But Smallchild had gone back to his earphones.

Scott picked them up and heard an advertisement for a second-hand car company. The advertisement finished and Scott heard the next caller being introduced. Ray from Tooting.

'Well, Smallchild,' he said, 'you got it this time. Someone who can argue the pants off of you. What do you think of that, then?'

Scott looked at the control room. The glass was crowded with people. The row at the front were standing still, some with their mouths open, some just looking glum. But at the back, in the second row, there was laughter. At one end of the line Scott could see Nicky, the woman he had met in court. She saw him look at her and began making gestures, lifting her hands at him. 'Go on, go on,' she was mouthing.

Scott turned and smiled at Smallchild, who said, 'Well, here's another record,' and he slid down one of the levers in front of him. Scott saw him listening. He was clearly being spoken to, but through a different line, so Scott could hear nothing. Scott spoke into the microphone. 'Can you hear me, Nicky?' She responded. Obviously the other line had been left open.

'What's all this about kissing in the street? You didn't say anything about that guff, nor about this man here.' He pointed across the desk. All the people in the back row turned to look, while the producer in the front still talked furiously into the other line. Nicky made a gesture of 'I don't know', but laughed as well.

'What happened to Ray from Tooting?' Scott said. 'He was on my side.' But he was speaking to nobody, or at least nobody replied. It was a funny feeling, how cut off he was, cut off because they had to throw a switch for him to speak to someone. 'What happened to Ray from Tooting?' He repeated the question when Smallchild looked up at him, but again got no reply. He was going to have to wait till the end of the record.

Just then there was a rush in the control room and a man appeared, out of breath, tugging at the producer's arm. Obviously it was the presenter who had turned up late.

'Here's the chap you're standing in for,' Scott said.

Smallchild didn't pause. 'Well, there you are, listeners, that's it for another day. I'm off. Here he is now,' he said as the presenter came into the studio.

'Goodbye, Mr Smallchild,' Scott said. 'It was nice meeting you.'

Smallchild walked past saying nothing.

'I'm off too,' said Scott, following him out of the door.

He had expected to find the presenter waiting for him outside the door, but he wasn't there. Scott could see him disappearing down the passage. He hesitated. Should he go to the control room? Nicky was there. On the other hand she was the person who had got him into this – not that it was her fault that Smallchild had been loosed on him. But then the problem was solved. The door opened and Nicky came out.

She was laughing and hugged him. Again Scott thought of Catherine. He suddenly realised that he wished it was she who had put her arm through his.

Chapter One

In the library of the bar mess of the Old Bailey, Jeremy Scott found a large leather book. It was the suggestions book. He turned the pages over. The paper was heavier and thicker than one would buy now. It was old – the first entry had been in 1935, and the book had last been used – he looked to see – ten years ago. There were no entries since then.

He read through it.

People objecting to the quality of the biscuits. Each complaint had been properly acknowledged with initials to show that the mess junior had noted the objection, but the complaints didn't go away and, from what he read, the biscuits didn't seem to improve. If anything they got worse.

He turned the pages.

At one stage a debate began about mashed potatoes, culminating in an entry by a man whose name he recognised, now a Lord Justice of appeal. But it was the same as with the biscuits; all the fuss made no difference. Six months later the potatoes were still being described as cold and lumpy, and, someone suggested with horror, powdered. Then the debate trailed off and the main point of interest became the disappearance of the mess newspapers so quickly after lunch.

Scott didn't suppose it was possible to complain about the bar mess food any more, and even if you could, it certainly wouldn't be the species of sporting activity that it seemed to be then. 'Bring back the cat,' someone had written, 'it was lovely.'

He put the volume aside.

The messroom was almost empty. By now everybody had gone down to court, save for a small group, deep in discussion, gathered at one of the long tables. Scott watched them. For the moment there was nothing he could do. He was floating. His case had not yet been assigned a court and he had to wait until a judge came free.

He stood up to look out of the window across the London rooftops. In the distance, to the right, in between the air-conditioning tanks, he could see the Telecom Tower, and over to his left Westminster Abbey.

He stared at the air over London, not taking in what he was seeing. He was examining over and over the story he had come to the court to tell. The whole case was ready, tethered, waiting to be released.

Being an actor must be like this, he thought, knowing the lines that were about to be spoken, ready for them to be brought to life. But this was crucially different. Unlike an actor, he didn't know which lines were going to be chosen, which direction the action was going to take. How would an actor feel, waiting in the wings with only a rough idea of what was going to happen, and then having to react on the instant to what did? If Ellie were convicted the judge was going to have to pass a sentence of at least seven to eight years. If they convicted her, she was going to be locked up for the best part of her youth, and it was a strong case, she was bound to be convicted. It didn't bear thinking about.

He tried to think about something else, but of course he couldn't. The same question returned. 'Are they going to be able to get the evidence out?'

Scott's full attention catapulted back to the trial.

There was a child who said he had seen what had happened, and had described it clearly: a man and a woman were in the road fighting with another man. The woman pulled the man to his feet and held him while he was stabbed.

The Scotsman – the man who had been stabbed – had told exactly the same story. He said he had been knocked down in a fight, then picked up by a girl and, as he was being picked up and held, he was stabbed.

It was a strong case, even though the prosecution weren't saying Ellie was the one who had used the knife. But if you pick someone up and hold him so he can be stabbed, that's as good as doing it yourself, and enough to convict you of attempted murder.

The court Tannoy crackled. 'All parties in Wilson, please go to Court Nine.'

Scott started to his feet then, realising it wasn't his case, he relaxed. The group round the table got up and began to gather their papers together. Scott could see Tim Spencer among them. He hadn't seen him before or he'd have gone over to chat. He waved as Tim went down the stairs.

'What is it?'

'It'll be a verdict,' said Tim as he disappeared from sight, fumbling at his pockets. Scott could see that he was about to light another cigarette, even though it would take only a moment to get to court, where he would have to put it out. It was the waiting that did it.

Scott got to his feet. If there was a verdict coming then there might be a court free soon. He'd better go down to see Ellie again.

She was in the cells and would be in a terrible state – at least, she had been when he visited her earlier. She had been in Holloway prison since her arrest. She had not got bail – the police had said there was a danger of her interfering with witnesses. Why they thought this had never really become clear, but just the suggestion of it was enough to frighten the magistrates into locking her up.

Scott put his wig and gown on and followed the group that had just left. He went down the short staircase to the lifts. Two of them pinged in unison and the doors opened. The recorded voices announced to each other that they were on the fifth floor. Scott hadn't yet got used to automatic voices in the lifts and still found them faintly disturbing.

The Tannoy above him asked Henry the carpenter to go to the main entrance. Scott got into the lift and punched the down button, lower ground. Someone had told him once that on a ship a request for the ship's carpenter meant an emergency. Was that true? Did it mean the same at the Old Bailey? The lift went smoothly downwards and stopped. The voice told him he was at the lower ground floor where there were cloakrooms. For some reason, probably good taste, the recording didn't mention the cells.

The moment he went through the large brown door towards the custody area the atmosphere changed. Here the floor was unadorned concrete; outside it had been marble. Outside there were men with waxy mops who polished the floor; here there were cigarette butts scattered around. There was no heating and the draught in the cold passage penetrated through his gown.

Just outside the cells, hanging on the wall in the waiting area, was the old prison door of the original Old Bailey, a desperate attempt at decoration. The metal grille set into the door at eye level had been completely worn away, where generations of people must have pleaded through it – it was as if language alone had the power to wear away the metal.

He rang the bell to the cells and settled down for the usual wait, looking at the gate. Perhaps he only imagined it, but it always seemed that the wait was designed to emphasise just who was in charge.

The main problem was the coincidence – the evidence of the stabbed man and of the child. They both said the same thing, yet had never met. Scott went over the problem again, standing at the door of the cells to the Old Bailey. If the evidence came out just as it had been presented in the statements, then there was going to be very little that could be done about it. And if the prosecutor was any good it would come out.

Unless the policeman interviewing the children had known what the victim had said? Perhaps the policeman knew that the Scotsman was claiming he had been picked up and held by a woman? The image of it would be unusual enough for him to have asked the child about it, in effect prompting him.

If the man had not been picked up, and Ellie said he hadn't, then that could be the only explanation for the coincidental descriptions – innocent contamination. But no officer would ever admit to prompting, even if he remembered or was aware of having done it. That kind of thing was impossible for the courts to investigate. They weren't subtle enough.

Oddly enough it would have been a simple thing to do, even by mistake. You want to put a child at his ease by talking about the incident. Did you see some people? Who did you see? Was there a woman there? Do you remember? She looked different, she had long hair and boots. Did you see a woman helping someone up? Then what happened? The officer could easily have said that, and if you ask the questions with the proper urgency the child will catch on to the idea.

But to suggest now that the child had been led into saying what he said, even if Scott tried to make it clear he wasn't saying it was intentional, would immediately set off a suggestion of police conspiracy and dishonesty. People would start getting itchy. Itchy wouldn't describe it. The prosecutor would become instantly indignant. 'Is my learned friend *really* suggesting . . . ?' That sort of thing.

Scott opened the case papers to remind himself of the names of the officers who had countersigned the child's witness statement, but of course he couldn't get at them. It had to be in the last file he opened, and immediately he found himself balancing on one foot, trying to get at the papers at the bottom of the bundle. He put his hand out against the door to steady himself and nearly fell over when it was suddenly opened.

He was confronted by a vast stomach straining at a white shirt, and above it a smiling face. It was Geoffrey the Gaoler. A great chain stretched from his belt to the door lock – if you wanted to run off with the door, you'd have to take all Geoffrey's seventeen stone with you.

'If you haven't read your brief by now, Mr Scott, then it's too late.'

'Hallo, Geoffrey,' Scott said, trying to keep his balance. 'I'm only trying to remember my client's name. Here we are. Ellie Johnson. Ellie Lamarck Johnson. Can I see her?'

'Oh, it's you looking after her, is it, Mr Scott? She's quite a handful, isn't she?' He turned away and pointed a stubby finger towards the cells. 'You're along the passage, Room Seven. From what I hear you're in trouble there, sir.'

'Thanks for the encouragement, Geoffrey,' Scott said, and he set off down the passage towards the women's section.

Ellie Johnson was trying to work out a new way of asking Scott what was going to happen to her. Scott sat looking at the girl in front of him. It was difficult to think of her as an adult. He knew her age, eighteen, or a bit more. As far

22

as the law was concerned she was an adult, but still pretty young, especially to be dealing with this.

'Look, Ellie. At the moment there's not much we can do. We've been over it, we've got it clear now. If we go over it again we'll only confuse ourselves.'

Scott had gone through the problems in the case again and again, but they weren't easy to explain. After all, if a client said something hadn't happened at all then it was difficult to discuss the quality of the prosecution's evidence to the effect that it had.

'You know I didn't pick up that man, Mr Scott.'

'Of course, you've told me that.'

'Well, if you believe me, that's good enough for me.'

Scott knew that what he believed wasn't relevant. If he believed every word she was saying was made up, he'd be just as much use to her, maybe more. He'd be able to see the weaknesses more easily. But where was the point in trying to tell her that? It was only another complication. No, it was worse than that. For her it would be a lie, since she didn't separate her feelings from her thoughts, as he did.

Scott looked at the girl.

Her normal prettiness had been affected by the worry, and there were lines beginning to show in her face. Her eyes were staring slightly, in the way Scott had noticed in other people who had suddenly been tossed out of a comfortable life into prison. She continually touched her face and her hair, shifting on her seat and tugging at her clothes as though they were too tight. She kept coughing, starting to speak but then subsiding into silence. She looked distraught.

She brought him back to the moment.

'But, Mr Scott, how can they not believe me? We were nothing to do with that man being stabbed. It was some other people who suddenly ran over. We were just standing nearby.'

Unfortunately her boyfriend hadn't said the same thing. He'd said to the police that they'd been out of sight, nowhere near the fight. That was a clear lie and the jury would be asked 'Why did he lie?', the obvious conclusion being he was guilty.

The jury wouldn't have heard as many lies as Scott had. Perhaps they didn't know how panic could make people do odd things. Anything, however absurd, could be said – and said to a policeman, whose job wasn't to stop and tell the man not to be silly. After all, why should the police do that? A policeman's job was to get a conviction, not to worry about the truth. Like Scott – worrying about the truth wasn't his job either.

He changed the subject, disastrously. 'Mum and Dad are here,' he said. 'We went through everything and they know exactly what's happening.'

Earlier Scott had been tannoyed to the door of the court to meet them. They had to go out into the street to talk. It was amazing. Their eighteen-year-old daughter was on trial and they weren't even allowed into the court, only up into the public gallery where Scott couldn't go. If they hadn't caused a fuss and demanded to see him, Scott might well not have known they were there at all. No one else would have told him.

He shouldn't have mentioned them, and he watched Ellie begin to crumple again, but he was saved by a knock on the cell door.

'The court's asking for you. C'm'on, then, miss, let's be having you.'

Scott saw Ellie stand up and move, like an automaton, towards the door. He wanted to say 'Don't worry', but that would have been pointless.

'To this count the prisoners at the Bar have pleaded not

guilty and it is your charge to say whether they are guilty or not.'

They had been given Court 2, one of the old courts, huge and dramatic. It was built on varying levels, each part of it fenced off from the others to emphasise the difference between the people there.

The defendants were in a box four feet above Scott's head. To speak to Ellie, Scott had to stand on tiptoe and she had to lean down towards him – the classic pose, the lawyer plotting with his client.

The judge sat even higher than the dock, behind a long bench which, typically, was studded with makeshift pieces of electrical equipment, most of them, Scott could see, completely useless.

The jury sat to the judge's right, squashed together in another box, with hardly room to move, let alone relax, concentrate and make notes. Scott had seen juries hundreds of times, and each time he had been struck by how they looked exactly like the Tenniel illustration in *Alice in Wonderland*. It wasn't just the situation, being crammed into the box, but they actually looked the same. The man on the right had the long nose of the griffon and in the front row there was a stout lady – as surprised at what was happening around her as a chicken.

Twenty feet above the jury, in a balcony jutting out over the court, was the public gallery, empty save for some tourists and Ellie's parents. Scott could see the strain on their faces. He stood up and smiled at them.

The moment they saw a familiar face they relaxed slightly, but then the tense looks returned. Scott knew he could do nothing for these people, except get their daughter acquitted.

The tourists watched the proceedings below in astonishment.

'Could those members of the jury panel who have not been selected go with the jury bailiff?'

The court clerk spoke vaguely into the dark space at the back of the court. There was a shuffling noise and some people pushed out through the swing doors.

For a moment attention was directed away from the jury, who took the opportunity to wriggle a little, trying to settle themselves more comfortably on the hard narrow bench. Several of the women looked around in the distracted fashion of people who know they are being looked at.

Suddenly the clerk, who had been watching the back of the court, swung back towards them. 'Members of the jury, the defendants Colin Jones and Ellie Lamarck Johnson are charged that on the . . .' He stumbled over the date. '. . . they did attempt to murder John Donald. It is your charge to say whether they are guilty or not.'

The jury looked surprised, for a moment feeling that something was expected of them immediately. One or two of them looked up into the public gallery.

There was a murmur from the judge. Unless you knew it was coming you wouldn't have caught it. 'Yes, Mr . . .' he said, his voice trailing away incomprehensibly, as though merely to mention someone's name was beneath him. Prosecuting counsel got to his feet.

'If it please you, Your Lordship,' he said, and then, raising his voice, he spoke loudly across the well of the court. 'Ladies and gentlemen of the jury.' He managed to include four syllables in the word jury, ending with a neighing sort of bray. The jury sat instantly to attention. 'I appear on behalf of the Crown in this matter. My learned friend Mr Benjamin Gribble appears for the defendant Jones and Mr Jeremy Scott appears for the defendant Johnson.'

The trial had begun.

Chapter Two

'At the moment Mr Scott is doing a trial at the Old Bailey. Yes, he's there now.' Scott's clerk, Harry, spoke into the phone and then listened to the reply.

'He can do that. Yes, at Holloway. Holloway prison. Five o'clock tomorrow. Thanks, Monty. I'll let him know.' He listened again and then said, 'Will you send the papers down?' Pause. 'He doesn't need any? Well, if you say so. What sort of case is it?' He listened for a while, said 'Oh' and put the phone down. He turned to his first junior clerk. 'Scott's got a conference tomorrow at Holloway. Put it in the diary. The case is called Forgan – the woman who was convicted of murdering her aunt, remember? You know, the one that Mr Gatling refused from Watkins and Jellaby. The one there was a fuss about.'

Barristers are not meant to refuse cases.

'Monty Bach said that the client was asking directly for Scott and I accepted the brief before I knew what it was.' He stopped talking and looked out of the window at the brick wall opposite, then he said, 'I can't imagine why she wants him.'

'Perhaps she wants to be convicted.' The junior clerk laughed. It wasn't a very nice thing to say. 'Well, that's what Cocks said when Scott lost that MP's case.'

'It isn't a trial, I told you, it's an appeal. Don't you remember Wethersedge prosecuted her in Winchester? It was all over the newspapers. Now she's sacked another set of lawyers and Monty Bach has taken the case over.'

'That's a good start,' said the junior clerk, and he laughed again.

The even tone of waiting continued in the clerk's room. Occasionally someone said something.

'Lewis still hasn't returned that brief.'

'That doesn't surprise me.'

Silence.

'Do you know the central taxation unit has taken nine months now over Glover?'

'Well, what can you do?'

Eventually the senior clerk said, 'I'm going down the Bailey.'

They all looked at the clock. It was getting on for twelve.

'I'll be back after lunch.'

Harry got up and buttoned his overcoat. 'Don't forget this.' He picked up a thin bundle of papers tied with red tape. It was a magistrate's court brief. 'Two o'clock at Old Street. Whoever rings in first can do it, otherwise punt it out somewhere. And get on to Lewis. We need those bloody papers back.'

He disappeared through the door and then, just as the atmosphere in the room was lightening, reappeared. He pulled an old scarf down from the coatrack which rocked slightly as the scarf came free from the tangle of clothing. 'I'll tell Scott about his conference,' he said, and then left. The others knew he wouldn't be back until at least three.

Harry had been working in the Temple for thirty-five years. He had started off earning just over a pound a week as the most junior junior there was and had never forgotten, or forgiven, the indignity of it, being pushed around by the barristers. 'Fetch this, do that. Carry the papers to court. Get this. I want that book.' In those days the clerks called the barristers guvner, and meant it. But it was different now. A good senior clerk earned five times what an ordinary barrister earned. And Harry was a good clerk, or at least he clerked a good set of chambers.

Now he was in control. But it didn't make him any happier.

He set off up the hill of the Temple car park, past the Clachan and up behind El Vino. He turned left at Fleet Street, and went along past Middle Temple Lane, across the front of the Law Courts and into the George.

It took a few moments for him to accustom his eyes to the dark, but then he saw what he was looking for – a group over by the far bar. As he walked towards them he unbuttoned his dark blue overcoat and put his hand in his inside pocket, so he had his money out before he joined them.

'Same again,' he said to the barman. It didn't do to show you were worried about what it cost or what you were buying.

A casual onlooker might have sensed that the others were faintly embarrassed by Harry's arrival at first, but they would soon realise that the movements of apparent discomfort – adjusting their overcoats, tugging nervously at their ties, occasionally swivelling and looking around the room – were habitual. It was the body language of the marketplace.

'How're things, then?' Harry said. There was a moment of silence as though the answer were a secret, then one of the youngest present said, 'Very slow.' More silence. This piece of information was digested, and one of the group, prompted by this seemingly extraordinary indiscretion, managed to turn full circle where he stood, pulling at his tie as he did so. But after a moment it became clear that it was generally accepted that the man who had made the remark had not, after all, given away anything too awful, and calm returned to the group.

A tall man with swept-back silverish hair, who stood leaning slightly forward on legs set a little apart to balance his belly, said, 'It's too damn slow altogether.'

He examined his foot, lifting his shoe up, considering the thin leather sole. The gilt buckle jangled slightly as he did so. His feet were tiny. He finished looking at his foot and then said, 'Monty Bach was looking for you, Harry. He was here a moment ago. He went to phone.'

There was a small laugh, instantly stifled as the group turned to look at Harry. He wasn't going to stand for this and he pulled rank. 'You may laugh at Monty,' he said, 'but I've seen worse.' He paused and then capped it, 'And he pays. What's more he pays everything, not like some I know of.'

The man who had laughed subsided.

'Monty's all right,' said the silver-haired man, who had decided to side with the stronger party. 'You just have to watch him. That right, Harry?'

'Watch 'em all, I say,' said Harry, who wasn't going to be so easily mollified. 'From the top to the bottom, because, mark my words, each of them'll screw you if they can. And don't think I don't include my lot either.'

He stood there and the group shuffled their feet.

'Because I do,' he said finally.

Over at the main bar, lit by the front door, Monty Bach leaned over and gestured at the bottle of single malt whisky on the shelf behind the girl. 'Some of that, my dear,' he said, 'and one of those little bottles of ginger ale down there.' He pointed at the rows of bottles nearest the floor. 'Now I don't need to ask what that will cost,' he said, and he opened a small leather purse, pulling out some coins. He took the drink and leaned against the bar, comfortably, his elbow at just the right height.

After a moment he pulled the small purse out again and from it he took a small tin. He opened it, tapped the side with his thumb and then placed a pinch of snuff on the back of his hand. He shut the tin with his free hand, put it away, looked around the room and sniffed the powder.

He didn't mind being on his own. He was a buyer and would soon be approached. He looked round at the groups. There was Vincent. He was from a set that specialised in banking and was currently having difficulties beating off a challenge for the appointment of a new chambers executive manager – the new word for a clerk. After all, one of the applicants had been a board member of an international company. Well, the job paid better, didn't it?

Vincent was standing with a group of other clerks. Monty knew one of them. Some of that man's barristers would be glad of a two-day trial in the crown court, let alone a commercial brief. Over by the machine there was another group. Two of them were women. He knew of two sets where the senior clerks were women. Didn't worry him, though he didn't brief them, he didn't need to. They did mainly modern work – immigration, discrimination, bus tickets for lesbians, funny stuff like that.

Harry saw Monty first.

'Did you say Monty was looking for me?' he said to the others, and then, not waiting for an answer, added, 'I'll see what he wants.' He walked over, deliberately, in no hurry.

'Hallo, Monty.'

'Your Mr Lewis did a nice job for me in Vannier,' Monty said. 'When I get something I'll remember him.'

Harry grunted. He had seen young barristers who were successful and others who weren't. They were all much the same as far as he was concerned, save some didn't return their briefs to the clerks' room quick enough.

'What about this Forgan business, then?' Harry said.

'Miss Forgan?' Monty said.

Harry said nothing.

'Well, she came to me after sacking her first solicitors. I don't know why. She tried Jellaby's but there was nothing doing there. She says that she's not guilty, and does she go on about it. Well, she rang me up two days ago and said she wanted Jeremy Scott to defend her.' Monty looked at Harry for a moment before continuing. 'And I said, "Are you sure?" He's not a Silk. And she said, "Yes. Jeremy Scott." So I rang you.'

Harry nodded and was about to speak, but Monty interrupted him. 'There's no money in it.'

'She's not on legal aid?'

'No, she had some money left her, by another aunt. Ironic, yes? The legal aid people refused, even though the cash has nearly run out now.'

Harry felt in his pocket for a match and lit a cigarette. 'You probably took what was left, Monty,' he said, grinning.

Monty didn't react to the remark. He said, 'It's a counsel-only application for leave to appeal, though they're sure to grant leave. It was only refused by the single judge because original counsel had said there were no grounds.' Monty leaned over the bar towards the girl and ordered another drink.

Harry had guessed right about the case. There must have been a reason for Gatling's telling him to refuse it when Watkins and Jellaby offered it.

'So what about this hearing?'

'Well, we can pay for a conference, but that's it. Say three hundred pounds and throw the preliminary application in for free?'

'Not much for a murder case.'

'It's all for the good of trade, isn't it, Harry?' Monty handed him the drink. 'Anyway, the press are sniffing around, so it could do your Mr Scott a power of good if he did well, couldn't it?'

Harry shrugged.

At about two Harry set off down Fleet Street to the Old Bailey. He had walked this street a thousand times.

When he was new, there had been a continual rush of people, the place had been packed. Messengers everywhere, boys about his age, sent out searching the pubs for journalists with messages from the newsroom. He'd got to know some of them in his lunch break and had got a glimpse of the tight world of printing. He had discovered it was only possible to get a job if you were related to someone. Once in the business, the messengers' main aim in life had been to become a driver for one of the evening papers. Five hours' work a day or less, and very well paid – what they could screw out of the system. What a life!

But that was all gone now. He had been on the other side of Blackfriars Bridge the other day and had seen one of the old union offices, dead and closed. He had had to explain to his son what a printers' union was.

What a bunch! Eventually they had screwed themselves out of jobs. Well, that was not going to happen to the Bar. They had more sense than that. For a start, money was in their favour. The basic pay was crazy. He had young barristers who regularly went out of chambers for seventy pounds a day and not necessarily every day. That was nothing, gross before expenses. Who was going to qualify and do that? But there you were. It was worth it if you succeeded, then you really made money. But not all of them could succeed.

Harry walked past the old *Express* building. He looked over the road to see if the man in the bowler hat and the umbrella was there preaching Corinthians. But it was too early. He carried on down to Ludgate Circus, then up the hill where the bridge used to be and left into the Old Bailey. As he passed the *Reader's Digest* offices on the right, there were little knots of smokers standing outside.

That was a real change. He remembered the old clerks' room when he had started. Sometimes the smoke was so thick that he had had to run out of the room. And the cigarettes he was sent out to get. Up to Weingott's to get Jimmy's Passing Cloud – no, not Passing Cloud, Sweet Afton, that was it. Sweet Afton, the pink package. Passing Cloud was the green one, wasn't it?

He arrived at the Bailey, and as he walked towards the main door he ran his hand over the marks on the stone where the bomb had gone off.

The police recognised him and let him through the side entrance. He checked to see which court Scott had been given and then took the steps two by two up the main staircase.

Chapter Three

'No, Mr Donald, you did not say that. You said something quite different. Surely you remember, it was only a moment ago.'

Scott stood quite still. He kept his voice clear and steady. 'Please remember there will come a time when your evidence must be considered by this jury.' He paused and looked up. The Scotsman stood in the witness box, which was at least five feet above him.

'You said that while you were still in the pub you called out, "He's got a knife." Now tell us again, did anybody react to what you said?'

'I didn't say I said that. I only said I may have said it.'

'Two minutes ago you said just those words to my learned friend Mr Gribble.' The witness transferred his attention to the other barrister, as if expecting to be attacked from another quarter.

'You said . . .' Scott picked up his notebook ostentatiously and read from it. 'I saw he had a wee knife, and I called out to my pals, "He's got a knife." Now you claim you didn't say it, or only that you may have said it. Why are you changing your evidence?'

Harry was standing watching from the back of the court.

From where he stood he could not see counsel, but the judge had seen him and nodded.

Scott continued.

'Come now, Mr Donald. We need to know the answer to this question.'

'You're huishing me.'

'I'm what? I'm huishing you?'

'No. You're pushing me.'

'Yes, Mr Donald, I'm certainly doing that. Now tell the jury why you have changed your evidence.'

There was a long silence.

'On this important point, Mr Donald, you have chosen to change your evidence.'

'I didn't.'

'But that's not right. I read out what you said,' Scott said quietly.

Silence.

'We can check the note if you wish, but of course I would already have been corrected if I was wrong.'

Harry, at the back of the court, thought, 'He really is very good.' Then he added, 'Sometimes.' He recited to himself, '*When he's good, he's very very good/But when he's bad he's* . . .' He wanted to change the last word of the ditty but couldn't think of anything, so he left it. Standing up to real opposition was another thing entirely, though.

Scott said, 'Mr Donald, you are accusing my client Miss Ellie Johnson of taking part in stabbing you, yes?'

'She did that right enough.'

'You say it all started in the pub?'

'That it did.'

'You say now you may have shouted out, "Look out, he's got a knife," referring to the man Miss Johnson was with.'

'Yes, that's so.'

'You may have shouted it out? You're not sure?'

'Well . . .'

'Let's see, then. Did anyone react?'

'Not that I'm remembering now.'

'You were there with two friends.'

'That's so.'

'What did they do? Did they respond to your shout?'

'No. I can't rightly say they did.'

'No. They didn't even turn around, did they?'

'Well, no.'

'That's because you didn't shout anything, did you?'

'I said just now I may have shouted out. Perhaps I did not.'

'Well, that's the change. Earlier you said you remembered doing so. Then you said you didn't. Now you say perhaps you didn't. Which is it? Remember, no one else seems to have heard you.'

'Mr Scott,' the judge warned.

Scott said, 'The learned judge is quite right. We have had no other witnesses yet. But will they come to court, I wonder? Did they hear you?'

'How could I know that?'

'Well, your friends might have turned around and said something in response.'

The witness said nothing.

'You never said it, did you, Mr Donald?'

Silence.

John Donald was not going to answer.

'You didn't say it because you had no reason to.'

The witness looked at the judge for help. The judge didn't even lift his eyes.

'I want an answer, Mr Donald. Miss Johnson wants an answer.'

Silence.

'We'll move on, then. Where are your two friends, the ones who might have heard you shout out? Are they outside the court?'

Scott knew they weren't. One was in prison near Glasgow and the other could not be found. Both had refused to make statements. They had not seen what had happened out in the street and had said nothing about what had happened in the pub. The barman who was giving evidence had not heard anyone call out anything about a knife, nor had any of the other witnesses. Scott knew he was on strong ground here.

Earlier, just after lunch, Scott had sat listening to John Donald's evidence and had realised there was only one way to defend Ellie properly. He was going to have to destroy the man. Not just set up the occasional contradiction in his evidence, but completely destroy him. It was going to be very messy, but it was what he was being paid to do.

Scott had watched while Ben Gribble cross-examined. Ben's client, Colin Jones, was the first on the indictment, so Ben had to go first. Ben was a nice enough chap, but cross-examining at the Old Bailey wasn't his main strength.

Scott tried to think what was. Personal injury pleadings – long pleadings setting out the multiplicands that had to be considered as against the multiplier, and then coming up with an enormous final figure for damages for some poor child in a car crash. He'd trust Ben to do that. But here he was only getting in the way.

He stopped himself.

That was unfair. Scott didn't do multiplicands because they were too damn difficult. Oliver multiplicands, Dawson regressive reductions, Amlot multipliers, all these odd names. They were extraordinarily complicated, and too bloody boring. Scott stopped apologising for himself. After all, if you weren't certain about what you could do properly then you weren't going to be able to do anything properly, and Scott knew he could take this witness apart.

He reflected on it and decided that in fact Ben Gribble's gentle questioning was making it easier for him to do that. The witness was becoming over-confident.

Now the witness was laughing at Ben. He was taking every opportunity to repeat his allegation, and in effect poking fun at him. 'If your client hadn't stabbed me, then perhaps I would remember better,' he said at one point.

The trouble was that *somebody* had stabbed the bloody man. Whatever Scott did to the witness, he wasn't going to be able to suggest he had stabbed himself in the chest. Just as Scott thought about it the witness said the same thing. 'What are you saying? That I stabbed myself?'

This was the point that had to be handled carefully, but Gribble fluffed it. 'Someone else came along,' Gribble said lamely.

John Donald laughed out loud.

'What? Someone else came along and stabbed me? Just like that?'

Scott waited to see what Ben would do. In Donald's witness statement there was a curious ambiguity when he got to this part. There was a reference to two other men, but it wasn't clear why he had mentioned them. Perhaps he was saying they had come to help him, perhaps not. There was just a reference to two other men who had got involved.

But fortunately Ben fluffed it, leaving it for Scott. After all, his case was that his client wasn't there at all, so why should he get involved in explanations of what happened to the man?

'Yes,' he said, 'I suggest there was someone else involved.'

'Oh. Tell me more,' Donald said.

'Are there people near this pub who don't like you?' Ben asked.

It was a simple question. All the best questions were simple, and for a moment it stopped Donald in his tracks. Scott could see there was mileage there. But Ben didn't press it. Donald said, 'No. No one. It was your man and the wee girl who did this to me,' and the moment passed.

Gribble didn't have the killer instinct. He was too nice. Scott began to ponder the implications of that. If Gribble was too nice, nice in court and out, what did that say about Scott? He knew himself only too well, he knew he could be fearsomely nasty when he wanted to be, inside and out of court. He had to control it, since he had been rude to most of the people he worked with at one time or other.

Gribble stopped and Scott got to his feet. The witness looked at him in a satisfied fashion. He didn't know what was about to happen.

Harry moved a little further forward in the court so he could see better.

'Now, Mr Donald, you say that the boy pulled a knife in the pub. We shall see if anyone else comes forward to say that happened.'

The witness was already slightly less sure of himself.

'He did not do that, did he? You're making it up.'

'No I'm not.'

'To justify your running after them.'

The witness made a mistake.

'I ran after him because he threatened me with a knife.'

Scott didn't pause at all.

'That's an odd reason, isn't it? If someone had a knife you'd want to stay away from him, wouldn't you?'

Donald was puzzled. It had seemed a good enough reason when he said it, and no one had questioned the idea before.

'You'd want to stay away, wouldn't you?' said Scott.

'That's what happened.'

'The real reason you ran after him was because he stood up to you in front of your friends and made you look stupid, isn't it?'

From now on the witness began to answer less and less.

'And you had to make up a reason to justify your doing so?'

'No,' said Donald. 'I . . .' then he said nothing.

'Even though the barman was trying to calm you down. He pulled you a pint of beer and you left it untouched?'

Scott was safe on this part of the case. There was no doubt that the Scotsman had left his beer and run after Ellie and her boyfriend. The only real argument was what happened when he had caught up with them. Sensibly the prosecutor had told the jury about the chase, attempting to lessen the effect of it, but there was nothing to match seeing evidence come out under cross-examination.

'You left an untouched pint on the bar in order to run after them, didn't you?'

John Donald started to look puzzled at what was happening.

'I don't suppose you've left a pint of beer untouched very often, have you?'

The jury laughed.

'Let's look at what happened in the pub to see whose fault this all is. Colin Jones was sitting with his young lady, Ellie Johnson. He left her for a moment and you spoke to her.'

Scott paused after each of these remarks, and when they weren't denied he moved on. Keep it simple.

'You spoke to his young lady. Didn't you?'

'I said something. Yes.'

'You walked over from the bar and breathed on her.'

'I what?'

'You walked over from the bar and breathed on her. How many pints of lager had you taken?' Make it sound like medicine.

'Not more than four.'

'Four pints at a quarter past twelve on a Sunday morning? And the night before? When you ended up waiting at the hospital for your mate?'

Scott had got the information from one of the taped interviews. Donald looked at him. How did he know that? He made no attempt to deny it.

'How many the night before? Two pints perhaps? Just a little bit. A small sherry perhaps?'

The jury stirred gently with amusement.

Scott knew that in effect this was a racist attack. Everyone carried a cartoon picture in their head of a fighting Scotsman in a pub. Perhaps it had some basis in truth. Often prejudices did.

Scott remembered defending a homosexual once, accused of importuning. The essence of the case against him was that the man was grossly promiscuous. The defendant had stoutly denied this, but eventually it emerged that his idea of promiscuous and other people's ideas differed somewhat. He thought four or five sexual encounters a week was quite restrained.

Scott went on, 'Well, five pints? Eight?' The witness said nothing, so Scott took a wild guess. 'Sixteen?'

Still Donald said nothing. So Scott took it he agreed.

'There'd still be quite a lot of that sloshing around in your belly when you went over to chat to Miss Johnson, wouldn't there? What did you want to chat about?'

'I asked her if she wanted to play billiards.'

'Why did you wait till Colin Jones had left before you went over?'

Either John Donald had waited or he hadn't. If he hadn't, his denial wouldn't amount to much. You didn't approach girls in pubs while their boyfriends were in the gents'. That's simple pub etiquette.

'I didn' wait.' Mr Donald's accent was beginning to show.

'She told you to shove off.'

'She didn't.'

'And then her boyfriend came back and told you the same thing.'

No reply.

'And you looked stupid in front of your friends. And then the couple left. It was clear they thought you were a drunk.'

Donald said nothing.

'And you went through this pantomime about a knife and ran after them, didn't you? That's what happened, isn't it?'

'No.'

'It did. They treated you like a drunk, didn't they?'

'No.'

John Donald decided to fight back. He turned to the judge and said, 'This man is trying to confuse me,' and the judge said, 'It seems perfectly clear to me, Mr Donald. What Mr Scott is saying is that you were pestering his young lady client. Were you or were you not? He wants an answer.'

Donald did what everyone does after finding no help in one place. He swung around to look for it elsewhere. He turned to the back of the court and looked at the defendants, and they looked back at him. He turned to the gallery – all he saw were faces looking back at him. He was alone.

Then he turned to the jury. 'Can't you see what he's doing?'

The jury said nothing. They looked at him impassively.

Scott said, 'What I am doing, Mr Donald, is asking questions about your behaviour.'

He was near to getting where he wanted to be, but he had to be careful not to overdo it.

'You thought you had been insulted, didn't you?'

Donald began to breathe heavily.

'You were thinking that they had treated you like dirt? That you weren't good enough for them?'

Scott guessed he was saying exactly what Donald had thought in the pub. Alcohol makes people very aware of being insulted. He looked at the man in the witness box. He could see he had hit the mark. If he could see it, so could the jury. He carried on. 'And you weren't taking that. So you ran after them.'

'I didn't run. I walked. A fast walk. I walked after them. It was they who were running.'

'Hang on. You've forgotten the knife now.'

This was so obvious that Donald couldn't say anything.

'I summed it all up and left the knife out. And you didn't correct me. Why not?'

'You're confusing me.'

'Am I?'

Harry caught the judge's eye for a moment and there was a flash of understanding. Harry had known the judge when he started at the Bar and still met him occasionally at boxing dinners.

'You ran down the road.'

'I did not.'

'Look, Mr Donald. Do yourself justice. There's a security

camera which shows you running quite clearly. We all know you were running. What we want to know is why you were running.'

Again Donald didn't reply.

'What were you going to do when you caught them?'

'They were arguing.'

'So what?'

'She was shouting at him.'

'So what?'

'She was angry.'

'Why shouldn't she be?'

'Well . . .'

'Well what?'

Suddenly Donald had run out of answers.

Scott said, 'You haven't answered me. What were you going to do when you caught them?'

'I wanted to sort it out. To see that there was no temper left. To make sure there was no understanding. I mean misunderstanding.'

Now the witness was beginning to gabble.

Scott felt like saying 'Shall we deconstruct that?', but it wasn't the kind of joke that would go down well in Court 2. So he said, 'Sort it out? What does that mean? How were you going to sort it out? A quiet discussion about their manners?'

'They stabbed me.'

John Donald retreated to basics. Scott was lucky. If the witness had accepted all the other allegations and then said, 'But then they stabbed me', it would have been much more difficult. You could behave badly but it didn't justify anyone stabbing you.

'That's another lie.'

'Why should I lie?'

'Why should you lie about the other things?'

No reply.

'You just want to blame someone else for your behaviour.' That was dangerous. What if he said, 'Am I to blame for stabbing myself?'

Scott adjusted it.

'You just want to find someone to blame for what happened.'

'They stabbed me.'

'How do you account for the fact that neither of them had blood on their clothing?'

'It's not for him to account for it, Mr Scott,' said the judge. He had looked as if he were fast asleep, but he was not.

'You knocked Colin Jones over from behind. You sent him flying.'

'I did not.'

'Well, did you see anything happen that might have torn his trousers like that? A long tear and dirt down the thigh?'

It was the same question as 'How do you account for it?' but put in a way the judge couldn't complain about.

'He attacked me.'

'What? How much do you weigh?'

No answer.

'Look at Colin Jones.' Scott gestured to Colin Jones to stand up. There was no doubt he was slim-built. Just the type to carry a knife, Scott thought.

'How much do you weigh, Mr Donald? Sixteen stone?'

'He ran at me.'

'Hang on,' Scott said, 'last time we heard you were running at him. Though of course you don't admit that, do you?'

'He ran at me and kno . . .' Donald trailed off.

'Were you about to say "He knocked me over"?'

It was clear that he was about to say just that. Donald said nothing.

'You were, weren't you?'

Donald began to breathe heavily again. Scott could see that he was really annoying him now.

'Why did you stop yourself, Mr Donald? Is it because it's obviously nonsense?'

The witness shouted out this time, to no one in particular. 'You're just crowding me with your clever questions.'

Scott said in exactly the same tone of voice, 'Is it because in your witness statement you say you slipped as you reached the couple, and fell over? That's what you said to the police, isn't it?'

Donald said nothing. 'You can look at the statement if you wish.'

Some judges would have stopped the flow there and made Scott produce the document. This one didn't.

'No,' said Donald.

'That couldn't be more different from "He ran at me", could it?'

'They stabbed me.' Donald was becoming very, very angry.

'We shall see about that in a moment, but first why were you about to pretend to us that they knocked you over?'

John Donald's face began to glow a bright red.

Harry had to leave. If he didn't go now he wouldn't be back by four. He had never arrived back later than that, and he still had to go upstairs to the list office. As he left he could hear the witness's voice rising in fury and the calm, steady tone of Scott's voice set against it. 'Go on, Mr Donald. Answer the question.'

Harry didn't stay in the list office more than five minutes. He got what he wanted and came back down in the lift. It didn't seem as if he was going to be able to speak to Scott – he'd have to get him on the phone later or hope he came into chambers. He glanced down the passage that led to the main hall outside Court 2.

A door opened and he could hear shouting. He recognised the voice. It was the Scotsman who had been in the witness box. The court must have risen. Perhaps he could speak to Scott. He pushed his way through the double doors and headed for the court. He was always astonished by the grandeur of the main hall. It was a huge tiled dome, echoing with light.

On the right there was a commotion. Harry could see the witness waving his arms about, trying to push past a man who was restraining him. He could hear quite plainly, 'That fucking little bastard.' Over and over again, and each time the word bastard came out it was spat out into the face of the man restraining him. Harry walked over.

A file of men and women came out of the court, walking past the argument, clearly apprehensive of the violence and anger. The policeman put his arm on the man's wrist but was shaken off as Donald turned and walked a few quick paces up and down. As he did so Harry could see him rubbing the tops of his legs and grasping the air with his open hands. His mouth was working hard. 'Bastard, bastard.'

Harry walked into the court.

The judge was just leaving. Clearly they had been discussing whatever it was that had happened. On the central table there was a mess of papers and a broken glass water decanter. The barristers were standing up and the usher was beginning to clean up.

Harry stood by the door. Next to him was a court attendant. Harry had known him for years.

'What happened?'

'He came right out of the witness box at Mr Scott there. Luckily his foot slipped as he went across the table or he'd have done him. I've never seen that before.'

Harry looked at Scott. He seemed quite calm.

'Well, your Mr Scott just stood there and there was a hell of a crash. And then Scott said, "Is that how you make your point, then?"'

Harry walked over to where Scott was standing.

'Oh, hallo, Harry,' Scott said. 'Come to join in the fun?'

Harry stood on his dignity and took no notice of Scott's remark.

'I'm glad I'm able to speak to you, sir. I've booked you up for a conference at five tomorrow at Holloway. Could you ring Monty Bach tonight after half past five? He needs to talk to you about it.'

'Monty Bach? Since when did he start sending me work again?' said Scott.

'Since this afternoon, sir. Don't you worry – I'm looking after your interests, sir. While you're here the clerks' room is working for you.'

Scott looked at Harry. He couldn't tell, as always. Was Harry laughing at himself or at him? Was it a joke, or did he really mean it? – 'the clerks' room is working for you'.

'Thanks, Harry,' he said.

The only way to deal with him was to reply perfectly straight without a hint of a reaction.

'I must be off, then,' Harry said, and turned on his heel.

Scott stood watching him. Harry had said nothing about the chaos in the court. Had he noticed it? Perhaps he thought it was always like that.

Scott began gathering his papers. He looked up towards the attendant at the door, who shook his head. He had better not go out there for a moment. It wasn't that he was nervous, though he was – he didn't fancy taking Mr Donald on in real life. It was just better to avoid any more fuss. He sat down.

Ben Gribble, sitting next to him, said, 'Well, you really got to him, didn't you?'

'What happened to the little spikes?'

'What?'

'The little spikes,' said Scott. 'I'm sure there used to be little spikes around the witness box to stop people doing that.'

'Were there?'

'I can picture them. So I must have got the idea from somewhere.'

'Taken off.'

'No doubt in the permissive sixties.'

Ben Gribble laughed.

'I think the jury have got the point about our Mr Donald, though.'

'He's not the meek type, is he?'

The court attendant called across. 'You're all right now, Mr Scott. You're safe now. He's gone.'

Scott picked his brief up and walked over, laughing. 'Safe now,' he said. 'What are you on about, Victor? We're all safe when you're around.' The attendant pushed the door open and they went out.

Outside the door there was a small group gathering. The court journalists had arrived.

'What happened, Mr Scott?'

'The witness got angry.'

'Can we print it?'

One of the great problems of being an Old Bailey journalist was that a lot of the stories could not be printed, for fear of contempt of court.

'I don't know,' said Scott. 'I can't see why not. After all, the jury saw it, though it's probably better not to say what the judge did after they left. Anyway, ask Ben here, he knows the law on this sort of thing.'

The group descended on Ben Gribble, who was pushing

his way through the court doors backwards, his arms full of papers.

'Mr Gribble, tell us what happened.'

He blinked at them in astonishment as he disappeared under the scrum.

Scott escaped down the passage. His solicitor had gone ahead, making for the cells to see Ellie. She had screamed when the witness jumped across the table, and Scott had seen the distress on her face. As he made his way down the corridor, he felt his gown being pulled.

'Are you Jeremy Scott?' He looked up. It was an extremely attractive woman.

'I'm new here,' she said. 'I don't understand.'

She couldn't have said anything more guaranteed to catch his attention.

'Understand what?'

'This contempt of court thing. Apparently it's contempt to hit or insult a lawyer in the court.'

'I think that's only solicitors and witnesses. For some reason it doesn't apply to barristers.'

She made a note.

'But check it,' he said. 'Surely you've got a book on it?'

'Can I talk to you?'

'Not now,' he said. 'I'm sorry. I have to see the client.'

'She's charged with attempted murder?'

'Yes.'

'Did she do it?'

'You are new, aren't you?'

'I watched you in court. No one could rely on that witness, could they?'

Scott looked at her again. Normally Old Bailey journalists only listened to the opening of a case. They weren't interested in the evidence – it was too problematic. Openings were simple – everyone was guilty.

'Why did you listen?'

'I was told you'd be good to listen to.'

This was getting a bit much.

'I have to go to the cells.'

'When can we talk?'

'I'll be here tomorrow.'

'I'm only here for the day,' she said.

'Why, who are you with?'

'I'm television. I'm from *Blind Justice*. Do you watch it?'

'I've seen it,' said Scott. He wanted to get away to see Ellie.

'I'll wait for you, then,' she said as he disappeared through the door.

Ellie, sitting opposite him in a cell, wanted to know why she couldn't go home now. What she had seen had been so obviously the behaviour of a dishonest man that she assumed everyone else would think so too.

'We have to go through the full procedure, Ellie. That was only part of the trial.'

'But the main part.'

'Yes, well . . . The main part, but not the whole thing. They can prove that a stabbing happened without even calling John Donald, and we've got the child to deal with yet.'

'You mean I could still be convicted?'

'Look, Ellie, I'm not saying . . . Yes, I am saying that. But what I am trying to say is that we can't rush it. There's still the other evidence to deal with.'

She turned her head away from him. She had been sitting in her cell for the last quarter of an hour assuming it must be all over and yet here it was, all starting up again. When she turned back towards him her cheeks were covered in tears.

'You'll get me out of here, won't you? I don't think I can go on any more.'

'I'm doing my best, Ellie.'

Chapter Four

Scott didn't want to talk to any journalists but the television woman was outside, and, of course, so were Ellie's parents.

'How is she, Mr Scott?' asked Ellie's mother.

'She's all right, Mrs Johnson.'

Scott included Ellie's father in his reply.

He was a tall, puzzled-looking man who expected his wife to speak first. Neither of them had the resources to control or understand what was happening to them. The police had arrived one morning at six thirty, got their daughter out of bed, told her father that she was a slag and taken her away. The once-benevolent face of a society in which they felt safe had turned against them.

Mr Johnson dressed and went to the local police station – nobody knew anything. It might as well have been the Gestapo. Of course, that was an absurd comparison, since everything had been done according to the rules. There had been a valid warrant. Ellie was an adult. The police had no duty to inform anyone any more than they had done. They were still looking for her boyfriend, who happened to be away, so Ellie was held incommunicado in case information should get back to him and alert him. For six hours Ellie disappeared from the face of the earth.

Then there was confusion about legal aid. Ellie had a good job and no real living expenses since she still lived with her parents. Her first bail application was made by a rushed and ill-informed duty solicitor, and failed. He hadn't had the time to sort it out.

The prosecuting lawyer, acting on a hurried note from a police officer, stressed 'the bad feeling in the area about the attack, and the very real danger', he said to the nervous magistrates, 'of witnesses being threatened. Some of the witnesses are children.' The police officer from whom this came was never seen in the case again. Ellie spent another two weeks in prison.

She didn't get a lawyer. The legal aid authorities, alerted by the popular press to the danger of helping people who didn't deserve it, were wary of giving legal aid until they knew it was absolutely necessary. 'No,' said the local office, 'being in custody is not a good reason. We are talking about public money here.'

It cost the state a thousand pounds a week to keep Ellie on remand until her trial.

That all seemed very odd to Mr Johnson. But at last he had found someone he could trust, even if it was the blind trust in someone who was paid to be on their side.

'What will happen, Mr Scott?' he said.

Scott allowed himself a little optimism. 'It's not been a bad start. After all, John Donald is the person who says your daughter attacked him. How much reliance can the jury place on him now?' Then he repeated what he had told Ellie.

What was awful about going through it again and again was not just having to do so – of course he had to do that – but the inadequacy of the explanations he had to offer.

There were so many variables, so many nuances. The main value of Donald's behaviour was not the effect on the jury, though that was pretty immense, but the effect on the judge and the prosecutor. For the judge this would now no longer be an ordinary case, meandering towards a conviction. Now it was a case where he had to make sure that the proper implications were drawn from what had happened.

And the prosecutor was on his back foot. Now he would always be arguing from a disadvantage. He would not be able to call on the jury's sympathy any more. In fact, knowing the pessimism of prosecutors, so much greater than defence counsel's, he probably thought the case was lost already.

But Scott couldn't explain this to the Johnsons. Or at least, if he did they would object, saying that people's feelings and reactions ought not to be allowed to interfere with justice. And they would be right, but there was no taking away from the fact that this business was theatre, as well as justice.

'Did you do that on purpose?'

The journalist caught up with him as he walked past the Rumboe pub. Scott was wondering, as he did every time he passed it, whether it was the origin of Rumpole's name. 'Do what on purpose?'

'Taunt the witness.'

'I didn't taunt the witness.'

'Of course you did.'

She settled into a walk beside him.

'All I did was ask him questions.'

'But it was the way you did it.'

'I was quite calm.'

'That's part of it.'

'Part of what?'

'Part of what upset the witness so much. He had come here to say something and all he got was someone prodding him.'

'But what he had come to say was lies, or at least those are my instructions.'

'Instructions. Instructions. What's so special about instructions?'

This was astonishing. Did she know nothing about this?

'That's all I've got. Instructions. My client tells me what happened and I put it to the witness. That's all I do.'

'Well, if you think that's all you do, you're kidding yourself. She didn't instruct you to make him jump out of the witness box, did she? You decided to do that.'

She had a point.

His explanation for what was going on was as inadequate as he thought hers was. He had often thought that lately. There was a rigid justification for what he did in court, but in truth it didn't begin to cover what happened. Since when had – it was the only word – humiliating a witness been part of the disinterested presentation of a client's case?

'Tell me about it,' he said. A good, hard-boiled remark, just on the way into El Vino.

Ronnie Knox said, 'But, young lady, you just don't understand.'

Scott smiled. Nothing could have been more calculated to upset someone like her, though Ronnie hadn't meant to do so, he was just like that. Scott could see the anger in her face. Ronnie's episcopal manner and florid language clearly epitomised everything she thought rotten in lawyers.

'When I defend someone I am not putting my opinion forward,' Ronnie said. 'Not, if I may be so bold as to say so, like you do when you write your stuff.'

She now felt insulted.

'No we don't,' she said. 'When I cover something I present a balanced argument.'

'Oh, come on,' Scott said. 'I bet the first question you ask when you decide to do a case is "Was this a miscarriage of justice?" If you say yes, you do the programme. If the answer is no, then you don't do it. You don't say to yourself, "Was this person, guilty or not, wrongly convicted on the evidence?" You're only interested in the shock of it.

'Take the Yorkshire Ripper case. That was clearly a miscarriage of justice. Here was a man who was obviously insane enough to be acquitted of murder. But the jury was bounced into saying he was sane, even though the prosecution had originally accepted the doctors' advice that he was barking mad. You don't see that one on television. Why? Because it doesn't fit your pattern.

'Us, we're not interested in patterns, we're only interested in evidence.'

'Sometimes evidence is not enough,' she said.

Ronnie began to cough – or laugh, it wasn't clear which. He could hardly get it out. 'For a trial lawyer there *is* only evidence – there *is* nothing else.'

Scott felt sorry for her. She wasn't arguing on her own ground.

By now Ronnie sounded as though someone was turning the handle on a barrel full of pebbles. She looked anxious. He intervened.

'All right, Ronnie. Slow down. You're here to order wine and for no other reason. Why don't you do what we expect you to do?'

He turned to the girl. 'That was Ronnie laughing. Don't be frightened. His breathing was perfected in early morning prayers at the monastery. He used to be a monk.'

She looked at Ronnie with even greater dismay, but Ronnie didn't notice. He was leaning back holding his hand up to attract the attention of the waitress.

'I don't know your name,' Scott said.

'Veronica, Veronica Vesey,' she said, wrinkling her nose. 'But they call me Nicky.'

'Oh,' said Scott. 'What do you do?'

'I'm a researcher.'

'On *Blind Justice*?'

'Yes.'

'What do you research?'

'I research the various cases we get sent.'

'To see if there is a miscarriage of justice?'

'Yes.'

'And then you make a programme about it.'

'Yes.'

'And then they get released in a blaze of publicity?'

'The films?'

'No, the people who've been wrongly convicted.'

'We hope so.'

'Oh.'

'You don't approve?'

'I didn't say that.'

'You didn't have to.'

'Actually that's not true. I think some of them are very good. What you do well is what we don't do well. You have the resources to re-examine our assumptions. I remember there was one which really struck me.'

'What do you mean, assumptions?'

'The things we rely on without even thinking about it.'

'Which one was it?'

'The case about the clock.'

'I don't remember that one.'

'It was about a defendant who had run an alibi. He said that at the time of the murder or whatever it was, he was somewhere – say Norwich, Norwich railway station. And he remembered the time he got there, ten to four by the station clock. The prosecution examined his explanation of his movements and were able to prove that he couldn't have got there by then, and they were right, he couldn't, so they argued the whole alibi must have been made up. He was never there at all, therefore he did the murder. But he stuck to the explanation – 'ten to four on the station clock, I saw it'. Anyway, he was convicted. The jury didn't believe his story about the clock and that was that. And what you did . . .'

'I don't think it was us,' Nicky said.

'Well, what the television people did was, they went to Norwich and asked about the clock. And guess what? The clock was broken – stuck at ten to four. Everybody assumed the clock was telling the correct time. That's pretty good if you ask me.'

'That wasn't us. I don't remember it. Perhaps it was the other lot – *Rough Justice*.'

'Oh, are there two of you? I didn't know.'

'What's this "rough justice", "blind justice" stuff?' said Ronnie, returning with a bottle of wine.

'Hang on,' said Scott. 'But it's got more to it than that. What was interesting for me, Nicky, was that the client was willing to stick to the truth. He could so easily have changed it and said, "I was mistaken, it was half past four, or ten to five" or something. You can bet his lawyers, once they'd seen the prosecution's evidence, asked him a number of times whether he was sure. And there's one simple rule: when your lawyer asks you more than once if you're sure, then that's exactly the time to change your story. And the real irony is that if he had changed his evidence about the time and then said, "Oh well, I was mistaken" and the truth about the clock had then come out, then he couldn't have relied on it. Truth is like light, it creates as many shadows as it does clarity – or whatever the opposite of shadows is.

'It depends where you stand in relation to it. All you can be sure of is that at the end of the case, the defendant knew he was innocent and the police knew he was guilty. And in a way neither of them was wrong.'

'What's "blind justice"?' said Ronnie.

'You'll have to explain. I don't think Ronnie owns a television,' said Scott.

'It's the name of the programme,' said Nicky. 'I'm a researcher on it.'

'Are you researching Jeremy?'

'No. Of course I'm not. Why should I want to do that?' She sounded startled.

'Who knows?' Ronnie said.

'Thank you, Ronnie,' Scott said. 'I have to apologise for Ronnie. He gets annoyed when I suggest that there can be different sorts of truth, or that honesty doesn't depend on truth. He has to since he spent many years teaching Catholic philosophy, where there is only one truth.'

Ronnie smiled and began to reply.

'Look, I have to phone someone,' Scott said before Ronnie could get going.

'Use my phone,' said Nicky. She bent down and rummaged in the multicoloured bag she was carrying. Scott looked at Ronnie over her head. Ronnie raised his eyebrows and smiled.

'Here you are.'

'Do you think I'm allowed to use one of these in here?' Scott said as he took her mobile phone.

'I doubt it. Use it discreetly,' said Ronnie.

'Of course I'll use it discreetly,' said Scott. 'What do you think I'm going to do? Stand on the table?' He looked at it. 'Which button do you press?'

'God, you two are out of the Ark.' She took the phone

from him. 'This one. What do you normally do when you want to call someone?'

'I use a public phone.' Scott fumbled at the buttons. 'I have to make two calls,' he said.

'Go ahead.'

The buttons beeped as Scott pressed them.

'Harry? Have you got Monty Bach's phone number?'

There was a scuffling noise at the other end of the phone and Scott was put on hold. Harry was transferring him to one of the other staff. Even if he knew the phone number he wasn't going to demean himself by telling Scott what it was.

All three in El Vino sat looking at each other.

After a moment Nicky said, 'Monty Bach? You should have said. I've got his number programmed in on the phone. Press END and then this one.' She reached for the phone and they held it together. Their heads were quite close. Scott could smell a perfume. Chamade? It was the one his wife had used and he felt slightly giddy.

'Then punch in number thirty-two. That's Monty.'

'You know Monty?' Scott said as the phone rang. But before she could reply Monty answered.

'Ah, Mr Scott. Good to hear from you again. I've got a nice little case for you.'

'That's very kind, Monty,' Scott said. He made a face at Ronnie.

'It's a lady who's been accused of murdering one of her relatives.'

Scott was surprised. A murder case from Monty? What was wrong with his usual counsel, Tozer or Ned?

'Well,' Monty went on, 'she's not so much accused. She's been convicted. It's an appeal.'

'Oh,' said Scott. This was a distinctly unattractive proposition. 'What's happened to her original lawyers?'

'Ah. Well, there's the rub. She's dispensed with them.

In fact they say there are no grounds to appeal, so she sacked them.'

'Oh Lord,' said Scott. 'Why me?'

'You're a fighter, Mr Scott. And you're not part of the Establishment, are you?'

'Only because they won't let me in.'

Monty laughed. 'Oh, very good, Mr Scott. Look, I arranged with Harry that you should see her tomorrow at five. I have no papers as yet, so I said we would just see her.'

'OK, Monty.' Scott's heart sank. This was just the kind of case that he did not want.

'This could do you a lot of good,' said Monty. 'If you don't mind a wise old bird speaking.'

'No, Monty, I don't mind,' said Scott. He pressed the button to end the call.

'He's impossible,' he said. 'You can't even be rude to him. He wouldn't understand if you were.'

Ronnie laughed. Scott handed the phone back to Nicky.

'Monty wants me to go to the Court of Appeal and say that one of his clients wasn't defended properly.'

'One of Monty's own clients not defended properly by Monty?'

'No. She sacked the previous lot and then went to Monty. God knows why.'

'Why isn't Tozer doing it?'

'Don't ask me. Why am I doing it? That's even odder.'

'Because you're a fighter,' Nicky said. He looked at her. Where had she got that phrase from?

'Well, that's all very complimentary,' said Scott. 'It's easy enough to be a fighter over a bit of grievous bodily harm in the crown court, but being a fighter in the Court of Appeal is a different proposition. Not quite my normal sphere of operation.'

'What's she been convicted of?'

'Murder.'

'What are the grounds?'

'Couldn't be worse. She's arguing with her previous lawyers.'

They sat for a moment, then Ronnie said, 'Well, here's one for you, Nicky. "Brave barrister briefed to attack colleagues at the bar."'

They looked at Scott.

'But does he have the stomach for it?' said Ronnie.

Even Scott wasn't sure about the answer to that.

Chapter Five

The next day the prosecution called the child's evidence in Ellie Johnson's case.

Ben Gribble hardly challenged what Darren, the boy, had to say at all. He didn't need to. His client was saying he wasn't there. All Ben did was emphasise the boy's evidence that the incident took place down a side road, some distance away from where his client said he had been knocked over.

That didn't help Ellie.

The problem was that the child's description of one of the people fighting in the road fitted Ellie exactly. Scott was going to have to deal with that – he wasn't going to be able to leave it alone as Ben had done. He either had to suggest that the boy was confused and had mistakenly thought Ellie was present at the stabbing, or that there was another girl dressed in long boots carrying a white handbag who was helping someone off the floor. That seemed pretty unlikely.

The oddity was that the white handbag was much better identifying evidence than any description of Ellie might have been. 'How many people,' the prosecution could say, '*were* there walking around with a white handbag in just that part of Hackney at that time?'

But who could know the anwer to that? Dozens perhaps. Maybe it was a local fashion. Scott remembered doing a case once in front of a particularly bloodless judge called Teflin. There the man the police wanted had been seen drunk in the centre of Brighton with a can of Special Brew. Later on Scott's client was seen drunk in the centre of Brighton with a can of Special Brew. There was no other identifying evidence – were they the same guy?

He had tried to point out that most of the drunks in the centre of Brighton, and there were a lot, drank Special Brew – either that or cider.

'But how can one know that, Mr Scott?' Teflin had said, looking at him through his rimless glasses. Scott wanted to say, 'You either know it or you don't, and if you don't you should keep quiet about it,' but couldn't. This was a court and Teflin had to be treated with respect – stupid questions or not.

But Teflin was right. It wasn't something that could be proved, and Teflin, who probably went to bed most nights at half past nine, had never been in the centre of Brighton. If he had been, then no doubt he would have averted his eyes from any drunk he saw.

The jury knew, though, and acquitted Scott's client in a minute. The story had some poignancy for Scott since it was Special Brew that he had drunk during a bad part of his life. Vicious stuff.

'Mr Scott? Do you have any questions for this young witness?'

'Oh, yes. I'm sorry, m'lord. I'm sorry, Darren. I was thinking about something that happened to me once.'

Scott didn't stand but stayed sitting and grinned at the boy who had been put on a chair in the well of the court below. He took his wig off. The little boy stared at it as he put it down, and on an impulse Scott said to the usher, 'Let him have a look.'

The usher took the wig, and the boy did exactly what all small children did with Scott's wig. He put it on.

The jury laughed. So, amazingly, did the judge. Now Scott had the boy's complete attention.

'There you are. Not so odd, is it? But, Darren, I still need to ask you some questions.'

Scott expected to have to tell the child to put the wig down in case he was distracted, but the boy transferred his attention to him so completely that he didn't need to.

'The fight you saw. OK? You definitely saw a fight.'

He had to take this slowly.

'Do you often see fights?'

'On the films.'

'Have you ever seen a fight in the street?'

'No.'

'Was it different from the films?'

The boy stopped and thought about it. And then said nothing.

'Who fights on the films?'

'The turtles.'

'Who?' said the judge.

'The turtles.'

'I thought you said that,' said the judge.

'When the turtles fight it looks like fun?'

'Yes.'

'Was this different?'

'Yes.'

'In what way?'

'It was. Dirty.'

'You mean they fought dirty, like in football some people play dirty?'

'No.'

'What, then?'

'It was horrid.'

Scott knew exactly what he meant. Fights on the screen had a balletic quality, lots of whooshing and leaping. Fights in the streets were squalid. Fights in the mean streets.

'You mean yukky?'

'Yes. That's it.'

'What does that mean?' said the judge.

'Squalid,' said Scott, and he went straight on. 'Was it quick?'

'Yes.'

'Didn't take long?'

'No.'

'Difficult to see what was happening?'

'I saw it.'

Scott felt the pressure of the experience the boy had gone through. He probably still woke up dreaming about it.

'Do you dream about it?'

'Yes.'

'Where did it happen?'

'Outside my nan's.'

Scott had discovered the confusion, but he didn't react.

'Where does it happen in your dreams?'

'Anywhere, especially in the streets.'

'Anywhere in the streets?'

'Yes.'

'Often?'

The little boy wasn't talking about dreams.

'When did it happen last?'

The little boy looked at Scott and his mouth snapped shut.

'You've got the talker's hat on now, so you talk about it and it won't hurt you,' Scott said.

The little boy looked up at the wig which had slipped down over his forehead and grinned.

'It's like a magician's hat. You can talk about it now and it won't hurt you,' Scott repeated.

He was careful not to look at the judge. What would he think of this? Across the court the jury was engrossed. There was absolute silence.

Scott said nothing for ten seconds.

'Where did it happen last?'

'Outside here. When I saw the car.'

'The police car?'

Scott understood it now. The Scotsman staggering past Darren standing with his little brother, blood dripping from beneath a hand clasped to his chest, and then the police car, a siren wailing feet away, huge men in dayglo suits pushing past them. The children engulfed in sound and light. Later the thrashing noise of the helicopter ambulance. Scott could see the children standing in the street unattended, drinking in the powerful images, images that it would be impossible to get out of their systems. Darren was sitting there in the court still in the grip of flashbacks, intrusive imagery, the lot – displaced memories, the whole post-traumatic stress syndrome.

The boy smiled with relief as he was able to describe what really mattered to him. He said, 'Yes. When the cars go by I see it.'

'Have you told anyone this?'

'Only my nan.'

'When?'

'I was crying.'

'Was that outside her house?'

'Yes.'

'Had you seen the fight take place again there right outside her house?'

'Yes.'

'Is that what you told your nan?'

'Yes.'

'Where does your nan live?'

'Southend.'

There was an audible release of breath in the court.

'Where did the first fight, the real fight, take place?'

'I don't know. All I know is that when I go to my nan's again I see it. And sometimes in bed.'

'So two things make you see it again? Your nan's and the police cars?'

'Yes. And bed.'

'And you don't know now where you saw it first?'

'No.'

Scott paused for a moment.

He had destroyed the evidence relating to where the boy had said the fight took place, but that was only one part of the case against Ellie dealt with.

The child took off the wig, put it on the head of the social worker sitting next to him and laughed. It was extraordinary to see such simplicity in the dark courtroom.

Scott had to push his questions further.

Ellie's instructions were that she had picked up her boyfriend, who had been knocked over by the Scotsman. She was saying that she had not touched the Scotsman, who, she said, had run off pursued by two other men.

'The girl who helped the man up?'

'Yes.'

'You're thinking about that now?'

'Yes.'

'The man she picked up?'

'It was the man who had blood on him.' Catastrophe. The boy had gone straight back to the story he had told all along. But Scott still had to put Ellie's case.

'She was helping the man?'

'Yes.'

At least that was something.

'And later you thought about it?'

'Yes.'

That mixture of times, the idea of *now* thinking back to what he thought *then*, was probably right at the limit of the boy's understanding.

'The one you were sorry for?'

'The one with blood on.'

'You thought it was he whom . . .' Scott stopped. Don't speak like that.

'I'll say that again. You thought it was he who she was helping?'

'Yes.'

'But it was the other man, wasn't it?'

'No.'

That was as much as he would get. He leaned back on his bench, and lifted his hand to the judge to show he had finished.

The little boy sat with the wig on his head and looked around.

The prosecutor asked one question. 'When the girl picked the man up, what did the other man do?'

'He hit him in the chest. There.'

And the little boy turned to the judge and showed where he meant.

It was exactly the position of the wound that nearly killed John Donald.

'That's screwed it,' Scott said to himself.

'What was the idea of getting that boy to wear the wig thing?' Colin Jones, sitting in the dock, asked Ellie.

She didn't respond. She didn't even look at him. She knew the jury were watching her. God, what a moron he was. Whatever had she seen in him? She knew what it was

– she used to let him tell her what to do. Well, that wasn't going to happen any more, she wasn't going to let any man order her around. Look at the trouble he had got her in. And those letters he had sent her in prison. What a fool.

In the first letter he was trying to get her to say things that had not happened. How did he know that the letter wasn't being read? She had thrown it away and hadn't accepted any more.

Then one of the girls on the wing came up to her and said she had a message from him. She refused to listen. She was lucky it was one of the sensible ones who had tried to deliver the message, otherwise there would have been another screaming match.

She had seen enough of those scrappy arguments to last a lifetime. They were over silly things, like 'You made a mark on my trainers.' My God, what a fight there had been over that. Two coloured girls. She couldn't say the coloureds were the worst, but when they really got going they were the hardest to stop. And everything, they did everything to each other. No wonder. They were really angry. Angry about everything. She could see it now. Some of them, the whites too, could hardly read or write. Just enough to forge a name, one of them told her.

She realised how lucky she was now. Her parents had made her stay at school. They had made her learn. Sometimes it even annoyed the teachers at that awful school how she had tried. She remembered once how one of them asked her, 'Who do you think you are?'

It was obvious to her now. Even the teachers thought they were deadbeats. No, that was wrong. The teachers themselves thought that the teachers themselves were deadbeats. It was all one big sink and anyone who tried to crawl out was resented.

She was intelligent. She knew she was intelligent. There

was no reason why she should not get ahead. Miss Forgan agreed with that. Miss Forgan had talked to her and told her things. Until she disappeared. Miss Forgan had been convicted of murder. She had read it in the paper. It was funny, such a nice woman a murderer, and she was so kind too.

Scott was getting to his feet.

He was nice. He was nice to her. He treated her with respect. He treated her like a real person. No, better than that, he treated her like an equal. That's why she didn't mind if he got angry or impatient with her sometimes. Because it meant he trusted her to be real. Not just a thing.

Respect. That was more important than nice cars, nice clothes. Respect. When she got out of here she was going to demand respect.

When she got out of here.

Her heart heaved inside her. Perhaps she wasn't going to get out of here. Perhaps she was going to have to sit in here for another five years, or longer. She squeezed her hands together till they hurt.

'. . . no evidence against Miss Ellie Johnson.'

What was this? Scott wasn't looking at her. The jury were not there. Lord, she hadn't noticed they'd left the court. That Colin Jones had distracted her again. She strained to understand what Scott was saying. He had said something to the judge about there being no case against her. Perhaps this was it.

'On the attempted murder charge, even if she was holding Mr Donald, there is no evidence of any intention on Miss Johnson's part beyond that. There is certainly no evidence of any intention that Mr Donald should be killed. Without evidence of that intention the Crown case on attempted murder fails immediately. There is no evidence to go to the jury.'

Of course not, Ellie thought. What was he on about? There never was any evidence.

'I make it clear, of course, for Miss Johnson's benefit, that at this stage I am speaking as if the jury accepted that she held the man. Even then there is no evidence of intention.'

He looked good.

He wasn't a handsome man and he was a lot older than she was, but he looked confident. Ellie was pleased.

'I am concerned for the moment with intention . . .'

The judge interrupted.

'But, Mr Scott, what about the *actus reus*?'

What was that? The *actus reus*? What on earth was that? Scott would know, though. She looked at him. He didn't! He was fumbling. She had not seen him fumble before. And the prosecutor was looking at Scott. He was just as puzzled. Something funny was happening. Then Scott stood up straight again.

'M'lud,' he said. 'You are right. I ought to have started with the *actus reus*.'

'Yes, Mr Scott, you should have done so. And in that case your submission also extends to the second and alternative count?'

'Of course it does, m'lud, and I apologise for not getting to it as quickly as I ought.'

'No matter,' said the judge. He looked angry. Scott had done something wrong. 'What does the prosecution say?'

Scott sat down. Why was he sitting down? Was he giving in on something? He'd given up. Ellie squeezed her hands together and craned her head round to look at her parents above her. They smiled, but Ellie could see they were worried as well. What was happening? Perhaps Scott was giving in. Had she been right to trust him?

'M'lud, the Crown says the events must be taken together.'

'But you heard the little boy. He said Miss Johnson was trying to help the man.'

That sounded hopeful.

'No,' said the judge. 'My mind is made up. I have listened very carefully. As, of course, gentlemen, I always do.'

The barristers were laughing. His mind was made up.

'Bring the jury back.'

'M'lud, may I?' Scott got up. Now he was going to fight back. 'May I explain what has just happened to my client?'

'Of course, Mr Scott.'

Scott threaded his way towards her. She sat in the chair which was bolted to the floor.

He leaned against the side of the dock. She didn't move.

'Come here Ellie,' he whispered.

She didn't want to speak to him. She didn't move.

'Come on, Ellie.'

She got up and walked the two steps to where he was.

He touched her hand where it lay on the rail.

'It's all over,' he said. 'You're going home.'

Chapter Six

'I was going to argue that there wasn't enough evidence to convict her of attempted murder at this stage. I didn't think that I had any argument at all on whether she was involved in the assault. I wasn't just going to argue about that.'

'That was obvious from the look on your face when the judge interrupted you.'

'I mean, it seemed clear to me that there was a case against her on stabbing him. It was only whether she intended to murder him that I could argue at this stage. So when the judge started suggesting that there was no evidence to suggest she had done anything wrong at all, I couldn't work out for a moment what he meant. Then I realised and had to switch.'

'So we noticed.'

'Well, if you noticed it, I hope no one else did. The judge must think I am a complete berk.'

'If it's any comfort to you, I didn't see it either. If someone picks someone else up in a fight and holds them helpless and bang, a knife goes in, that sounds like a guilty act, whether you call it an *actus reus* or use ordinary English. But then he turned to me and said his mind was made up. What was I to do? Lie on the ground and kick my heels? No, give in gracefully, I say. Do you think he fancied her?'

'Well, I was astonished. What do you think the jury thought when the judge said, "Since when has helping someone up been an offence?" I'm withdrawing this case from your consideration.'

'I don't think he cares. He's doing what he thinks is right. He's good enough not to care. And too old to fancy her.'

'One or two of the jury looked surprised.'

'I don't think they were – after what you did to Donald and what the little boy said.'

'What the boy said is that she picked him up and the man stabbed him just here.' Scott put his finger just above his heart. 'A little lower and he would have been dead.'

'Yes. Well, there is that,' the prosecutor replied. 'But we can't get it right all the time, can we?'

'I understand you were seen kissing, sir, outside the Old Bailey,' the junior clerk said.

Scott had pressed his nose up against the glass of the clerks' door before he came in to see who was there. He found them all there, looking at him.

'How did you know that so quickly?' Scott had walked back from the Old Bailey to chambers only moments ago.

'Some achieve kissing and some have kissing thrust upon them,' said Brian. He was standing there opening his mail and looking at Scott over his glasses. 'Our understanding back here at the nerve centre is that you had kissing thrust upon you.'

'How on earth do you lot know what happened?'

'We have our ways, sir,' said the junior clerk, tapping his nose. 'This is a small town and you can't make a public display of yourself without us knowing.'

Harry was leaning back in his seat enjoying this.

Emma walked in. 'Even I have never been kissed outside the Old Bailey for everyone to see,' she said.

'Who told you?'

'Everyone in chambers knows.'

Scott was amused. Five years ago he would have been angry to be teased like this, and might have walked out. But that was another set of chambers, and another country. Living with Catherine had changed him.

Philomena came in smiling her lopsided smile. 'What have you been doing, then?'

'His gorgeous client kissed him outside the Old Bailey in front of all the cameras.'

A phone rang and was answered.

The first junior said, 'Tosswill's are on the phone. They want to know who kissed you outside the Bailey and can they have a copy of the photograph?'

'What photograph?' Scott said.

Everybody laughed. The junior clerk said, 'One of those photographers who hang around outside the Bailey rang. You know, the evil bunch who know everything that's going on. He rang and asked about you. He wanted to know all about you.'

'Well, I hope you said nothing.'

'Only to Tosswill's.'

Harry intervened. 'You do remember, sir, you're meant to be at Holloway in half an hour.'

'Oh God,' said Scott, 'I'd forgotten.'

'Well, we don't want you throwing away the work that the clerks' room got you, do we, sir?'

'I wouldn't dare do that, Harry,' Scott said.

Monty Bach was there before him. Scott could see him waiting in the area by the thick plate-glass window. He stopped his car at the barrier and waved. A prison van pulled up behind him. Scott could see the women who ran the entrance office looking at him through the window. Monty was talking to them.

Still they wouldn't let the barrier up. Scott sat there for a moment, then Monty made a sign for him to come over.

He had to get out of the car and walk over to the office. 'We can't just let anyone in, can we, sir?' the prison officer said when Scott gave his name and what he wanted. Why they couldn't take Monty's word for it I don't know, he thought, as he went back to the car. There were now two prison vans and a taxi waiting.

The prison service always managed to set the precise tone of a prison visit within seconds of one's arrival. 'This is not a free place and you're only here under sufferance,' they were saying, and they would go on saying it all the time he was there. Since it was true, Scott reasoned, they had a right to say it. But there was no doubt that some prisons enjoyed making it as difficult as possible for lawyers to see their clients. Perhaps they thought that if they let too many lawyers in the prison population would drop, which of course was contrary to official Home Office policy.

Scott said nothing and grinned cheerily as eventually the barrier was raised.

They walked through the entrance hall, a strange room, obviously designed for a specific purpose, but in which Scott had never seen anything happen. Clearly whatever did happen there happened away from any prying eyes. They signed themselves in. Monty surrendered his mobile phone and they ended up in a small glass booth waiting for the client.

Scott and Monty looked at each other.

'This is a difficult woman, Mr Scott,' Monty said.

After a while there was a shuffling noise. The door opened

and a woman wearing what looked like a dressing gown appeared. She clutched it tightly to her throat and at the waist.

She stood at the door and looked around.

'Is it just us?' she said.

Monty looked around the small room, no bigger than a large lift, and said, 'Yes. It's just us, Miss Forgan.'

'Are there any tape recorders?'

'No tape recorders, Miss Forgan.'

'Who is this?'

'This is Mr Scott. You remember we spoke on the phone and I said I would be coming with him tonight?'

The prison officer had stood patiently behind the woman, holding the door handle while this conversation took place in the open door.

'Come on, Hilda,' she said. 'These are the ones you wanted to see.'

The effect was astonishing. The woman spun round and snarled into the officer's face, 'I won't be hurried.' Her voice had gone up at least three octaves.

For all the time that Scott knew her after that he never saw her do such a thing again, but he always remembered it.

'OK, Hilda.' The prison officer didn't take the woman's reaction as an opportunity for confrontation. That was good. Scott had seen officers do that, putting themselves and the prisoner on the same level. Instead she merely contained the anger. 'All right, Hilda,' she said, raising her eyebrows at Scott and Monty, 'take your time.'

The woman moved into the small cubicle. 'I won't be rushed,' she repeated, now talking as she had before in a low monotone. 'I allowed myself to be rushed before and look where it got me.'

She sat down opposite Scott at the Formica table. She didn't look at him. From her dressing gown she pulled a sheaf of notes. Scott could see that they were covered in intense, tiny handwriting.

'This is Mr Scott, Miss Forgan,' Monty repeated. He tried to sound normal.

'I hope he's not like the other ones.'

Monty said nothing.

'You got Ellie off.'

Scott was astonished. How did she know?

'Ellie was a friend of mine. She said you were all right.'

'All right' was one of those expressions like 'ignorant' that had a much stronger meaning in prisons and courts than they did in a world where relationships were much less intense. It was a word for a world where you sometimes had to trust people whom you barely knew, and trust them totally.

'Ellie didn't come back on the bus. We all expected her back. I was only told about it, since I don't see her any more, now that I'm a murderess. But word gets round quickly here.'

Scott had barely time to take in what she was saying. When Hilda Forgan started talking, she didn't stop.

Scott sat and waited. It was getting very hot. He scratched his knee under the table, took out a pen and a notebook and made some marks on it. None of this disturbed Hilda Forgan.

Scott turned to Monty, who made a face at him. It was in full view of the woman but she took not the slightest notice and carried on talking. At one point Hilda Forgan turned over the notes in front of her, though she didn't seem to be reading from them. Her speech was more like a recitation.

Scott guessed she carried this monologue in her head with her, all day, every day. Wherever she went it would be flowing just beneath the surface, ready to be voiced.

He had to sit and listen because any interruption would seem like an assault to her. He had to keep his eyes on her and wait for the exact moment. There would probably be only one short instant to get through. If he missed it he would have to wait and wait again.

After a long while, still talking, Hilda Forgan raised her face and looked at him. Her eyes were uncertain. Until then she had kept her eyes on the table and Scott had not seen them. They were rimmed with redness and she was blinking regularly.

She met Scott's eyes fully. For a moment there was hesitation, and then she held his gaze. At last she was speaking directly to him. She continued talking while Scott held her eyes with his.

'On one side attacking me there's the great I AM, who walked around with that stupid grin on his face. I watched him. And on my side I have a lawyer, who tells me what to do. Why should I listen to to him? Because I'm new. I've never been in a court before and of course I listened to what he had to say. Who wouldn't?'

Scott seized the opportunity. 'Ellie said she had met you. She said how much help you had been to her.'

The sharp change of subject cut through the stifling monologue. Scott had guessed who this woman was as he had sat listening to her.

He said, 'She said to me that there was someone who had made it possible for her to survive in here – that was you. She sends her love. She wishes she could see you again.'

'Ellie. She was such a sweet child.'

Hilda Forgan looked at Scott.

He reached out his hand towards her. He didn't touch her – that would have been too much. 'I'm here to help you, Miss Forgan,' he said, 'but you have to be strong.

Please try and listen to me. I'm going to try to put right
what has gone wrong.'

She stared at him. She had no words for this.

For a moment Scott had her attention. 'I need to know
what has happened. I need to know everything. And then
we need to work together. But first I have to ask some
questions. If you can, please, just answer the questions.
Later you can tell me everything as you want to.'

She nodded at him. Her eyes were full of tears.

'You were charged with murder?'

'Yes.'

'And convicted?'

'Yes.'

'Who was it they said you killed?'

'My aunt.'

'How did she die?'

'A hairdryer in the bath.'

'I understand from what you said earlier that she was
very ill?'

'Yes. She was crippled. Disabled, they call it now. Those
social workers and people come round and tell me . . .'

'Miss Forgan, please, you're leaving me behind. Please
slow down for a moment.'

Scott held his hands up and then said, 'She couldn't leave
the wheelchair?'

'No.'

'How do you think it happened?'

'She killed herself.'

'How?'

'She got the hairdryer while I was out of the room.'

'Did you say this at your trial?'

'No.'

'Why not?'

'Because he wouldn't let me, that's why. Because I wasn't

allowed to. He used expressions just like you're using. He said, "Please don't go on, Miss Forgan. Don't go on." He decided that she wasn't able to move to get the dryer.'

Scott risked contradicting her. 'But you just told me yourself that she couldn't move.'

'You're doing it too. Of course she couldn't move. You're doing it. But this time she did move. Just because we believe something is so, it doesn't mean it is so.'

Scott sat still. This was a bit too much like the station clock at ten to four.

'You mean you think your aunt moved and managed to kill herself?'

Hilda Forgan wept.

'We talked about it. I loved my aunt. We used to read the articles by all those people who talk about it. You know, Ludovic Kennedy and the like. We so admired them. They were strong people who made decisions about their lives. We said why can't we? Of course, I couldn't talk about that to the court, and my lawyer didn't want to listen. "It's not relevant," he said. "She couldn't move, the doctors say so, so if you didn't do it, it must have been an accident. The prosecution are going to have great difficulty in proving it was not an accident. So let's not confuse the jury with other possibilities." '

She suddenly set off again: 'Confuse the jury! Why should the jury be confused? It was the truth. How could the jury be confused? If the thing were in a play then they would sit and accept it. None of them would get up and go out of the room saying, "This is nonsense, everyone knows a cripple can't move." No, they would have accepted that there are things happening that we don't understand. What about those people who wake up after years of being in a coma? What about them? What does that say about doctors?

'She wanted to end it all. She really wanted to and when

you really want something you can do it. I've been teaching that to children all my life. So why can't I stand up and say so in court?'

Scott locked his eyes on her again.

'I need you to stop now, Miss Forgan. I want to ask you some questions about something different. The papers. We haven't got any case papers.'

He turned to Monty to confirm this. 'Mr Bach hasn't got any yet, he's trying to get them out of the previous solicitors. But, Miss Forgan, you've got some, haven't you?'

Scott put his hand out gently to where he could see a court transcript in the confused bundle of papers in front of her.

'Can I take this for a moment?' He looked Hilda Forgan in the eyes directly again. 'May I just look?' He knew how precious these documents became and he was prepared for an outburst. But she let him slide the paper away from under her arm. He picked the document up. It felt warm.

The pages were covered with dense writing, at first in a neat italic but then overlaid with wilder and wilder printing in Biro. There were heavy underlinings and exclamations in the margins. 'No! no! no!'

Underneath the frenzied additions, the transcript of the judge's suave summing-up marched down the numbered and lettered pages. Scott knew it was suave since Mr Justice Savlin's summings-up to the jury were always suave. He needed only to read the first few paragraphs to remind himself of the man's style. The beginning set out in balanced eighteenth-century prose the various things that he, the judge, was about to say, almost as though it had been written in a classical study surrounded by books, maps, globes and quill pens – which, of course, it had.

The trouble was the jury wouldn't have been able to understand a word of it.

'*Ladies and gentlemen of the jury: I am the judge of the law and you must take the law from me, as I set it out for your consideration. If I am wrong then you may be sure I shall be corrected in another place.*' It was almost possible to hear the mocking inflection conveying the utter absurdity of such a thing happening, as though he could possibly be wrong! '*You yourselves, and you only, are the sole judges of fact.*'

It wasn't that it was unclear. Of course it wasn't. In fact, it was the standard direction. It was just that by the time the jury got used to such ideas, by the time they had chewed up the cadences and swallowed them, the judge would have been half a page further on.

What would have been wrong with saying, '*In order to come to a proper decision in this case you need to know the law. My job is to tell you what it is*' . . . ? But of course High Court judges didn't see what they did as a job, more as a state of being.

Scott ran his eye down the document. It was a full and careful rehearsal of the case. It was clear that the facts themselves were not immensely complicated. The medical evidence was summed up in a few lines – '*it is agreed on all sides that this unfortunate lady could not move unaided*'.

This was OK. Scott was going to be able to get a good overview of the case from the summing-up alone – but how was he going to get it away from Hilda Forgan?

'You've done this really well, Miss Forgan,' he said. He was amused to see that she had caught the judge out on a split infinitive.

'Ellie told me you were a schoolteacher.'

'Yes, I was,' she said.

'You can see that by the care you've taken with these corrections. Look, do you think I could borrow this? It will give me lots to be going on with.'

89

'I want it back. It proves what has gone wrong with my case, you know.'

'I'm sure it does, Miss Forgan.'

And she was right.

Because if there was anything in the medical point, if he could prove the dead woman could have moved, then it would certainly help her.

'You're right, Monty,' Scott said when they got outside. 'A difficult woman hardly begins to describe her.'

Monty laughed. 'Just your sort of client, Mr Scott.'

Scott was amused. That was a better estimate of what he was good at than the idea that he was a great Court of Appeal lawyer. It was only the clients who were interesting in this job.

He said, 'But what about the medical evidence?'

'I've got a doctor coming in to see you tomorrow.'

'Who was in the case? Who were the solicitors?'

Monty was buttoning up his huge black astrakhan coat, the collar framing his face like a ruff. Scott looked at him. Dressed like that, Monty could get mugged, right outside Holloway prison. Or perhaps some animal rights group, worried about unborn Persian lambs, would descend on them and tear the coat from his back.

Monty said, 'I wanted you to meet her before you finally decided whether you would do the case. She asked for you.'

He was clearly about to say 'I tried to dissuade her', but he didn't.

'Well, of course I'll take it, though I don't give it much chance. It depends. Who were the solicitors?'

'Munro Wilson's. A bit of a doubtful bunch, I always feel.'

That was a bit rich coming from Monty.

Scott said, 'But they get good counsel.'

'So do we,' said Monty sniffily.

Scott nearly made a joke about Tozer, who regularly acted for Monty, but then remembered that this man was one of Tozer's friends.

'Who did they get for Miss Forgan?'

'Galbraith.'

'Galbraith! Bloody hell! You mean I have to go in front of the Lord Chief Justice and tell him Galbraith got it wrong?' Scott rocked on his heels. 'The Lord Chief Justice was Galbraith's pupil. Galbraith pretty well taught him all he knows.'

Scott spun round, looking up at the night sky over north London, a dirty orange colour. A huge truck clattered past, and a big, incurious bus lumbered by on its way to Hornsey.

'I've never even been *in* a case with Galbraith. Good God, I might as well go back in and tell her to get on and do her fifteen years or whatever it is. Monty, Monty . . . where do you find them?'

Monty was pulling on a pair of black gloves, but changed his mind and unbuttoned his coat and jacket. He started rummaging in his waistcoat.

Scott said, 'Monty, what are you doing? Are you going to sniff that dreadful stuff here? Don't.'

A Securicor van pulled up at the barrier near where they were standing.

'Don't, Monty, the only thing that's sniffed like that in this part of London is cocaine. They'll drag you away and beat you with clubs.'

'Well, if they do,' said Monty, taking an almighty sniff, 'they'll have a big bill for damages.'

Whooomph. He sneezed with pure joy.

'Galbraith. Galbraith,' Monty said. 'I made Geoffrey

Godfrey Twistleton Galbraith. I made him. All those years ago.'

The London traffic roared past them.

'What goes around comes around,' said Monty.

He sniffed again and followed it with another shattering sneeze. Scott gazed up towards the Hubble Deep Space Telescope and wondered.

Chapter Seven

Scott shook hands with the doctor across his desk and then sat back to look at him.

Monty Bach, on one side of the desk, was fussing around. For an instant his hand went to his waistcoat snuff pocket but then, being in Scott's room, he changed his mind.

Dr Wilson wasn't dressed like a doctor, though why Scott should think that he couldn't work out. How were doctors meant to dress?

Dr Wilson was smart, though he was not wearing a suit. He looked more like a film director or a journalist than a doctor, slightly happy-go-lucky, wearing the kind of clothes that would suit an airport or some town in a war zone. The effect was heightened by the metal case he was carrying. It was the kind of case photographers carry, ribbed like an American trailer. It was open on the floor and he was getting his papers out. Scott wondered whether the confusing uniform was intentional.

He glanced at the doctor's qualifications again. FRCPsych and FRCP. A fellow of the Royal College of Psychiatrists and the Royal College of Physicians. That was pretty good, especially at his age. He couldn't be much more than, say, early forties.

Then Scott realised this was another thing that was wrong

about him, if you could call it wrong. He was much older than he looked. He was nearer fifty, even fifty-five. Yet he was dressed like a man of thirty-five.

People, and by people Scott meant judges, didn't like that. They might not even realise what was 'wrong', but a judge listening to Dr Wilson wouldn't have the feeling of security that should go with being lectured by an expert. His mere presence would present a challenge to the normal order of things.

Scott wondered for a moment what would happen if he asked him to put on a pair of half-glasses. That would cure everything.

Dr Wilson finished getting his papers out of his brief-case. 'Well, here we are, then,' he said lightly. 'What a cock-up.'

'Is it?'

'Of course it is.'

Scott was immediately wary. Finding an independent person who agrees with your case, especially if he is an expert, can be dangerously intoxicating.

'Tell me about it.'

'Where do you want me to start?'

'Wherever you want.'

'One of the first questions I would ask if I walked into this situation is why the old biddy was in a wheelchair in the first place. Was it because she wanted to be there?'

This was different. Scott said, 'Go on.'

'The problem may well be not whether she could get up and walk, but whether she wanted to get up and walk.'

'You mean she might have been quite capable of moving all the time?'

'No, I didn't say that. I don't know. But it is the first question I would ask.'

'Presumably her doctors asked that?'

'Not necessarily. I'm a psycho-geriatrician, so it's my job to ask these questions. General practitioners don't ask those questions, they haven't got time. They certainly don't ask us, not if the matter seems straightforward.'

He smiled at Scott. 'Many doctors are as ignorant of psychiatry as you are of the law of trusts. They know it exists but they haven't much use for it.'

Scott's suspicion mounted inexorably.

'How can we tell whether this question was asked?'

'We can't. Unless we see the notes.'

'Well, we've already asked for them.'

'Yes, I know.'

'But what do you mean? She wanted to be in a wheel-chair?'

The doctor spoke more seriously.

'This is my guess,' he said. 'I don't know if I am right. I would have had to talk to her. But my guess is that she felt she was useless, of no use to anybody, of no use for anything. She'd probably been feeling that way for some years, perhaps since her husband died.'

The force of the doctor's experience communicated itself to Scott.

'She had no grandchildren so there was no role for her there. And, feeling she was useless, she decided to *be* useless. In the old-fashioned phrase, she took to her bed.'

'But all the tests, clinical tests . . .'

'Tests, shmests. Rubbish. Of course there are tests. Tests are designed to explain what is the case, not why it is the case. We know bits of her were atrophied, but who atrophied them? She did.

'But then when she came to the conclusion that she was really useless, all her self-worth gone, every drop of it, something more important came along, more important

95

than the need to act useless – the need to die. So she gets up and walks. And dies.'

This was extraordinary. Scott was astonished.

The doctor continued, 'She was lucky, she managed it. She might have fallen over a few feet from the chair and then none of us would be here. If she had been found out of her wheelchair it would have gone down as one of those inexplicable things that sometimes happen – anecdotal information, the kind of stuff that gathers on my desk. And because no one needs to do anything about it, there is nothing done about it. The kind of stories nurses tell over their cocoa.'

Scott didn't say anything. It was clear that Dr Wilson was beginning to enjoy the effect he was having. That was another reason not to trust him – there was too great a desire to shock wrapped up in his opinion.

'What is really paradoxical is that since this sort of thing is in itself inexplicable, it's not included in the literature. It's not accounted for since no one needs to account for it, so it's not the sort of thing for which you can have a control study. If all the odd things I hear about had to be accounted for, then I wouldn't have the time for anything else.'

Scott looked at the man. He would never do in the witness box, and certainly not in the Court of Appeal. The doctor carried on talking, looking straight at Scott, almost laughing at him. Scott wondered, 'Is he teasing me?'

Dr Wilson said, 'But in this case the inexplicable thing happened and the one group of people for whom nothing can ever be allowed to remain inexplicable is the police. Detective Inspector Whatsit and his jolly men. For them, if something is odd, then there's only ever one real cause: someone's bad behaviour. So they look for a motive. Who inherits? they ask.

'There's nothing policemen enjoy more than attributing

bad motives to other people. Of course, they're not to blame for that, they do it because it justifies their existence and so on and so on . . . down to us. You and me. And that's why we're sitting here now.'

Scott tried to get him back on the subject.

'You mean you've known people with this illness get up and walk?'

'Dozens.'

'Really?' Scott was shocked.

'Look, by that I mean I've seen dozens of things happen that are not explicable in terms of a person's particular illness. This woman's illness *was* not getting up and walking. The illness changed, that's all. In fact, if it happens enough then eventually you change the diagnosis. It's not what happens that is odd. What's odd is our belief that we can provide a complete explanation for everything that happens. We can't allow ourselves to remain in a state of indecision, where paradox is normal.

'Modern physicists are happy with that. Poets do it all the time – Keats did. But not the rest of us – and especially not judges. For a judge a paradox is something that's got to be flattened out and explained. They love doing that.

'I've seen deaf people who have heard things. And what is just as interesting, I've seen people who have good hearing who haven't heard something. But of course, as a lawyer, your only reaction would be suspicion, especially of the second group. Even though these things happen in your work, you don't notice them.

'Think – have you worked in a shop? How often do people leave what they've just bought on the counter?' Dr Wilson answered his own question. 'All the bloody time. I've worked in a shop, it's a real pain in the neck. And of course we think nothing of it. But turn it around. If you take something and then forget to pay for it, why, that's not forgetfulness, that's dishonesty. You're a shoplifter. Hocus-pocus, let's make an arrest.' He moved his hands around, let the remark hang in the air and then said, 'Of course, it's complicated by the fact that there are lots of people who *are* shoplifters.'

At last, a bit of reality, Scott thought.

'And further complicated by there being people whose job it is to catch them, who don't believe in the notion of forgetfulness.'

Dr Wilson was determined, it seemed, always to say the thing that would make a judge immediately turn away and refuse to listen.

Scott had to see if it was possible to make any of this information useful.

'Dr Wilson, have you been told the precise situation we have here?'

'I have an outline, but it's not complete. I know she's been convicted.'

'Yes. She's been convicted. We're now in the Court of Appeal, renewing our application to be allowed to appeal. The only basis for an appeal is to argue that the jury ought to have considered if this woman could have moved or not. That was never considered.

'Let me get the passage for you from the judge's summing-up.'

Scott got out a photocopy of the document he had received from Hilda Forgan.

'Here we are, page six at D . . . He says, this is Mr Justice Savlin speaking, *"Here is the crux of the matter. Was it an accident or was it the deliberate intentional act of someone who knew that, if the hairdryer went into the water, it would kill Mrs Beatty? In short, was it the act of the defendant, since the defendant was the only person with access to the house at that time?"* Mrs Beatty is the aunt,' Scott said looking up.

'I assumed so,' said Dr Wilson.

'It is also agreed on all sides that Mrs Beatty could not have done this herself. You do not therefore have to consider that possibility. Thankfully, therefore, you do not have to consider whether that unfortunate lady intended to commit suicide or to kill herself in this awful way, a prospect, I think you will agree, members of the jury, almost too dreadful to contemplate.'

'Well, of course, Savlin is a Catholic.'

'Is he?' said Scott. 'How do you know that.'

'I just know. I think I read it somewhere.' Wilson laughed. 'Why is the possibility of the lady committing suicide "almost too dreadful to contemplate", while being murdered by her niece is perfectly contemplatable? If there is such a word.'

Scott refused to get caught up in this. He said, 'But that's the situation. The possibility of the lady doing it to herself was just not an issue in the case. "*Agreed on all sides*": that's a way of saying that the defence chose not to call evidence on the subject, nor to contradict the Crown doctors.

'Now, the general rule is that you cannot call fresh evidence on appeal if that evidence was available to you at the first trial. So, even if we can produce evidence that the aunt could have got up and danced, they can refuse to hear it.'

'You don't mean that?' The doctor looked more surprised now than at anything Scott had said up till then.

'Yes,' said Scott. 'After that the only path of appeal would be a request to the Home Secretary to refer the case for an appeal. If he thinks there was a miscarriage of justice, that is. Different rules apply then.

'This evidence was clearly available to the defence, they just decided not to go with that argument. The only thing we can do now is to show that it is so convincing we ought to be allowed to call it on appeal.'

Dr Wilson said, 'You always have to blame someone, don't you? What if it was just a mistake? What if counsel's decision was wrong? After all, even judges make mistakes. That's the whole point of the Court of Appeal itself.'

'I'm sorry, Dr Wilson, there's no point in debating that side of it. I was just trying to say that even if we can find good medical evidence to show she could have killed herself, we may not be able to call it. But we do need a statement to put before the court, at least for the judges to look at, so they can begin to consider whether counsel was wrong in not calling the evidence. We have at least to demonstrate to them what we're on about.' Scott hesitated. 'Now what you tell me is very interesting, but . . .'

The doctor was on to the hesitation immediately.

'But the Court of Appeal wouldn't think so?'

'No, or rather yes.' Scott decided to tell the truth. 'You must know what they're like. They don't like generalities, they hate generalities, and they certainly don't like grand concepts. Grand concepts make them act like old men sitting in a draught – they get all fidgety. We've got to put it in order. We need research references, we need examples, we need an analysis of the medical notes, but most of all, Dr Wilson, we need support from a neurologist or someone. A hands-on doctor. Someone whom the court will like, someone who thinks all psychiatrists are as mad as you think lawyers are. They might listen then.'

The doctor had been perfectly pleasant all the time. He just thought lawyers were absurd and had enjoyed saying so.

'He won't do, Monty. At least not just him. We've got to have someone with a bit of gravitas, someone the judges can feel at home with. You know they are going to be jumpy with this case, especially if people start talking about counsel's mistakes. Dr Wilson doesn't realise that. Judges are allowed to make mistakes, but barristers aren't. If a barrister makes a mistake in a trial you can't appeal on it unless you show it was grossly incompetent. This clearly wasn't that – it was a simple decision. No one is to blame for it, it was just a decision.'

Monty said, 'Well, we're going to have to talk about that.' Scott could see he wasn't convinced.

'Was that little Monty Bach?' a voice boomed out behind Scott.

It was Douglas Gatling, the head of Scott's chambers.

'Hallo, Douglas. Yes, it was, and his doctor expert.'

'I didn't know Monty came here any more.'

'I don't think he does. This is a one-off,' Scott said.

'That's good.'

Unaccountably, Douglas didn't move away. Normally Scott and Gatling didn't have much to say to each other.

Gatling looked down at Scott from his enormous height. 'You know Monty's reputation,' he said.

'I can't refuse to work for him,' Scott said, staring at Gatling's waistcoat. Why did the man have to wear waistcoats that were embroidered along the hem? Especially when the top button was at most people's eye level.

'Of course not. Scott, have you accepted this Forgan case?'

Scott was amazed. Since when had Douglas been interested in, or even aware of, what work he did?

'You must know,' Gatling said, 'I refused the brief. Watkins and Jellaby offered it to me. But I thought it better to turn it down. You must know that.'

Scott was divided between curiosity as to Douglas's reasons for refusing the work and annoyance at the man's self-satisfied assumption that everybody would know about what he did.

'If I thought it advisable to turn it down' – Gatling was beginning to repeat himself; Scott expected his hand to go to the lapel of his coat – 'then it would be better if the brief were not in chambers.'

'I can't help that,' said Scott. 'Harry tells me he accepted the brief before he knew what it was. Anyway, the lady, for some reason, asked for me personally, so I'm stuck with it.'

'Ye-es,' said Gatling, almost as though he were going to turn away in despair. But he didn't. 'May I enquire what you intend to do with it?'

For once in his life Scott saw the clever thing to do. 'Well, I was going to ask your advice about it,' he said, unctuously.

For a moment Gatling was shaken. 'Well, of course. I suppose if you are going to do it, at least we can talk about it. Why don't we go into my room. We can't really talk here, can we?'

He turned and went to his room. Scott saw that he almost had to duck to go through the door. He must have been at least six foot two tall, maybe more, and everything else about him was in proportion.

Gatling padded over to his desk, his long arms hanging motionless by his side, pulled his chair out, and sat down.

'Good to see you, Jeremy. We don't see enough of you. You and' – he paused and then took a guess – 'you and Catherine ought to come to lunch some time. Please take a seat.'

He waved a hand grandly at the room. All the chairs were against the far wall and Scott had to go to collect one. As he picked it up, he looked at the table beside the chairs. On it there was a series of silver-framed photographs – Gatling's wife, Lady Marjorie, and several other smaller photographs of children. The Spratlings and the Gatlings, as he had heard Douglas refer to them heartily. The man's confidence in the reality of his existence was all over him, like lather on a racehorse.

'This brief was touted round the Temple for weeks. Didn't you know that?'

Scott was carrying the chair, so he didn't need to answer.

'The woman is quite mad. She wants to say that she was incompetently represented. And everyone knows she was not. She got the very best of representation.'

The way he emphasised 'the very best of' as though it were one word told Scott that he was about to hear about 'Rolls-Royce treatment'.

Douglas suddenly shot out a drawer. He pulled out a packet of cigars and started to unwrap one of them. 'She got Rolls-Royce treatment,' he said, 'and she knows it, Scott. Oh yes, she knows it.'

It was extraordinary. If Douglas had been parodying himself he could not have made a better start.

Scott watched as Gatling began to rotate the huge cigar in his mouth, occasionally giving off little inchoate cries of pleasure as he expelled the smoke.

'Mwah', twist, 'mwah', another twist. 'She doesn't know just how well off she was. Munro Wilson's defended her, and you don't know, mwah,' – his voice skittered up and down an octave – 'mwah, just how damn good they are when they really try.'

Gatling held out the used match towards Scott, who nearly took it from him, but was prevented from doing so when Gatling dropped it straight down into a large ashtray sitting on the table between them.

'She don't damn well know how well off she was, Scott.' He sounded like Mr Sponge on a Rural Ride.

A long pause, then he barked out, 'Galbraith. She had

Galbraith, for heaven's sake. You can count them on your fingers: Durand. Hutchinson. Gilly Grey. Jimmy Comyn. And of course Galbraith.' He threw five fingers of an outstretched hand out towards Scott.

'The best advocates of their generation.' Another pause. 'You can't even brief Geoff Galbraith now. He just comes to court now and again. He appears.'

Scott stared in front of him. He had obviously stumbled across an atavistic loyalty. To suggest that Galbraith was wrong wasn't just unlikely, it was an attack on the very foundations that supported people like Gatling.

He ventured a remark. 'So that's why people refused it?'

'Damn right it was.'

'What if I don't attack him? In fact, why should I? The way he decided to do the case was probably the right decision at the time.'

'The court will assume you are attacking him whatever you do. And if they don't the prosecution will make it seem you are.'

'Why do they have to think about it? It's whether the conviction was right that matters, isn't it? Not people's feelings.'

The tension was becoming so great for Gatling that he got up to slough it off. He walked out past the desk, for a moment blotting out all the light in the room, and went over to where the photograph of his wife was.

He picked up the silver frame and looked at it, then set it down with a bang. He started to move away but, realising that he had not put it back in the correct position, he readjusted it. Scott watched as the huge man bent down to realign the picture, just so. He doubted whether Gatling was even aware of his presence any more. He was more concerned with propitiating his gods.

'And now she is whining to the Court of Appeal about something she fully agreed with. She' – Gatling searched for the word – 'she concurred,' he said explosively, as though he were now able to describe the ultimate act of obeisance. 'She concurred,' he repeated in a frenzy, 'in what Geoff Galbraith decided. And now she is whining that she didn't understand.'

Gatling transformed his voice into what he thought was a woman's whining voice and shook his head from side to side in imitation of a middle-aged spinster.

Scott was flabbergasted, what could he say? He tried to be conciliatory. 'This was all round the Temple, was it?'

'She insulted him. She demanded to see him. Geoffrey G. went to Holloway and she insulted him and sacked him. Galbraith said, "I don't have to take this from you, madam" – Munro said he was very polite, you'd expect nothing less from Geoffrey – and she said, "You don't have to. I'm sacking you."'

Scott suppressed a huge bubble of laughter.

'And she went to Jellaby's. And they couldn't cope with her. So she sacked them too. And now she's gone to Monty Bach, and he's gone . . .' Gatling stopped himself a split second before he said 'and he's gone to you'. He changed tack. 'And now the brief has come to these chambers. My chambers.

'I need a drink.' He turned and made for a small cupboard behind where Scott was sitting. Scott looked around him. The room had clearly been furnished from Peter Jones, lock, stock and barrel. There were fresh flowers on the drinks cabinet. Did chambers supply those? he wondered.

He sat quite still. It wasn't clear whether Douglas was going to offer him anything, but when he turned round the man had two whiskies in large thick-cut glass tumblers. Scott took his and felt its weight in his hand.

A man of substance, he thought to himself. Here is a drink of substance from a man of substance. He put the glass down. It made a solid clunk as he did so.

Gatling looked at him as though he were anxious that Scott was about to behave really badly, and said, 'Well, what is to be done?'

This scene must have been acted out in the past, acted and re-enacted in dozens of studies, colonels' rooms, messrooms and senior common rooms throughout the country – whenever a damn mess had had to be cleared up.

And it could be cleared up, of that there was no doubt, as long as everybody played the game and didn't let the side down. Gatling was about to tell him that.

Chapter Eight

' "Right-thinking people." Did he really say that? Did he add anything about all men of goodwill?'

'He said "right-thinking people", yes. The rest he didn't say out loud, but that's what it all meant. He said he would approach Galbraith and tell him how the brief came to me.'

'You mean he's going to apologise for you?' She laughed.

'No.'

Scott looked at Catherine. She was getting at him again. This seemed to be happening a lot recently.

'Why do you hate me?' He dramatised it.

'I don't hate you. That's only your paranoia talking. Don't be silly.'

She held him for a moment, though perfunctorily. He could still feel her annoyance. She said, 'I just wonder why you get yourself into these situations. You're entirely the wrong person to take on the Establishment. You're not the brave, rebellious sort, you like an easy life.'

'I'm not taking on the Establishment. I'm merely saying her conviction was wrong.'

'Of course you're taking on the Establishment. Things don't exist in a vacuum.'

'Well, it wasn't my fault. The bloody woman chose me

to act for her, I didn't go looking for her. I'm not some crusading lawyer.'

'But you should have known about what you were taking on.'

This was Gatling all over again.

'How should I have known?'

'Because, as he said, it was all over the Bar. Of course it was. Why were you the only person not to know about it? You're always saying you find out changes in the law by osmosis, by meeting people. Why couldn't you find out about this?'

'I don't know. How does one find out about these things?'

'Talk to people. Gossip, for God's sake. Chat about other people, who's who and what they're doing. Some people do nothing else. Look at Tozer. But you, you never talk to anybody, you never even talk to me, and you certainly never talk to the people you work with. You've got no small talk.'

'I do talk.'

'Oh yes, to your friend Ronnie Knox in El Vino, but not to anyone else, and you only talk to him because he lectures you on Catholic philosophy.' She sat down with a flounce. 'I've seen you. If anyone speaks to you, you either think they're insulting you or laughing at you.'

'They generally are.' Scott tried to stop the argument with a half-joke, but it didn't really work.

Catherine said, 'Well, what's going to happen, then?'

'Douglas Gatling is going to speak to Galbraith and tell him how I got the brief. Wait . . .' he said as she opened her mouth. 'He's not going to apologise. I told him there's nothing to apologise for, but to tell him how it happened and to ask for his help.'

'No chance,' she said.

Scott moved away and started rummaging in the drinks cupboard in the hall. He couldn't remember – was there a bottle of wine there?

He went on, 'If Galbraith decided not to call a doctor then he must have had reasons. Perhaps when I see those reasons the whole thing will become clear. He must have written an advice, especially on a matter as important as that.'

He found three bottles, all three a quarter empty.

'Even Douglas, who thinks the sun shines out of Galbraith's backside, agrees on that.'

There wasn't an unopened bottle in the cupboard. Scott began wandering around the flat distractedly.

'When I see the advice I'll probably agree with it. Remember, if I think the case can't be argued in law, then I have to advise against it, which means returning the brief.'

'What are you looking for?'

'Where is it?'

'What?'

'The wine. I had a bottle of Beaujolais.'

'I hid it.'

'Where?'

'What would be the point of my telling you that?'

'Come on.'

'In the kitchen with the pans.'

He went to get it.

'You're drinking too much,' she said.

For a moment Scott was annoyed, but then he remembered that this was what living with someone was like. They were allowed to criticise you.

'You'll get fat,' she said.

But they didn't have to do it all the time.

Later in the evening he said, 'There's a dinner, a formal

dinner, to say goodbye to my old clerk, Bill. You know, the chambers I was in before I moved? Dinner jackets, wives, everything.' She looked at him. 'Significant others as well as wives,' he said.

'You mean you're suggesting we should go to it?'

'Yes.'

'You've never gone to one of those things before. You've always said you'd rather die than go to the criminal solicitors' dinner.'

'Yes, well . . .'

'You're trying to humour me.'

'Yes,' he said.

'I haven't got a thing to wear,' she said.

'Good Lord,' he said, 'we sound just like Horace Rumpole and his wife.'

Catherine went to bed and Scott sat watching the television. Then he remembered and got up. He went into the bedroom.

'Did I tell you about the phone call?'

'Are you coming in to make love to me?'

'No,' he said, and sat down next to her. 'I came to tell you about a phone call I got.'

He stopped and thought about it. How could the man have got his number?

'What, then? If you're stopping me from reading, at least tell me what it is.'

Scott looked at her book. Simone de Beauvoir: *The Second Sex*. That was a dangerous book to bring into a placid relationship. Maybe that was the reason it wasn't so placid any more.

'I got an anonymous phone call at chambers.'

'How did that happen?'

'Harry just put it through to me.'

'What did the caller say?'

'He said: "Don't think you're going to get away with it, helping her get off." '

'Is that all?'

'Yes. I said all the obvious things, like "Who is this?" "Who are you?" But that was all.'

'Good God.'

'I spluttered a bit and then he, it was a man, said it again. Same words.'

She pushed her spectacles up on to her forehead.

He said, 'How did he get my number? And how did he know I was going to do the case?'

'He gossiped with people.'

'Well, he didn't seem the gossipy sort to me.'

'There's gossip and gossip,' she said.

'You haven't asked whether it was frightening.'

'Well, was it?'

'Yes.'

Silence.

'You haven't asked why.'

She hadn't taken her eyes off his face and she was beginning to laugh.

'Why?'

'Because the idea of being disliked by someone completely anonymous is frightening. Let alone being threatened.'

'But you expect everybody to dislike you.'

'But that's for a reason.'

'What's that?'

'That's how it's always been.'

'Oh, give me a break,' she said, and went back to her book.

He watched her. She really was very beautiful. Suddenly she tipped her tongue just out of her mouth on to her lips.

'Why did you do that?'

'What.'

'Put your tongue out.'

'Did I?'

'Yes.'

'Don't know.'

Scott touched her on the neck just where her hair became wispy. She arched her shoulder slightly. Their grumpiness with each other was ebbing.

'In *Zorba the Greek* – have you seen *Zorba the Greek*? – Anthony Quinn gives Alan Bates a piece of advice. I remember wondering whether it would be of any use to me.'

He stopped.

After a pause she said 'Yes?' and looked at him. He leaned down and put his mouth near her ear. She couldn't see him, but was watching out of the corner of her eye.

'Did they allow *Zorba the Greek* to be shown where you come from, or was it un-American?'

'America is full of Greeks. Spiro Agnew was Greek.'

'Well, Anthony Quinn is an old Greek and Alan Bates is a young English Greek who doesn't know owt from barleycorn. What's that in American?'

'He doesn't know piss from pimento.'

'Very expressive. So Alan Bates has this woman fall for him. She wants to go to bed with him. Probably Melina Mercouri, or was it Sophia Loren? A woman who acted only with her mouth. And he doesn't know what to do.'

He stopped again.

'So?' She tapped her nail on the book. 'Is that it, or do I have to pay for another instalment?'

'And Anthony Quinn says, in a deep, deep voice, "If a woman calls you to her bed, you must go."'

'And?'

'That's it.'

'That's all? You stopped me reading for that?'

'Oh no. I was wondering whether Mrs Sartre had anything to say about that. Look in the index. Has it got an index?'

She lay there, holding the book.

He said, 'Maybe it's under "Bed, invitations to: women's rights" . . . A man may not refuse.'

She still said nothing. But Scott could see she was no longer annoyed with him.

'If it's a rule in Greece, maybe it's a rule in France.'

Nothing.

'It's certainly a rule in this country.'

She lay there. He could see she was waiting.

'I'm going to get into bed sideways. Like an existentialist,' he said, burrowing under the duvet.

Chapter Nine

Scott drove down to Sussex, where Mrs Beatty had lived, and where she had died in the bathroom. He had not known what to expect. Perhaps a red-brick cottage covered in roses?

The reality was much more ordinary. A side road turned off the major road into Upper Meadow, itself once just a large field, but which had now been covered in a series of tarmac loops and banjo-shaped closes. Obviously the shapes were designed to allow houses to be dotted about, to prevent anxious buyers thinking they were being fitted into the neat rows of a housing estate.

Some houses must have had four or five bedrooms and he guessed others had only two. These looked cheaply built, brick below, giving way to a wooden facing above. Some looked smart, others a little scruffy. Perhaps this was a highly desirable place to live? He was interested to see that he couldn't make the judgment, normally so easy to do. Maybe it was because he knew so much about the complex life that had been lived out in one of the houses. It made things seem less obvious.

Eventually he found the turning he wanted, Briar Close, and stopped his car. There were about six houses set around the loop, again some a little larger than others. All were of the same design, though the way in which the mixture of flat

115

roof, clapboard facing and tile had been used was different in each.

Each had a car parked, either in the garage at the top of a slope, or on the sloping drive outside the house itself. On the drive of the house to his left two small children were playing, with a tricycle and a plastic toy. For a moment Scott could not see what the toy was, then he saw it was a submachine-gun.

He had stopped outside number eight, Mrs Beatty's house. It wasn't unkempt. In fact the small front garden was perfectly well looked after, the winter flowering jasmine at the end well pruned into a tight ball, but the house itself was clearly not lived in. The varnish on the clapboard had darkened and the paint was beginning to peel in places.

There was no car outside. This was the only house with no tarmac, only paving designed to allow grass to grow up through it. This had the effect of setting the house apart. He sat outside and waited. He had arrived much earlier than he needed.

After a while he became aware that a man was approaching his car from behind. He didn't pass but tapped on the window. Scott wound the window down. The time it took to do so allowed him to adjust his usual spontaneous reaction, to one of simple politeness.

'I do hope you don't mind.' The man spoke in an educated, pleasant voice. 'We have had one or two problems here recently, and one can't be too careful. Can I help you? Are you looking for something?'

Scott was surprised at himself. He found it easy to be perfectly friendly towards this man. 'No, no,' he said, getting out of the car. 'As you say, nowadays you can't be too careful. I'll tell you who I am,' he said, shutting his car door.

By now the man would have noticed his formal suit, his

stiff collar, and perhaps relaxed a bit. Certainly the uniform set people at ease.

'I'm concerned with the unfortunate case that occurred at number eight.' It sounded like a line out of Agatha Christie. 'I'm meeting a policeman here to be shown some things.'

'I thought as much,' said the man. Scott could see him clearly now. Cavalry twill trousers, a checked wool shirt and a rough tweed jacket, precisely Sussex.

'We have had so much coming and going. But I thought now . . .' He paused. He clearly wanted to talk about it, yet he finished, '. . . it would be all over.'

Scott took the opportunity of getting the man to go on. 'No,' he said, and he fluttered his hands in the air in a way he knew would set the man at his ease. 'It isn't.' His hands demonstrated just how these things are difficult to explain. 'There's still a bit to go yet.'

'You mean the appeal?'

How far was this chap involved? It wasn't Scott's job to investigate the case, in fact the time for that was well past, but he was curious to know more.

'Yes, the appeal. Can I ask, did you know Mrs Beatty?'

The man was reluctant to speak immediately. 'Why, yes,' he said. Clearly embarrassed at being so forward, he asked, 'Look, may I know? You understand the press have been here.'

'Of course, of course, how rude of me,' Scott said, smothering the man's concern with understanding. This was how the middle classes communicated, by picking up the signals immediately and sending the right ones back.

'How foolish. You can't go chatting to just anybody. I am a lawyer. In fact I myself am a barrister. I have become involved in the case.'

The man had the old-fashioned respect for barristers. 'How nice,' he said.

But Scott had opened the door to the subject and was able to go on, 'Can I ask, did you know Mrs Beatty?'

'Why, yes. I knew her. Of course, my wife knew her very well. She used to sit with her sometimes. I can't say they were good friends, but my wife liked to help her. She was, you may know . . .' He paused, embarrassed, but his confidence in Scott's credentials was growing, '. . . she was a bit of a difficult woman.'

There was that phrase again.

'Well, I ought to tell you,' Scott said, knowing what he was doing now, 'I'm what you might call on the other side.' He smiled as he used the childish phrase to take the sting out of his words. 'I represent Miss Forgan, who was convicted . . .' He didn't finish the sentence. 'So I will understand if you feel . . .'

He stopped. The man's mouth had dropped open.

'You're on Hilda's side? You're looking after Hilda?' He looked away. 'Joan! Joan!' he shouted. 'Look, excuse me. Please don't think me rude. Could you wait a moment?'

He turned and ran.

Scott watched him hurry down the close and up one of the drives behind a car. He could hear him calling, 'Joan, Joany. Come quickly. There's a gentleman here.'

Scott was left standing on the pavement. He felt someone behind him. He turned slowly and found one of the small children threatening him with the submachine-gun.

'Ah, ha ha ha ha,' said the small boy, in imitation of rapid machinegun fire. 'You're dead.' Then he turned and walked away.

The man returned. He was carrying a sheet of paper in his hand, which he was waving. Behind him walked his wife, obviously hurrying, obviously flustered. 'Joan,' the man said, 'this is Mr . . .' He stopped.

The nature of the occasion had driven the ordinary formalities out of his head.

Scott helped him. 'My name is Scott. Jeremy Scott. I am a barrister from the Temple in London.'

He used the advantage of his calmness and his shadowy position to force himself into control. He held out a hand, pressing good manners on her, knowing she would not be capable of resisting.

'Dalrymple,' said the man. 'This is my wife, Joan Dalrymple. I am Guy Dalrymple. It is a pleasure to meet you.' They shook hands.

Guy Dalrymple went on, 'It is such a pleasure to meet you. We didn't know what to do. We have this sheet. We have had no contact with the defence lawyers at all. And now she has gone to different lawyers. We just didn't know.'

Scott was obviously going to have to stop this.

'Now, Mr Dalrymple, things are getting confused. You must excuse me if I seem impolite, but I am going to have to slow you down a little. Was there something specific you wanted to say?'

At first Scott thought he had gone too far, but then he saw the effect he had produced and knew he hadn't. Guy Dalrymple suddenly stiffened. Unbidden the phrase 'braced up' came into Scott's mind. He had often been told to brace up when he was much younger.

'You must excuse us. I am sorry, Mr Scott. We have been in a state of such indecision that it has affected us. Not what I am used to, I am afraid.' He turned and looked at his wife. She smiled at him. It was a look Scott had seen before, one of pride.

Guy Dalrymple said, 'I will be direct. We have a few things to say about the trial and we didn't know who to say them to, but you are obviously the right person, so if you don't mind, we will say them to you. You see, Hilda

Forgan was a good friend of ours. I might say a very good friend.'

He wanted Scott to know that the distinction was important.

'Indeed, she is a good friend to everybody in the close. We think it's all wrong, and no one has allowed us to have our say.'

He stopped. He was about to look foolish again. It had been as though this ringing declaration were all there was to it. But then he gathered himself together.

'May we speak to you for a moment, Mr Scott? Could you please come in? Come into our house?'

'Why, of course,' Scott said. He glanced through the window of the car at the clock. 'I have plenty of time. I should be most pleased to come.'

He opened the car door, took the keys and then, remembering, slid one of his counsel's notebooks out. Holding this, his badge of office, he followed the Dalrymples into their home.

'Now, Mr Scott . . .'

Scott had been taken into the drawing room of the house. It was much larger than he thought it would be. There was a grand piano at the back of the room covered in photographs, and yet at the other end there was enough space for a sofa and two chintz-covered chairs to face the large brick fireplace.

In the fireplace there was, despite it being a pleasant day, a good fire. Two large windows looked out over the street. On the window sills there were four silver pheasants. It must have been through these wide windows that he had been spotted lurking outside Mrs Beatty's house.

'Mr Scott. I should tell you again, we are very good friends of Hilda Forgan.'

In the background Scott could hear Joan Dalrymple on the phone. 'Vera, Vera. Could you come round? It's about Hilda. And bring George if you can. I'll phone William.'

She put the phone down and started dialling again. She stood listening to it ring. After a few moments, she shouted out, 'It's no good, Guy, William's not there.'

Over his shoulder Guy Dalrymple said, 'He'll be at the club, dear, try the club.'

'Look, Mr Scott. I'm sorry. You've tumbled into something you probably had not expected.' He had obviously gained control of himself. Scott became aware of a slightly military inflexion. Dalrymple went on, 'Can I ask you to wait for a moment? Vera and George Thompson would like to be here, I know. And we're trying to get Bill Scott-Williams to come.'

He looked up at his wife, who was now speaking into the phone. 'The secretary, yes. If you could fetch him, please. It is urgent.'

'Mr Scott, would you take a cup of coffee or something? If you have time. I do hope you have the time?'

Scott glanced at the clock which sat on the mantelshelf surrounded by more pheasants. He had time. Hilton had said 'between twelve and one', so he could take an hour and still be all right.

'Yes, coffee would be fine.' Again Scott smothered the man with goodwill. 'Mr Dalrymple, I am Miss Forgan's lawyer. You have my complete attention for as long as you wish.'

Dalrymple sighed. He got up and said to no one in particular, 'What a relief,' and left for the kitchen. There were banging noises.

Joan Dalrymple came into the room, her hands clasped, and sat down. 'It is such a relief to see you, Mr Scott,' she said. 'We just didn't know what to do.' Scott noticed they talked as though they were one person.

'Now Hilda has been convicted we can't get in touch with her. One of us tried to go to the prison, but they wouldn't let us see her without an order, a visiting order or something. Apparently she has to send us that. We've written to her but got no reply.

'We've written to her solicitors. They were very polite but have said that there is nothing that can be done. We even wrote to our Member of Parliament, at least Bill did. But he said he couldn't interfere and that we should write to the solicitors.'

She stared into the fire. There were reassuring noises from the kitchen. Scott almost expected to hear a Hoover start up in the background. The atmosphere of complete domestic calm enveloped him, and yet in front of him this woman was wringing her hands in distress.

'Mr Scott, you hear of these things. You read of them. Do you remember those frightful Irish bombers? But you don't think it can happen to you, do you?'

'Mrs Dalrymple, I'm a bit lost, I'm afraid. But what? What has happened?'

'But you know, don't you? You're on her side. You must know. Hilda didn't murder her aunt. She couldn't have done it.'

Chapter Ten

The policeman's car came round the corner just as Scott returned to Mrs Beatty's house.

'Been here long?' the driver said through the open window.

Scott grunted.

'I'm Hilton,' the policeman said. The first impression Scott had was the smartness of the man. He got out of the car, took a coat from a hanger behind him and slid it on. As he began to speak, he smoothed it down and adjusted it. The coat was cashmere.

It was his smartness – he was even wearing a stiff collar – which made Scott realise he had seen him before.

Hilton said, 'You remember me. I was in court at the time when there was all that fuss over the drug smuggler.'

It was a gentle way of putting it, and Scott did not want to be reminded.

'Oh yes,' he said.

'Been here long?' Hilton repeated. The policeman had noticed that Scott had not answered his original question.

'Not long.'

'Sorry I'm late. I got held up. I rang to see if you had a mobile, but they said you don't carry one?' It was a question.

'No,' said Scott.

'I thought all smart lawyers had them.'

'Perhaps they do,' said Scott.

'I would think so,' Hilton said, and he set off down the path to the front door. Scott followed, watching the chains on the man's shoes jiggling to and fro. Hilton reached the door and rubbed his feet on the mat, though there wasn't a trace of damp outside. As far as Scott could see his shoes were much cleaner than the mat.

Hilton opened the door and the burglar alarm went off. They both stood there.

'Now what was the number?' Hilton said. He did not seem at all disturbed. Scott waited. How long did they have before the full alarm went off? Forty seconds? Forty seconds was a long time, or so it seemed, for they stood there an age. Then Hilton said, 'Oh yes.'

He punched a number in.

'She didn't tell you the number, then?' he said.

'Who?'

'Our Hilda.'

It didn't seem right to call someone you have had convicted of murder 'our Hilda', so Scott only grunted again.

'She didn't tell you the number, then?' Hilton clearly wanted all his questions answered.

'No,' said Scott. He could see this was going to be a difficult occasion.

The house had a slightly musty smell, mixed in with – Scott had to concentrate a moment to work out what it was – the sweet smell of an invalid – unopened windows, undisturbed rooms.

It was small, much smaller than the Dalrymple house, and somehow, from lack of use perhaps, it had taken on the air of an imitation of itself, as though it had been decked out to represent a house that might be lived in by an invalid, merely to demonstrate what such a place would be like.

'We haven't touched it, hardly,' said Hilton, apparently responding to what Scott was thinking. Scott felt slightly eerie, until Hilton demonstrated that he wasn't a mind-reader. He went on, 'You should see what places are normally like when we've been through them.'

They stood in silence, then the policeman said, 'You'll be wanting to see the bathroom. Have you seen the photographs?'

Scott said, 'No.'

'Well, let's go through the motions, then.'

What did he mean by that? Scott could feel the constant pressure. Hilton was telling him that his time was being wasted.

'Your Mr Bach said you wanted to see everything.'

It was the other way round. Monty had particularly asked Scott to go to the house – for no really good reason, Scott had thought, but he wasn't going to tell Hilton that.

'We haven't touched anything,' Hilton repeated, 'save the fingerprint man, he went over the lot. So don't you touch anything or you'll get dirty. Magnesium whatsit.'

They climbed the stairs. There was a chair attached to a rail set in the wall. It was a lift. Scott imagined the scene, hauling the old lady into the chair.

'She never used this,' said Hilton. 'It was installed about the time she became unable to move, and after that she didn't go downstairs at all. The doctor told me that he thought it may have been this which set her complete immobility off.'

'Which doctor was that?'

'Her GP.'

'Was there a statement from him at the trial?' Scott couldn't remember any reference to it in the summing-up.

'No.' Hilton stopped on the stairs and said, 'Are you saying there should have been?'

'I've no idea,' said Scott. 'Why didn't the doctor make one?'

Surprisingly Hilton did reply. Scott had expected more stubbornness. 'The GP refused to make one. He didn't certify death, and he said the consultant was a better judge of the particular information we wanted.'

Scott wanted to say 'Surely it didn't need a consultant to say whether she could move or not', but he restrained himself. If everybody else knew what the appeal was about, and by what they had been saying to him they obviously did, then you could be sure Hilton did also. But still there was no point in opening it up entirely.

As he watched Hilton fiddling with the chair mechanism he considered what the doctor had said. If it was the installation of the chair which had set the old lady's immobility off, then the whole thing must have been more complicated than an ordinary illness. The chair began to make a buzzing noise and then chugged up the stairs. Hilton looked at Scott with pleasure. 'There you are, sir,' he said. 'Full demonstration.'

They followed the chair up the stairs.

'It is the bathroom you want to see?' Hilton stopped outside one of the doors with a direct question.

Scott said, 'I've come to see what there is.'

After a fraction's delay, Hilton opened the door.

'Why have you come, Mr Hilton?' Scott said.

'What do you mean?'

'Well, I hardly expected to see an inspector here.'

'I always like to know what's going on, sir.'

They left it there.

The bathroom was a small room – to be expected in a house of this size. The sink had clearly not been used much, since blocking it was another chair, this time attached to the bath. Scott recognised it from advertisements – another contraption. It would have enabled a nurse to get Mrs Beatty in and out of the water.

The machinery took up most of the floor space in the room. At the end, where the bath did not fill the length of the room and there was a gap, there was a wall covered with pegs. On the pegs, still hanging there, were an old lady's clothes, her night things and a dressing gown. That was where the hairdryer had hung. He remembered Hilda Forgan's description in the police interview.

To reach the dryer whilst sitting in the chair contraption would have needed a long stretch. He looked at it. It could have been done, a mobile person could easily do it. Perhaps if she had used all her strength to reach out? Then if Mrs Beatty had worked the controls on her bath hoist holding the dryer, she would have been lowering herself to her death.

Again Scott imagined the scene: the heat, the distress, the arrival of the police, the doctors. Although in his own life he dealt regularly with the aftermath of such things, he had never been there. He had never stood in his boots in a ditch at night, examining the body by torchlight. Did that lack of real experience put him at a disadvantage, or didn't it matter? Who knew the answer to that? He had to act as though it didn't.

He looked around. As he might have expected, there were no sockets in the bathroom. 'Where was the hairdryer plugged in?' he asked.

'There was an extension lead. They ran it from out here,' Hilton kicked the skirting board outside the bathroom in the landing, where there was a socket. 'Asking for trouble,' he said.

This was a rather unnecessary remark, Scott thought.

'The whole connection went into the bath, extension

lead, socket and all. There must have been a hell of a bang.'

'Where was her wheelchair?'

Hilton didn't reply for a moment. 'I dunno,' he said. 'It wasn't in the photographs.'

Scott wondered. If she had been lifted from a wheelchair on to the hoist, where would the chair have been left? Out in the hallway where they were standing? Or would it have been left squeezed into the bathroom? He looked. The chair could probably have been got into the room, perhaps projecting into the area at the end, between the bath and the wall with the pegs on.

If the ducking-stool – a name for the contraption for getting the invalid into the bath forced itself into his head – swung around, it would be parallel with the wheelchair. It would surely be designed for that. If the wheelchair was in the room, could the dryer have been plugged in and then left hanging on it, just in reach of Mrs Beatty?

Then he remembered. He was, out of force of habit, looking at the whole thing as if it were a trial about to happen. It wasn't. The facts were established. Hilda Forgan said that she had left her aunt in the lifting contraption, with the bath running. She said the hairdryer had been hanging on the peg and that the extension lead was in the doorway, the dryer plugged into it. She hadn't said whether or not it had been switched on.

'How does the lifting contraption work?'

'Once you're on it, all that happens is you press the buttons and then the machine does everything else. Up, across, down.' Hilton indicated with his hand. 'It swings round too. But you have to push it.' He smoothed his hair back. Then he said, 'No, she couldn't have managed it.'

'Managed what?'

'Reached the hairdryer. That's what you're here to look at it, isn't it?'

What could Scott say? He could hardly answer, 'I am not at liberty to discuss that.' In fact, what would be the harm?

He replied, 'Well, it's one of the things that I need to look at, yes.'

'She couldn't move on her own, that's for sure. Do you think we would have charged your Hilda if we thought she could?'

Scott didn't reply.

'I mean suicide is the obvious answer,' Hilton said.

'Why obvious?'

'Well, an old lady. Bedridden.'

'Bedridden old ladies don't commit suicide.'

'This one might.'

'Why?'

'She was a member of the Euthanasia Society, or some such organisation.'

Scott tried hard not to react strongly. This was what Hilda Forgan had said. He tried to cover up his reaction. He said, 'Well, that's common enough isn't it? They probably target people.'

As soon as the words were out of his mouth he realised how ridiculous they were. Of course these societies didn't target people. How could they? What would be the method? 'We see from the electoral register that you've been around for a long while. May we enquire, please, what your plans are for the future?' But amazingly Hilton took the remark seriously.

'No. We checked. She applied off her own bat.'

'This wasn't mentioned in the hearing, was it?'

'No. But it was all there for the defence to find in the boxes of papers. The boxes in the squad office. The defence could have looked. It was unused material, we had no reason to keep it secret.'

The exchange had changed their relationship slightly. 'Would you fancy a cup of tea?' Hilton said. They went downstairs to the kitchen.

As they got to the bottom of the stairs, Hilton pointed. Scott could see his shirt cuff almost sparkling with starch. 'That's what all the fuss is about,' he said. There was a mark on the wall. Clearly a large picture had hung there once.

'She had a picture by Sargent. You'd know about him – John Singer Sargent. It was a portrait of her aunt's grandmother, all decked out in the smartest gear. Worth thousands and thousands, apparently, more than the house, by at least ten times. It's in storage now.'

In the kitchen Hilton started opening and closing cupboards energetically.

'It was called *The Hon. Mrs Wallace Beatty With Her Favourite Cocker Spaniel, Fart.* He looked at Scott, his face full of pure pleasure. He had found the tea.

'Now, I don't know, you'll have to tell me. Is 'fart' a modern word? Did Mrs Beatty's grandma know what she had called her dog? Perhaps she didn't know what a fart was. Like Queen Victoria never knew what lesbianism was, so they couldn't make it a crime.'

He searched for teaspoons. 'Perhaps Mrs Beatty had never farted, or if she did she never absorbed the act of farting into her consciousness sufficiently to need a word for it. The opposite of the Eskimos having one hundred and thirty-eight words for snow.'

He found the cups.

'I believe modern French philosophers are intrigued by this sort of thing. Anyway, for me it's much the most interesting part of the case.'

Scott listened, then he said, 'It's an old word. Queen Elizabeth said to someone, "I have forgot your fart." '

'Shall I be Mum?' Hilton said.

'Yes.' Scott nodded and Hilton poured the tea out.

'I'm told it could double the price.'

'What could?'

'The title of the picture.'

'You're kidding me, Mr Hilton.'

'No I am not, sir.'

'So you say this murder was committed out of greed?'

'Yes.'

'But everything the old lady had was Hilda's anyway, or almost. She was the only relative.'

'Pretty nearly.'

'She could just have moved in.'

'Would you fancy moving in here?'

Hilton looked around. Scott followed his look and saw the lists and instructions pinned up round the kitchen, timetables, recipes. The atmosphere of anxiety and hysteria clung to the place still. He looked back. Hilton was brushing the sleeves of his jacket.

'No, perhaps not,' he said.

'Powdered milk, sir?'

The detective was looking at him, a tiny apostle spoon containing milk powder in his large hand. Scott could see that his fingers were manicured.

'Was she much liked? Yes, please,' he said.

'Who?'

'Mrs Beatty.'

'I don't really know. I don't think many people round here knew her.'

'What about Hilda Forgan?'

'Was she liked? Oh, I think she was liked locally. Though again I don't think the people here knew her much.'

Scott was interested to see what Hilton would say. He asked, 'You didn't get much local interest, then?'

Hilton looked at him. Scott wondered whether he could

see what he was doing. You never really knew whether you were being utterly transparent, until people actually told you they could see right through you.

'Not much,' Hilton said, 'but remember, we're not the local police station.'

'But did the local people rally round? Did they have an opinion?'

'You'll have to ask them that, sir. That's not my job. Opinions. Not much use to me.'

'But the vicar gave evidence for her.'

'Well, he would, wouldn't he? That's his job. He's in the business of forgiveness. After all, that must be a major source of trade for him, forgiveness. If he didn't forgive everyone there'd be no congregation left.'

Scott tried again.

'Has there been anyone else interested? Other people?'

Hilton looked at him, slowly taking a sip from his cup.

'Who might you mean?'

'Other people. You know, third parties?'

How weak he sounded. Then Scott remembered. 'You said there was another relative.'

'Did I?'

'I think you did.'

'I don't think I did, you know.'

'Well, anyway, are there any other relatives?'

'Oh. I see. Yes, there is. A man in north London. He'll inherit the lot. I've seen him here once. He came the moment he heard we had charged her. And I saw him at the trial, every day.'

Hilton took another sip.

'He's the one who insisted on the picture being taken away somewhere.'

'Oh,' Scott said. He thought about it and went on, 'But there's no one else who has shown any particular concern.

I mean, sometimes you get other people who have it in for the arrested person, dislike them for some reason.'

'No, nothing like that, sir. This one didn't cause any ripples.'

'Look, Mr Hilton. I've got a reason for asking. I've had an anonymous phone call.'

Hilton didn't react. He said, 'A threatening phone call, sir?'

'No. Well, not quite threatening. It was a man. He said, "Don't think you're going to have her get away with it." '

'Not threatening to you, then.'

'What could it mean?'

'Well, it could mean they think you're a jolly good advocate and that you might well get our Hilda out of prison. And they don't want that.'

Hilton was laughing at him.

'Or it could just be a crank call. Which do you think it is?'

'It would hardly be the first, would it, Mr Hilton?'

'Here they are now,' said Hilton, looking out of the window.

Scott looked up. A large Jeep-like car was pulling up outside. It was corrugated all over and had huge metal bars attached to it. It seemed entirely out of place in Briar Close.

A slim young man jumped out of the driver's door and started unloading equipment, mainly in shiny metallic boxes. Scott recognised them. It was camera equipment.

While he was doing this, another man, tall, quite the size of Gatling, strolled round from the driver's door and stood on the pavement, gazing up at number eight.

He was dressed in corn-yellow corduroys and an old green waisted jacket. From his sleeve there protruded a khaki handkerchief.

'Who are they?' Scott said.

'The TV,' said Hilton.

'The TV?'

'Yes. Didn't you know?'

'No.'

'I thought you did.'

'No.'

They both stared out of the window. The younger man had joined the elder and was staring up at the house as well. They both started to walk backwards into the road, at the same time turning to their right and left in unison. It looked like a dance by the Dutch Ballet. Perhaps they were planning camera angles. Did people do that?

'What do they want?'

'They want to know what happened.'

'It's a bit late, isn't it?' said Scott.

'They're investigative,' Hilton said, as though that explained everything.

Scott looked at him. He was surprised at the detective's naïveté. 'Are they on your side?' he said.

Hilton looked at him as though he didn't understand. 'What?' he said, and Scott realised he was right. He hadn't understood.

'You don't think they are on your side, do you?' he said, but Hilton was on the way out of the front door.

Why worry? It wasn't his problem. Scott rinsed his cup and put it on the draining board.

He watched carefully for the right moment, then he slipped away. He thought he hadn't been noticed, and when last he looked back down Briar Close, Hilton was being lined up in front of the door of the sad house.

Policemen had become so obsessed with standing on the steps of the courts giving the press an easy story, saying how evil the defendant was, that recently they seemed to have lost all touch with what they were meant to be doing.

Hilton looked pleased with himself. If the television people were doing what Scott guessed they were doing, then he might regret that.

'She was an exceptionally cunning woman,' Hilton said. 'Oh, yes. For some considerable time we believed her explanation, that the whole thing was an accident. Then of course we realised that she had been fooling us.' He looked down and shook his trouser leg so that the crease hung just so, breaking on his shoes. His father's suit. Would he be able to say how much he loved opera?

'But she never admitted that she killed her, did she?'

'That, as far as I am concerned, only confirms it.'

The interviewer adopted a puzzled expression. 'That's a little odd isn't it? How can a denial of guilt be proof of guilt? An innocent person would deny guilt just as much as a guilty man would. Perhaps more.'

Hilton looked amused.

'You haven't seen what I have seen. When you've seen that then you can lecture me on who did it, and who didn't. This one did it.'

'And the fact that she denied doing it is added proof that she did do it?'

'In the twisted world of the criminal mind it is.'

'The criminal mind?'

'We shall never understand it. All we can do is combat it. With all the forces at our command, without being shackled by outmoded ideas of fair play and suchlike.'

Hilton watched the camera looking at him and swelled up in its gaze. 'You know, at the beginning she looked genuinely distressed, very upset. Now of course we know it was all an act. A clever act.'

The camera sucked up his personality and he felt compelled to continue, 'I might almost say a fiendishly clever act.' He stopped speaking and there was silence. It felt awkward, and when he was asked another question he plunged on.

'Did she plan it?'

'Almost certainly,' he said. 'It would have to have been planned to have so nearly tricked us into believing her story. She was driven by greed.' Hilton's mind went back to the *Sun*'s headline about the case.

'What if she did it in one mad moment of anger and hate?'

'There is that too,' said Hilton. 'It was either one or the other.'

'Not forgetting greed,' said the the man in the corn-yellow corduroys. He could hardly keep himself from laughing.

'And greed,' said Hilton.

The interviewer gave a signal and the cameraman lowered the camera. 'That was terrific, Detective Inspector. Just what we need.'

Hilton relaxed and stepped down from the doorstep of the house. 'You've seen enough?'

'Everything. Perfect. We're finished here now. Save this perhaps.' The interviewer paused and went to speak to the cameraman, then he turned and said, 'Are you going now?'

Hilton looked slightly disappointed that his part in the filming had ended.

'Yes,' he said, adding hopefully, 'If you don't want anything more?'

'No, nothing more, thank you, Inspector. You've been very kind.'

Hilton was being dismissed.

'Nicky, have we got everything we need from the inspector? All the phone numbers?' She appeared from behind the Jeep where she had been rummaging in a filing cabinet.

'Yes, Toby, we've got everything.' She looked up at the policeman. 'Thank you, Mr Hilton. We'll be in touch.'

'Can I see the programme before it goes out?'

The film crew's friendliness evaporated instantly. 'No, we can't do that, I'm afraid. Company rules. Editorial control.'

Hilton was taken aback by this. It was the first time anything he had said or suggested wasn't instantly agreed upon and greeted with admiration.

'One more shot,' called the cameraman. 'Just a continuity shot. Could you walk to the car, Mr Hilton, then stop and look back at the house. Then get in and drive away towards me? Thanks.'

'Shake your head as you look back at the house,' called the man in corduroy. 'As though you were despairing over the wickedness of mankind,' he added.

Hilton did what they wanted.

'There's only one mercy,' Toby Beyt said as Hilton disappeared. 'At least he doesn't boast that it's his father's suit he's wearing.'

They watched for a moment to see if the policeman returned, then the cameraman, at the top of the road, waved to confirm that he was gone.

Toby said, 'Don't look now, Nicky, but the people next door but one are watching us. Take your time and then go up and see what they have to say.'

'Which side of the road?' said Nicky, not looking around.

'Our side. One up, behind the curtains. She's been watching all the time.'

'OK.'

After a few moments Nicky turned and walked straight up the road, as though she had always intended to call at the house. As she approached the door the curtain in the window twitched.

Nicky rang the bell purposefully. She could hear it pealing and held her finger on it for a moment longer than necessary. The door opened, almost too quickly. 'My name is Veronica Vesey,' Nicky said, sticking out her hand. She spoke with such assurance that Mrs Dalrymple was completely taken aback. She took the girl's outstretched hand.

'Hallo,' she said.

'We're doing a programme.'

Mrs Dalrymple rolled her eyes and Nicky played her trump card. 'About how badly the press behaved.' She saw immediately she had got it right. The woman at the door turned and called, 'Guy, Guy, dear. Can you come here?'

She turned back. 'Well, it is interesting to meet you. My name is Joan Dalrymple. We would be very pleased to speak to you. Yes, we would. Guy, dear,' she called. 'There's a young lady here.'

'Toby. Toby Beyt. I am the producer. Veronica is our researcher. Veronica here hit on the good idea of asking people who have been harassed by the press about their experiences.'

Toby Beyt was strolling about the Dalrymple drawing room with the assurance of someone used to much grander rooms than this. He went over to the window and picked up one of the pheasants. Mrs Dalrymple watched in dismay. Never had her things been touched in this fashion, and at the same time never had she felt so powerless to object.

'We know that the press descended on you after the terrible thing next door.'

'Yes,' said the Dalrymples.

'We know that in one house they even got into the bathroom without permission.'

'Did they really? We didn't know about that, Joan, did we?' said Guy Dalrymple.

'They probably respected you a bit more,' Toby said. He stopped examining the Dalrymples' ornaments and sat down on the sofa. His long legs stuck out towards the fire. 'So they pestered you?' he said.

'They were dreadful,' said Guy Dalrymple. 'All they wanted were stories about her.' He obviously wanted to tell the story but he was stuck at the start. 'I don't really know how to put this.' Toby realised that meant he didn't want to say it in front of his wife. After a moment Mr Dalrymple summoned up the courage.

'She was a spinster, you know. They both were. But the press, they wouldn't have that. They weren't having anything of that. They said, "She must have a man. Surely." It was extraordinary. They couldn't believe someone could live a normal life without some . . .' He looked at his wife, reassured now that he had got it out. '. . . some sort of scandal attached to it.'

Mrs Dalrymple suddenly began to get angry. She obviously knew precisely what her husband was saying. 'I got really annoyed with them. Or at least with one of them. And do you know what he said to me? 'The *Sun* doesn't need you, love. We don't need you at all. We could chew you up and spit you out.' And the odd thing about it, Mr Beyt, was he obviously thought this was important or something. I was meant to mind that the *Sun* newspaper didn't need me.'

She turned to her husband. 'I told you, didn't I? Don't you remember? That was the oddest thing of all. It was as though he had tried to curse me in some way, but he'd done it with a curse that had no reality, like . . .' She searched for a comparison. '. . . it was as real as a child's complaint. "I'll tell on you." That sort of remark. It was very odd indeed. I felt like sympathising with the poor man.'

Toby Beyt looked at Nicky, who dropped her eyes. He had, in almost less time than it took to sit down, convinced the couple that he was entirely on their side. The odd thing was that he had started on the *Sun* himself. That was where he had learnt how to do this.

'I don't suppose they showed any sympathy at all, did they?' he said.

'For whom?' Guy Dalrymple tried to follow his thinking.

'For her.'

'None,' said Joan Dalrymple. 'They treated her as though she was guilty from the start. They didn't say so out loud, of course, but the reporting of the trial was incredible. They had got hold of that video of her with her aunt, at the party where she kissed her, and had taken a frame from it and printed it. The "Judas Kiss", they called it.'

Guy Dalrymple got up and went to his mantelpiece. He took a pipe from a bowl and started stuffing it with tobacco.

Nicky had seen people do that in moments of tension in films. Who was it? Basil Rathbone? In moments of high tension the hero stuffs his pipe. But she had never seen it done in real life.

'And then the pictures of that dreadful police officer, standing on the steps of the court, saying how evil Hilda was. He'd never really met her.'

They paused, then Guy Dalrymple said, 'Well, you know that. You've just been talking to him. We saw you.'

His wife interrupted him. 'And he's the one I told. I told him Anna Beatty was perfectly capable of moving about. He knew because I told him. But he told me it was unimportant. Now you tell me if that is unimportant. I think the word he used was irrelevant. Well, is it? Is it really?'

Nicky was watching with astonishment. How was it that Toby always managed to stumble on the real story?

'That seems important to me, Mrs Dalrymple,' said Toby Beyt. 'Look, would you mind repeating that in front of the camera?'

140

Chapter Eleven

Mrs Dalrymple said, 'I remember when she came here. She was a bit standoffish. At first I thought it was her illness that made her difficult but, as I got to know her, I came to realise she was like that anyway. Maybe she was a snob.

'Whatever she was, it was also clear she was an intelligent woman. She made me feel a bit ordinary – all those books, a lot of them in foreign languages, and the pictures on the wall and hundreds of classical records, and the concert programmes to go with them.

'She saved the programmes of everything she went to. And she had been to the lot. Glyndebourne. Everywhere. The Festival Hall, the Albert Hall, the Wigmore Hall – more places than I knew there were. And she had all of them, some signed by the people who had performed, and of course photographs, signed photographs. Photographs of herself with people and with her parents.

'There was even a photograph of the Queen Mother meeting her father, or rather the other way around, and a lot of musical stuff in the background. I never asked about it directly but there was the photograph, put on the piano just so, right in the front. Of course, the Queen Mother was the Queen then, wasn't she?

'Anyway, I got to know Anna, Mrs Beatty that is. We all

did. This is such a small close that it isn't easy to remain apart. It's more like a village, actually, a village atmosphere at least. Especially later on, when she fell more ill, a number of us used to pop in to help her and get things for her. She could hardly refuse that, could she? We didn't force ourselves on her, no. Nothing like that. At least, I hope not.

'Eventually she gave in. I always laugh about that, that way of putting it – "she gave in". She gave in and got quite friendly and in the end there were people popping in and out all the time and she became one of us.

'And then Hilda appeared. She was like a breath of fresh air. She wasn't just like it, she *was* a breath of fresh air. She opened all the windows, cut back that spriggy plant at the back and got a bit of light into the place. Of course, cutting back wisteria makes it bloom. You have to cut them, you know, and the harder you cut the better, so there was this amazing scent, though maybe that was from the jasmine. It was so heavy it made you feel faint sometimes. But Hilda, she swept through all the must and the dust and her aunt's house was different. Completely different. Fresh and clean. She had so much energy.

'Do you know how I put it? Hilda was a pre-television person. Do you know what I mean by that? She was always *doing* something. Not watching, but doing – bottling something, making something. Some people would call her bossy, in a Mrs Thatcher kind of way. What I always call a Peggy Pulvermacker way. But it didn't matter. Hilda was Hilda. And then we found out that she gave tuition, extra tuition. Well, then we got to know a different side of her. Of course, everybody was interested, since a lot of the children needed to get into the better schools, and if you go to the state primary, which saves you a lot of money to begin with, you need to catch up. So, regularly, Hilda would have the children.

'It was quite a shock to them, to be told to sit up straight for the first time, to be told to do their work neatly. To speak when asked to and not before. It was a real shock to their system.

'But the effect of it was amazing. In the end people used to say when they were talking about a child, "Has Hilda seen him yet?" And if the answer was no, then they would laugh because it meant that the shock was still in store. But they came back. The children came back. They used to come back to see her. My Thomas came back to see her. I remember. He wanted to see her as much as he wanted to see Dad and me.'

Mrs Dalrymple looked distant and then shook herself free from the memory.

'Anyway, that's how she appeared, and she became everyone's friend. I'm trying to be reasonable and balanced about it, but I have to say it. No one had a bad word to say about her. No one. She was here and there, always helping, talking, chatting, and when she moved closer – she came to live over the fields at the back near the main road – everyone was pleased. And pleased for her aunt. Because there's no doubting her aunt was a difficult woman and in the end the only one who could handle her was Hilda. Of us that is. Of course, she had professional help, but I mean of her friends.

'She would call every day and she was always cheerful. At least in front of her aunt and most other people. I know the whole business used to get her down sometimes, because I got to know her very well and occasionally she would let on to me. It was so *draining*, that was the word she would use. Draining.

'Because by then her aunt had taken to her bed. And she was becoming impossible. Not always, mind, but often, making life a misery for everyone. Eventually I organised a rota to help Hilda so that one of us would guarantee to be around for two hours early most evenings. Not all evenings but enough to make a difference, and also if you did your two hours you didn't feel guilty if you didn't go in otherwise.

'There was me and Mrs Pottock and Mrs Ableson and some others. But mainly us three. We would go in and get her what she wanted, and then Hilda could arrive later in the evening and put her to bed properly. Of course, she was always in bed, but put her to sleep I meant.'

Mrs Dalrymple paused. 'Well, you know what I mean.' She laughed nervously. 'Put her to sleep – silly expression.

'And it was then I noticed the differences. That's what I want to tell you about. Little differences. At first I didn't take any notice. Let me tell you about it properly. I would go in, help with one or two things, and then I would say I'm popping home, I'll be back in twenty minutes or so and I'll sit with you till Hilda comes. And I'd go out. And sometimes when I came back I'd notice things had changed. Not big things, but a glass or a jug would have been moved. Before, where it hadn't been near the bed it had now moved, say, from a table *to* the side of the bed. Or she would have a book she didn't have before. Little things – a cardigan on.

'I didn't say anything. I didn't know what to think. But one day I mentioned it to Mrs Pottock. And do you know what happened? Bessie Pottock, she just sat down. Now Bessie Pottock is a big woman. But she just sat down there and then and said, "Joan, you've taken the wind out of me." Because she had seen the same thing and hadn't mentioned it to anyone. She had convinced herself it wasn't happening, because she didn't want to upset anyone. But she'd seen it too. Not things that she could swear to, but when I said I had seen it, then she was certain. You know, it was like when you're not sure about something and because you're not sure, you ask someone else and they say "Funny you should say that" – then you are sure. It was like that.

'She'd seen things moved. Right up to the end. Only a few times, mind you. And even I couldn't give exact examples, but it came to be one of those things you know is the case. You can't prove it, you just know it is true.

'So when I heard that the prosecution were saying that she wasn't able to move at all, I knew it was significant. I had already told that stupid young man from the solicitors and he had said it wasn't important. I doubt if he even understood me. So I've been looking for someone to tell.'

'Well, there it is, Mrs Dalrymple's statement. Monty Bach eventually got someone down there to write it up, and there's another statement on its way from Mrs Pottock too – you know, the woman she mentioned? But apparently it doesn't say as much. This one is better.'

Scott took Mrs Dalrymple's statement back from Ronnie Knox, who had read it slowly, sinking in the depths of his armchair, the gas fire puttering.

Ronnie looked at Scott sitting opposite him and said, 'Well, it's something to start with.' Then he got up. 'Where did I put the whisky?'

He went to the bookshelf and started pulling books out at random. Scott watched him despondently. 'What's happened to the book on the cy-pres doctrine? You used to keep the whisky behind that.'

'Young Miss Farson borrowed it. I don't know why.' Ronnie transferred his attention to another shelf. 'She's pretty cy-pres herself, I think.'

'What on earth do you mean by that, Ronnie?'

'Well, we went out to dinner . . .'

'Ronnie, are you starting on another one of your adventures?'

'I don't know what you mean.'

'If young ladies start borrowing your book on the cy-pres doctrine, then it sounds as though something is about to happen. Where did you go?'

'Wild Bill Hickock's . . .'

'Where?' Scott was amazed.

'. . . Wild Bill Hickock's Wild West Saloon in Romford. Line dancing and boot scoop a speciality. Everything we ate was covered in bar-b-q sauce.'

'Why on earth . . . ?' Scott was astonished. Ronnie's usual haunt was the dining room at the Travellers Club.

'Ah, here it is.' Ronnie pulled the whisky out. He got two glasses and started pouring out the drinks. He explained, 'I was listening to the radio in the car and I heard this song. It was about a man who was saying that he admitted that he had not loved his wife enough – at least I suppose she was his wife – but in mitigation he was saying that despite all that, "You were always on my mind." It reminded me of a sermon of Margerison's. "You are always on my mind." ' He repeated the line contemplatively.

Scott said, 'I know the song, Ronnie, and it never sounded much of an excuse to me. Just the kind of thing some self-indulgent slob would say to his wife when he's taken no notice of her for years. She gets up and leaves him, so he starts feeling sorry for himself. What's that got to do with Romford?'

'It was a country music station and then there was an advertisement for Wild Bill's Wild West Saloon.'

'Yes?'

'I was with Miss Farson at the time, and she said she had always wanted to go line dancing.'

'What is line dancing?'

'Well, you all get in a line. It's what it says it is.'

'And you did that with Andy Farson?'

'Yes.'

'You mean the really pretty one? The one with frizzy hair?'

'You've noticed her?'

'Of course I have, I'm not blind. But I haven't taken her line dancing. What are you up to, Ronnie?'

'Nothing,' said Ronnie. 'We talk about things.'

'What things?'

'Well, Margerison, for one.'

'How did that start?'

'I saw her at Farm Street once.'

'Where?'

'The Chaplaincy.'

'And now she's borrowed your book on the cy-pres doctrine?'

Ronnie nodded.

'It sounds pretty passionate to me.'

Ronnie smiled back at him and said, 'Do you want another whisky?'

'No,' said Scott. 'One's enough.'

They both sat in the half-light. The phone rang. Neither of them moved, then a voice spoke at them out of the telephone intercom. 'Mr Scott, line one, please.'

'What's this?' said Scott, and he got up and pressed the button on the phone. 'Hallo.'

A bright voice at the other end of the phone said, 'Mr Scott?'

Scott didn't recognise it. He said, 'Yes.'

'It's Nicky Vesey here. We're doing a radio programme on the law, and I was wondering if you would be interested in coming on? It's about the criminal courts.'

This was a surprise. Scott raised his eyebrows at Ronnie. 'Why?' He hesitated.

The bright voice cut across him. 'There'll be a fee, of course.'

'When would this be?'

'Well, we're trying for next week. The twenty-fifth, in the morning.'

'That sounds fun. OK. Give me the details.'

Ronnie took another drink and picked up Mrs Dalrymple's statement. He read it again slowly. It looked pretty good to him.

Scott came off the phone. 'What was that?' said Ronnie.

'I've been asked to appear on the radio by that girl. You remember, the one we met in El Vino.'

'What's it about?'

'Criminal law. The courts.'

'Well, you'll have to be careful, won't you?'

'Why?'

'Because you're so indiscreet. You'll start sounding off about Meadowsweet or Teflin – whoever your latest gripe is.'

'I'll be the soul of discretion,' said Scott. 'What do you think of it?'

'The statement? It's all right,' Ronnie said.

'No it's not,' said Scott. 'You don't know the Court of Appeal. They won't believe a word of it. The Crown will tear it apart.'

Ronnie looked surprised. 'Why? What's wrong with it?'

'Ronnie, you've spent much too much time arguing about rights of way and demurrages and things. This is the criminal law, for heaven's sake. Once the criminal courts have got hold of someone they don't let go. Not on this sort of evidence. They'll call the statement "tittle-tattle" – or at least counsel for the Crown will, and the court will agree with him. He'll point out that neither of the women were sure of what they'd seen till they convinced each other, and anyway they can't remember what happened exactly or when. I doubt they'll even allow me to call the evidence.'

'Don't they have to?'

'Not if they don't think it's credible.'

'And they won't?'

'No.' Scott threw the statement on the table. 'And what's so awful is that any reasonable person reading that statement would be convinced by it. It's so normal. But it's the normality of it that defeats it.'

He sat down and picked up his whisky glass again.

'What she's describing is a quite normal thing to do. Imagine you weren't sure that you had seen something. You might easily discuss it with a friend, and if he came up with the same idea independently then of course you would be convinced. That's how people work. And as for her inability to remember exactly what happened, again that's just what would happen. The first thing you'd say to yourself is "I've made a mistake about that" and then forget it. These people aren't experts, for heaven's sake. They're normal, ordinary people. But that will be used against them in the Court of Appeal.'

Ronnie looked at him over his glass.

'And there's no premium on being an ordinary person in the criminal courts,' Scott said. 'Unless it also turns out you're a multiple murderer, and then everyone really does get excited about how ordinary you seemed to be before they found out you were a multiple murderer. Normality is just a cloak for depravity in the criminal courts.'

'See what I mean?' Ronnie laughed. 'Say that sort of thing on the radio and you'll get your licence to sit as a judge endorsed.'

Chapter Twelve

At home an hour later, still slightly affected by Ronnie Knox's whisky, Scott stood in the door of the kitchen. Catherine had her back to him. She was working at the sink. This was what happened.

Scott said, 'I asked if there was anyone who was involved in the case who might have a motive for these anonymous calls. There is – some relative. Apparently he inherits the lot if she remains convicted of murder, so maybe it's him ringing.'

Catherine turned a tap on and began to rinse a pot, but didn't speak. Scott went on, 'I told the policeman about the calls and he just laughed. He didn't take it seriously.'

'Why does this person stand to inherit?' asked Catherine.

'You can't inherit anything from someone you've murdered, so this man will get it instead of Hilda. He's already taken one valuable picture and put it in storage.'

'A picture?'

'The picture of Mrs Wallace Beatty and her dog Fart.'

'What?' The story woke Catherine up and she turned round to face Scott.

Until then she had barely reacted to what he was saying, but had continued preparing the food at the sink. She was making spaghetti. There was a smell of anchovies and olives.

'Yes. Really, that's what it was called. Some sort of joke, I suppose.'

'Is the picture worth a lot?'

'Apparently it is, and all the more because of the dog's name.'

Catherine turned her back on him again. Scott felt cut off once more.

'So I asked him about the phone calls,' he said. Again Catherine didn't reply. 'I thought he might have something to say, but he just laughed.'

Now she was peeling garlic, and the smell of it rose up towards him over her shoulder. Scott put his arms round her waist, but she didn't respond. He stepped back.

'When did this happen?'

'When I went down to Sussex that time. I'm telling you now because I've had another phone call,' he said, 'from the same man. This afternoon.'

Scott found himself still talking to Catherine's back. Why were they falling out? What was all this about?

'This time he did threaten me.'

'Did you do a phone trace?' She didn't turn around to speak, but just talked down into the sink.

'No, we couldn't. It came through the switchboard. But I told Harry not to put calls straight through to me any more.'

'Are you going to tell the police?'

'I did. I just told you that.' The moment he said it, Scott felt bad. He hadn't meant to be rude or aggressive. It just came out that way. She shrugged her shoulders.

'I'm sorry,' he said, and put his arms around her waist again. She turned round, still holding the garlic and a knife. He was close to her, but she was pulling back from him, so he let her go. The knife seemed appropriate for what was happening.

'I'm going to Holland,' she said.

'Why?'

'I want a break.'

'What do you mean, you want a break?'

'From you,' she said.

'Why?'

'Look,' she said, turning away again, 'you never talk to me. I never know what you're thinking. It's like living on my own being with you.'

'I do talk to you. I was talking to you just now.'

'You might as well be talking to yourself. You don't talk to me about me. I thought you would change, but you haven't.'

There was silence between them, and she continued preparing the food, cutting strips of bacon.

'I think of you a lot,' he said.

'A fat lot of use that is,' she said.

Scott thought of the song Ronnie had mentioned, 'You were always on my mind', and what he had said about it. Out loud he said, ' "Thus the whirligig of time brings in its revenges." Do you want a drink?'

'Back home we say, "What goes around, comes around," ' Catherine replied. 'I'm going on Saturday.'

Then she looked at him, and laughed. 'Don't look so fed up. Do you want to come? You can stay for the weekend.'

He felt frustrated. He was used to this sequence by now. First annoyance, because he could do nothing to control the situation, then anger, then feeling sorry for himself just like the stupid guy in the song. And the only way he could deal with it was to walk out of the room, but that left everything unresolved. 'Typical man's behaviour,' she told him. It was a fixed pattern of behaviour and once the pattern was triggered off then he found it almost impossible to break.

'Yes, I'll come,' he said. He tried to brighten up. 'Where are you going?'

'To stay with Marina and Jeroem in Amsterdam.'

'How long are you staying for?'

'I don't know. I'll come back when I feel like it.'

At least she was expecting to come back. That was something.

'Stop feeling sorry for yourself,' she said. This time she moved towards him, not holding the knife. He could smell the garlic on her. He pushed her hair away from her face.

'Of course I'm feeling sorry for myself. You won't be here.'

'Well, you can always think about me, can't you? You can have me on your mind.'

'I've been asked to appear on the radio.'

'That's nice.'

'Next week.'

They were eating the spaghetti and drinking wine.

'What's it all about?'

'Something to do with the criminal courts.' He dropped spaghetti on his shirt and started brushing at it.

'Don't do that,' she said, 'you'll make it worse.'

'It's going to be live.' He found the idea rather exciting.

'Don't you want to talk about us?'

He didn't really. Conversations like that were difficult. He said nothing.

Catherine looked at him. 'Why not? You can't go through your life being unwilling to talk. Just because you think it's like reading a woman's magazine. It's not, it's important.'

'In a moment you'll be asking me to get in touch with my feelings,' he said. He went on, 'And I don't think that's something I want to do much. My feelings are best left alone, I think.'

'Well, if you want to be left alone, you're going the right way about it.'

'I don't want to be left alone. I enjoy being with you, but I don't want to talk about it all the time.'

'You don't talk about it at all.'

'What is there to talk about?'

'We can talk about the fact that we never talk.'

'But if the only thing to talk about is whether we talk enough about talking enough, there doesn't seem much point, does there? Why don't we just sit here quietly?'

'I think you've got a problem,' she said.

'You always did think that,' he said.

They went to Holland together.

Scott liked Holland. He thought that in Holland people lived a different and a better life. If you wanted to go and see a friend you got on a bicycle. It didn't involve an expedition across miles of unfriendly territory as in London. If you wanted to sit in a café at a long table, drink coffee and read the paper, people didn't think you were odd. Instead they provided fantastic coffee and lots of newspapers. You could walk along roads that were better for walking on than for driving, although cars could still go along them. It was just that cars hadn't won. People were still winning.

Scott dropped a stone off the bridge into the black canal beneath him. It made a reassuring plop in the darkness. He said to himself, 'Just like it ought to.' The very act of being abroad was a pleasure, even if you were only looking down into a canal.

A cat on the bank to his right looked at him for a moment, then got up and walked off, jumping on to a barge. Behind him, a tram, lit like a huge moving cinema screen, pulled up, spilling light over the whole area. Some people got off, talking to each other.

Dutch. It was a strange sound. At first it seemed comprehensible, as though with only a little more effort you could understand it, but when you listened closely you couldn't work out what they were talking about. All you could understand was the intonation – at least you knew they were not angry. When Chinamen spoke, you couldn't tell if they were laughing or crying.

Two people walked past him and the tram pulled away with a satisfying clatter. Scott turned back to the water. The cat was now sitting on the barge cleaning itself.

A voice next to him said, 'I followed you.'

At first Scott didn't grasp what was being said, then he didn't think the voice was speaking to him. It was as though he had suddenly begun to understand Dutch and had overheard something not meant for him at all.

But then it happened again, the words quite distinct in a conversational tone. 'I found out where you lived in London and I followed you here.'

There was no aggression, which made the words more compelling. Scott thought he could hear the trace of a Scots or North Country accent, and that he knew the voice. He turned. There was a man standing next to him, tall, but Scott could make out no detail, only a dark outline against the sky. The man was looking the other way, his head turned away from him, as though the words were nothing to do with him.

It was odd enough for Scott to react, an Englishman standing on his dignity. 'Are you talking to me?' he said. The man turned to face him. He was wearing dark glasses and a hat. Scott could hardly see his face.

He said, 'Of course I am, you pompous git. And the next time we meet I won't just be talking.'

The man turned away, stepped on to the tram tracks and crossed the road, away from where Scott stood. He disappeared behind the advertisements on the tram shelter. The voice was the voice Scott had heard on the phone, though now the man had a stronger accent. Or was it just nastier?

Scott watched the shelter behind which the man had gone. No one appeared from behind it. He wasn't sure that he wanted him to come out. What would he do if he did see him again? Run over and accost him?

A tram pulled up, a large parcel of light. He saw a figure get on and make its way down the centre of the carriage. It was the same man. He stopped. He couldn't have been further than twenty feet from him, the width of the narrow road, not even that. Maybe less than ten feet. He turned to face Scott, looking out over the heads of the people sitting with their backs to the windows. His scarf was pulled away from his face, and for a moment Scott had a feeling that he had seen the man before somewhere. But almost immediately his face became unrecognisable. Then he opened his mouth and yawned at Scott. He continued holding his mouth open, until the gesture became one of utter contempt. Scott found himself watching, trapped by the movement.

Then the tram pulled away, rocking slightly, and slid into the night.

Marina and Jeroem's house opened directly into the street from a bare front room. Of course, it wasn't bare, it was just minimally furnished. On the walls there were photographs, grainy, black-and-white, of a yacht crashing through waves. The photographer had used a long lens to foreshorten the background, bringing the sails right up under the lee of a church on the far shore. It was as though the boat were clawing its way from under the threatening bows of a great stone ship. They were pictures of an inland sea.

At the back of the long room there was a metal stove standing isolated, on a slate base. Scott could feel the warmth immediately he stepped in. Opposite it, in an L-shaped corner, he found Marina and Jeroem sitting with Catherine at a computer.

'We're going to go dancing,' Catherine said over her shoulder.

Scott felt like saying 'Can I come?' but stopped himself. Merely thinking of asking to come made him realise how detached he had become, as though he depended on her permission.

'Where?' he said.

'At the Belgrade.'

Jeroem said, 'Look, if you put this in, press carriage return, then . . .' Scott could see the screen break up into a dozen different images. A car floated off a street, a bus was swept away into the background.

'And then you can colour it.'

The little arrow began to trace lines of colour on to the car which now filled the foreground.

'What's carriage return?' said Catherine.

'It's what we call "enter". On typewriters it was always called "carriage return",' said Jeroem.

After a moment Marina turned to smile at Scott.

'It's the new programme. We can deconstruct photographs,' she said.

It was amazing. Scott watched as another photograph was brought up on the screen. It was a picture of a group of people. Marina covered one of the figures by stretching the background over it, as though the image were made of rubber. The figure disappeared.

'We can put someone else there instead,' said Jeroem. Marina punched a key and a number of other photographs appeared on the screen. She scrolled through them and then stopped. It was a picture of her and Jeroem. She clicked on it and the figures were lifted out of the photograph and drawn down towards the original.

'Let's get the size right.' Marina manipulated the image. 'There.' She hit a key and the new picture came up on the screen. Scott recognised the original photograph. It was one of himself and Catherine standing with a friend on the banks of the Thames at Putney. At least it had been. Now where he had been standing were Jeroem and Marina instead.

'And we can print that.' At the touch of a key a menu dropped down and Jeroem punched in 'Print'. The machine next to them started to chatter. Slowly, line by line, the photograph appeared.

'There we are. A new life,' said Jeroem, handing the paper to Catherine. 'We've rewritten your past.'

'Maybe the future too,' said Catherine.

Scott looked at the photograph and saw another certainty disappear.

'Let's go,' Marina said.

Catherine and Marina disappeared up the stairs to the upper parts of the house.

'Marina likes to dance the kolo,' said Jeroem.

'What's a kolo?'

'It's a Yugoslavian dance. Marina is Serbian. You'll see.'

They stepped out on to the dark road and turned left, back towards the bridge where Scott had stood earlier. When they reached the corner they crossed the road and stood at the same tram shelter.

There was silence, then Scott said to Catherine, 'You won't believe this but the man who was telephoning me in London has followed us here. He spoke to me just now, while I was standing by the railing there.'

Her reaction was just what he thought it would be. 'Come on! You must have been mistaken.'

'I wasn't mistaken. He spoke to me.'

'What did he say?'

'He said he had followed me.'

'And then?'

'He walked away.'

'He didn't do anything?'

'No.' He walked over to where we are now and got on a tram.'

'Oh. Sounds a little tame.'

'Then he . . .'

The tram pulled up and they got on it. It rattled off. They all turned towards Scott, waiting to hear what had happened next.

'Then he . . .' Scott stopped. It sounded so silly. 'Then he yawned at me.'

'He what?'

The tram stopped. Directly opposite the stop there were some steps leading down into a half-cellar. They followed Marina down and found a table.

Jeroem looked at Scott and said, 'Yawning is infectious. You'll see.'

Behind a small dance-floor, not much bigger than ten steps across, three men were playing music on a squeeze-box and two guitars. The waiter brought white wine, fizzy water and beer.

It was foot-tapping music, and soon everybody in the room had turned to face the sound. A girl got up and was joined by another girl. They held each other's hand at shoulder height, stood for a moment, absolutely still, and then, precisely on the beat, started a rhythmical stepping dance. Two steps forward, one step back, a kick; one foot forward, one foot back. Slowly they began to circle the dance-floor. Others joined and the line became longer, but always moving slowly along.

'That's a kolo,' said Jeroem. 'They dance like that in Belgrade.'

'Come on,' said Marina. She broke into the group and Scott followed. Immediately he was taken over by the insistent beat transmitted through the dancers.

The line started to curl in on itself, forming a spiral as the dancers led each other and the line into a tighter and tighter corkscrew. What would happen when it became too tight? The spiral became denser and denser and then, just when it seemed the dance would have to stop, the leader turned round and started to unwind the circle. All the time, the same insistent beat continued, two steps forward, one step back. The small area became a mass of people all making the same movement, all connected, all part of one piece.

When the leader emerged from the spiral, she set off threading her way through the tables. Slowly Scott found himself winding after her through the restaurant.

He was half mesmerised by the music when he saw a man who was sitting at one of the tables throw his head back and yawn. Scott's attention snapped back to the present. The hand leading him turned him away from the man and Scott had to twist to see him. But he could not. As he turned, the man got up and joined the dance.

Scott found himself yawning too. Yawning was infectious.

Catherine came with him the next day to see him off. It wasn't until they reached the railway station that they argued. Catherine started it. 'How can you be so indifferent?'

He said, 'What do you mean, indifferent?'

'Well, do you want me to go off on my own or not?'

'Of course I don't want you to leave.'

'You've said nothing.'

'I don't need to say anything. You know I don't want you to go away.'

'Well, you might say so.' For a moment she was calmer, but then almost immediately started again. 'It's like living with a snowman. You never touch me.'

Scott said, 'Is that why you're painting me out of your life?'

'What do you mean by that?'

'It's obvious, isn't it? That stuff with the computer last night.'

'What on earth are you on about?' She looked genuinely puzzled. Scott realised that he had exaggerated what was happening. Easy to do when you were feeling raw.

'That picture, when they cut me out of the picture.'

Now she was genuinely angry. 'Cut you out? I'm not cutting you out. It's you who's behaving as though we don't even know each other.' She turned away and walked a few paces towards a flower stand selling large African daisies. Scott could see the wire holding their heads up. They looked improbably bright.

'How on earth do you think we can have a relationship when I might as well not exist for you?'

'That's not right. You do exist, you are important to me.'

'You're not getting the message. That's not what I feel. You care more about your stupid law cases than you do about me. And you don't care about them much. They're all brain games anyway.'

A tall Dutchman was buying two flowers, which were being carefully wrapped in clear cellophane. Two flowers only?

'You're not even listening to me now,' she said.

Scott felt an urge to admit this. Certainly her temper

seemed just as unreal as everything else around him. Probably she was right. He wasn't much good at relationships.

'Catherine, I do want you to be with me. What can I say? I'm like I am. Even if I said I would change, it wouldn't be much help. I don't even know what it is I'm meant to be changing.'

'I thought I could help you,' she said. She laughed. 'Women always think they can be the one to get through to a man. But you. You're completely impossible.' She turned and walked away. Scott watched her disappear into the crowd, then he picked up his bag and headed for the platform.

He had to go to London to do the radio interview. He wished he hadn't agreed to it now.

Chapter Thirteen

Nicky Vesey slipped her arm through his. She was so full of words that there was no time for Scott to react.

'I don't believe it,' she said. 'You saw off Simon Smallchild completely.'

She set off down the radio station corridor at speed. 'It's a disaster in there. Gary's furious, but at the same time he's pleased. He doesn't know what to think. The phones are going crazy. And that's how they measure everything here, how often the phone rings.'

She stopped to laugh at the memory. 'You asked him to tell you how much he earned. How did you know that was his weak spot? That's the one thing he's notorious for. He's so mean, he'll never even buy a drink.'

Scott wanted to say that he hadn't known, but she carried on, not waiting for a reply. 'And telling him on air that he was sweating. My God, you should have seen his face! It was a picture.'

'I did,' said Scott, but she wasn't listening. 'And they said he was going to eat you up.' She went through a door and Scott found himself at the back of a shop. After a moment of confusion he worked out it was the bookshop he had seen while searching for the radio station. Even in here the radio was playing.

Nicky said, 'You were great. You really can handle yourself, can't you? I told them you'd be sensational. I told them they should see you in court.'

This was heady stuff.

'Oh no,' Scott said, 'I just responded to what he was doing.'

Nicky laughed. 'But that's the point. Nobody usually does. He doesn't expect people to stand up to him like that.'

Of course Scott had responded, and as for standing up to the man, where was the courage in that? It was just a matter of being able to talk quickly.

'C'm'on, we're going out to lunch. Are you free?' she said as they burst out on to the street.

'And now,' he heard the radio say as he walked away, 'after all the excitement, a change of speed with some music from James Last.'

'Yes, I'm OK for lunch,' said Scott, thinking of Catherine.

'I sometimes wish I had gone into a profession like yours, rather than being a journalist. It's so much more valuable and important.'

Scott wasn't sure, but it sounded as though Nicky Vesey was coming on to him with a chat-up line. He looked at her but there was no hint of it in her face.

She had amazing blue-grey eyes. One of them was slightly flecked with a different colour. It was the epitome of an attractive blemish. There were worse things than being chatted up by an attractive woman in a bar in Soho.

'Not so important perhaps,' he said, non-committally. 'You know, most of the people I defend are guilty, and I'm not doing much of value by getting them off – if I do.'

'But you're standing up for them.'

He laughed. 'Come on . . .' Then he stopped. She looked hurt.

'Don't laugh at me, I mean it,' she said. 'People always laugh at me when I say I want to do something serious. It's always been the same.'

He didn't know how to handle this.

'Well, what you do is serious, isn't it?'

'Not really. Your friend the other day, Ronnie, was right. It's all rubbish.'

'He didn't say that.' Scott thought, Ronnie hadn't said that, had he?

'No, but it's what he thought, isn't it?'

She was right there.

'I don't know what people think. How can one know what people think?'

'Of course you can. You only have to talk to people. That's the trouble with men.'

She looked away from him. This was extraordinary, the female version of his telling her that his wife didn't understand him.

'Are you married?' she said.

'No,' he replied.

'I thought not,' she said.

Scott felt guilty. Should he tell her about Catherine? Except that would be like telling her his wife didn't understand him. What should he say?

'I'm on my own nowadays,' he said.

'Where do you live?'

'In Chelsea.'

'Just you, no sharing?'

'Yes.'

'Let me imagine, a smart little flat with a porter and an old-fashioned lift?'

'That's about it,' said Scott.

'Campari,' she said.

The barman had arrived. That was what Catherine would

have ordered. For a moment Scott wondered what he was doing here with another girl, but then he was only having lunch. This wasn't part of his life at all really.

They were in the bar of the Groucho Club. He had never been there before but had always been curious. It was *the* place for writers, journalists and the kind of actors that writers and journalists liked. At least, that was what they said. But of course it looked completely normal – one or two people leaning on a long bar and, further over, some tables. Perhaps he had expected a big sign, flashing, saying, 'Here you are, right now you're where it counts.'

The girl who had welcomed him to the radio station suddenly arrived, out of breath.

'He wants you to come on the programme again. Gary's really pleased after all.' She didn't wait for a reply. 'It's really worked out well. You were quite right, Nicky. David! David! Did you hear it?' She was speaking to a small man in a white suit with thick spectacles. Scott saw that he was carrying a handbag with the strap wound around his wrist.

'Did I hear it? My dear, it was sensational. Is this him?'

The man stuck a hand out towards Scott. 'Dave Pannick. 3HC Radio. You know my programme? "Press the Pannick button." ' He made little quotaton marks in the air. 'All the news, on the hour and from the hour. I heard you. Fantastic.' He turned away, not waiting for an answer. 'Spritzer, Milly, please.' He waved at a girl behind the bar.

That was it. He started talking to someone else.

'Hi, Wallace.'

'Pansy, David. Oh, hallo, Nicky.' Another man joined the group. 'Is this him?' Scott heard a voice say.

Despite being the subject of these introductions, Scott felt detached and rather irrelevant.

What he noticed most about these people, other than

their complete indifference to him, was how beautifully dressed they were. Scott spent his life in a three-piece suit, and he had no other presentable clothes to speak of. He certainly had no other clothes to go out in during the week. He felt ashamed of his creased jacket with the small red stain where a felt-tip pen had leaked.

Another voice addressed him. 'I'm Toby Beyt.' Scott turned to see a large man looming over him. He was dressed in corn-yellow corduroys, beautiful brown brogue shoes and a hacking jacket. He looked slightly out of place here among the soft fabrics and the rumpled linen coats. 'I heard you deal with that man Smallchild.'

'I didn't think so many people listened to the radio,' Scott said.

'Yes. That's right, isn't it? When you listen, it always feels as though you're the only one.'

The man spoke slowly and softly with no emotion or inflexion to his voice, as though words, being important, shouldn't be let loose unnecessarily. Throughout, Scott had the feeling he had come across him before.

'Smallchild really is frightful,' he said, 'but one's not allowed to say that out loud. It's strange. Criticising him is like laughing at a *Sun* journalist. The faintest criticism is like a challenge to their manhood. What manhood they haven't sold, that is.'

'Who does Smallchild work for?'

'Once he worked for the *People*, or at least I think he did. Maybe not. It's funny how he just arrived in our consciousness unannounced.'

'He rose without trace,' Scott quoted.

Toby Beyt smiled at Scott from his great height. 'Perhaps you've started the sinking,' he said.

'Oh, I don't think so,' said Scott. 'A thing like that has no effect really, does it?'

'From what I've heard you're willing to pick an argument with anybody.'

Scott looked at him. Heard what? Did he know this man?

The tall man interpreted the look. 'I work with Nicky,' he explained. 'Or at least, to be honest, she works for me.'

'Oh. What do you do?'

'I make films. Sometimes about the law.'

Scott said nothing.

'That's why Nicky was talking about you. I heard how the witness jumped out of the witness box.'

So that was it.

'That must have been unusual, or at least I hope it was.'

'Oh,' said Scott, reacting to the curiously flat tone of voice himself, finding it difficult to pitch his words properly. He kept noticing that his voice sounded absurdly enthusiastic in comparison. 'Unusual, I suppose,' he said.

He realised as he said it that he had even repeated the man's words.

'Do the people you cross-examine ever try to get back at you?' Toby Beyt said.

Scott thought about it. 'I've never come across it, or at least only that once,' he said. 'I think the funny uniform protects us.' He added unnecessarily, when there was no response in Toby Beyt's eyes, 'The wig, the gown.' This lack of reaction and emotion was difficult to deal with. It was disturbing, as though one of his senses had been lopped off and he was having to grope in the dark without it.

There was silence. In the end Scott filled the gap. 'The governor of Wandsworth was once strung up on Wandsworth Common. By his thumbs, I think. But I don't suppose that counts. His son was a High Court judge.'

Toby Beyt smiled down at him impassively. Scott soldiered

on into the silence. 'There was an argument in court I heard about. Two barristers got into a fist fight at the Old Bailey. One of them accused the other of being a shit and knocked him over.'

Silence. Scott felt as though he were signalling messages over a large chasm. He carried on. 'The police officer who was there had to look the other way quickly.'

'Was he a shit?'

'The police officer?'

'No, the man who was knocked over.'

'Oh, I should say so, yes. I once had an argument with him in the off-licence part of El Vino. Nasty piece of work.'

Silence.

'How about lunch?'

'No, I was buying some wine.'

'I meant how about having some lunch.'

'What, me?'

What a stupid remark. They might almost be speaking completely different languages.

'With Nicky and whoever else sits down.'

'Well, OK. Thanks a lot. Yes, I will.'

'What was it about?'

'What?' Scott was beginning to feel completely disorganised. Everything he said was received so impassively that he felt the subject had died. Then, it seemed an age later, a response came, not unlike one of those telephone calls where you have to wait for your voice to get to the other side of America, and then wait for the reply to get back.

'What did you fight with the shit about in El Vino's?'

'It was silly really . . .' Again the conversation was going nowhere, and Scott stopped speaking. He was beginning to bore himself.

Toby Beyt turned away towards a table. Scott followed. They sat down. Beyt ordered straight away. 'Chicken liver

salad. Aubuisson dressing. Fleurie, please.' Clearly the whole
ritual of sucking his teeth at the menu had passed him by.
Either that or he was a Martian.

He said, 'We're doing, Nicky and I are doing, a programme
on the law at the moment. Would you like to help us make
it?' Toby looked at Scott, who by then was trying to deal
with a piece of lettuce. He nearly said 'There'll be a fee,'
but then he changed his mind and said, 'It'll be fun.'

Scott looked at him, not understanding anything he was
saying, and Toby Beyt had to repeat himself. 'It'll continue
your media career,' he said.

'Oh,' said Scott.

Outside the club, John Donald stood, leaning against a wall.
Though it was a warm day he felt cold. He was hungry. He
hadn't eaten since yesterday and he had been standing or
walking since early morning, when he had taken up his
usual position outside Scott's flat. He was tired.

The wait outside Scott's flat had been longer than normal.
Usually Scott left at about nine, but today he hadn't appeared
till at least half past ten. Donald had nearly given up, but he
knew that if he waited long enough he would get what he
wanted. He also knew that if he went away then surely that
would be the one day it would have been possible to act.

At last Scott came out of his flat and John Donald followed
him across London. During the Tube journey he stood right
next to him. Once he touched him while the train swayed in
the tunnel, but Scott didn't notice. To Scott, John Donald
was just one of the anonymous crowd of people by whom
city dwellers are surrounded – faceless, normally benign.

Scott didn't go to court that day. Instead he ended up
at a radio station. Donald had watched as Scott searched
for the place. Clearly it was his first time there, but after a
while he saw him disappear through an unmarked door.

He stood in a shop doorway, next to the passage he had seen Scott enter. He listened to a radio playing inside. Then he saw the Zap radio sign. He waited in the doorway, occasionally attempting to disguise his presence by walking a few yards away and then back. Then he heard Scott's name announced. He was right. Scott had gone inside. He was pleased at the accuracy of his guess. He was finding that he was becoming better at this as he continued.

Then he heard Scott arguing. He recognised the tone. It was the same tone that had been used on him in the witness box. John Donald had heard the presenter of this show before. Simon Smallchild. He was the one who put people down, especially if they thought they were smart. What was he called? A shock-jock. He'd get Scott.

John Donald waited, but Smallchild didn't do it. Why not? It was as though Smallchild were just giving in. John Donald remembered how in the witness box he himself had slowly given in to that voice and those questions.

Then it finished. Scott came out of the shop with a young woman. They walked south towards Oxford Street, across the road down towards Soho. John Donald followed. Eventually they went through a rotating glass door. He was standing opposite it now.

At first he couldn't work out what it was. There was a steady stream of people going in and out, mostly young, well dressed people arriving in taxis and one guy who got out of a chauffeur driven car. It wasn't a pub, or a restaurant, though it looked like one. Tentatively he approached the door, as if to go in, but he realised immediately that they wouldn't let him in. He decided it must be a private club.

Normally he wouldn't stand for that. He wasn't going to be treated like some piece of filth who didn't count. But this time he had something else to do, something more important. He could always come back later. For a moment he looked at the entrance of the club, imagined the chaos and smiled. Then he turned back to the present.

He stood waiting. He wanted to get away, to get a sandwich or something to eat, but he had to stay and wait. He'd only get his chance by waiting.

The level of noise had risen inside the club. Now all the tables were full. There were people constantly coming and going between the tables, sitting down with other people, putting their arms around them, kissing. Scott watched the strange air kisses that the women offered, and some of the men too, but what stood out was how full of themselves, how confident, these people were.

There were lots of famous faces. He noticed a comedian sitting in one corner with another man he recognised from television. At the front of the room, at one of the prominent tables, there was a film star sitting with a journalist. A stream of people went to and from the film star's table. Every time there was an interruption the journalist scribbled busily, and, while his guest – Scott supposed that film stars didn't take journalists out for lunch – was occupied, he surveyed the room, enjoying sitting in the limelight.

The table where Scott sat was busy too.

Pansy and Nicky had arrived from the bar accompanied by another group, and eventually there were eight of them. It was strange, because although they were all eating, they weren't doing so together. They seemed merely to have gathered.

Toby Beyt was almost completely occupied by people who came up to him. Whoever he was, he was much in demand, at the centre of the marketplace. The feeling Scott had experienced on entering became much clearer. This place existed to be a centre of things and was all the stronger because of its exclusivity. Just being in the room reinforced people's idea of themselves.

174

Scott looked out of the window at the street. He supposed there had always been this scene, people inside looking out, people outside looking in. What was really surprising was that the people who were excluded agreed to put up with it. After all, places like this could only operate because people allowed themselves to be pushed around. It always astonished Scott that people did allow it, that there weren't more people who answered back. After all, the provocation offered was great enough. He'd done enough of that himself, provoking people. The Scotsman jumping out of the witness box at him, for instance.

'This is Jeremy Scott,' Toby said to someone arriving at his shoulder. 'He's a barrister. He works in the real world. Not like us.' Toby's latest acquaintance glanced at Scott and laughed complacently. Scott didn't count in his world – real or not. 'But Toby,' he said, 'we have to get together to talk soon or the whole thing will go off the boil.'

'Let's have lunch,' said Toby.

'I know you can't talk about specific cases,' Toby said to Scott. 'I understand that, but we shan't be asking about particular cases. What we're doing is looking at the overall picture. We may support it by reference to particular examples, but of course you won't necessarily know about them.'

'Well . . .' Scott was doubtful. 'I'm quite happy to talk about things. But going on camera is a bit difficult. We have fairly strict rules.'

'We won't relate what you say to particular cases. It'll all be general stuff. That's right, Nicky, isn't it?' Scott became aware that Nicky had stopped chatting to the man near her and was watching their conversation.

He got the impression that they were trying to handle him. The idea was ridiculous and the moment it entered his head he disregarded the thought. He wasn't some sort of hot property, after all. What could they want with him?

'Well, OK. I'm sorry to sound unenthusiastic, but when you are as nervous of authority as I am . . .'

They laughed.

'No, I mean it,' Scott said. 'One of the problems of our job is how easy it is to look as though you're being sharp. Sharp is the worst term of abuse there is at the Bar. And looking for publicity, going on television and talking about a real case, is the kind of thing sharp people do. It would be dreadful, as well as being against the rules.'

'I want to know about the appeal system,' said Toby. 'How does it work? Start at the beginning.'

Scott said, 'You really want me to tell you? Law is very boring.'

'Yes?' said Toby.

'It's incredibly difficult to appeal a conviction successfully. People often say, "I'll appeal if I lose," but you can't just appeal if you're convicted. People think you can, but you have to get permission from the Court of Appeal.'

'But that's astonishing. Why should you have to get permission?'

'Because of the number of appeals there would be otherwise. Look, be reasonable, you've got to have some way of stopping everyone appealing.'

'Why? Isn't that what the courts are there for?'

Scott hesitated. That was the kind of comment you couldn't answer. He said, 'But an awful lot of appeals are rubbish.'

'How do you know?'

'Well, I don't, I just presume they would be.'

'What happens if you don't get this permission?'

'If you are refused you can go along to the court and argue for it. Oddly enough I've got one of those tomorrow. I'm appealing on behalf of a woman who was refused permission to appeal. I'm going to argue that she should be allowed to appeal.'

'Could Nicky come along and watch you do it? Just to see what happens? It may give us a better idea.'

'No problem,' said Scott. 'It's quite an interesting case, actually. I should imagine I'll get leave to appeal on this one.'

'What happens when you've got permission?'

'Then the prosecution get instructed and the whole thing is put off for a full hearing later.'

'And in your case?'

'Well, this is a bit more complicated since we're asking to have new evidence heard.'

'No specific questions, but is that difficult, calling more evidence?'

'Almost impossible. Appeal judges hate new evidence. Asking them to hear it is like asking a professor of engineering to get under a car and get oil on his hands. Professors don't do that. Everything in the Appeal Court is totally detached from reality. New evidence is a bit too much like real life.'

That sounded a bit harsh.

He went on, 'It has to be. The Appeal Court is dealing in general principles, you see.' It was always difficult to describe courts to someone who had never been in them. You always had to leave so much out.

'You're apologising for them again.'

Scott realised Toby was right. Whether or not he was leaving bits out, he was certainly apologising for them. Well, perhaps they needed it.

Chapter Fourteen

The Court of Appeal is like a church. Three judges who, although they weren't very old, all affected incredible antiquity filed in, their hands folded calmly one on top of the other, like monks at compline.

Scott couldn't quite see. Was one of them carrying white gloves? He thought probably he wasn't – that was an Old Bailey ceremony. Maybe it wasn't merely ceremony here. Perhaps the judges walked up and down the broad private passage behind the courtroom, fully dressed in their robes with white gloves on, nodding slowly and graciously to each other.

He knew that at night they were put away to sleep in rows, in tall, dark cupboards. So anything was possible.

It had been pouring with rain when Scott crossed Fleet Street to the High Court, and the damp had infected the whole building.

In the main hall, cavernous as a cathedral and shimmering with crystal light, there was a miasma of steam rising from the patient queue at the X-ray machine. For a moment Scott jostled with persistent litigants, errand boys, people about to be divorced who had lost their way from Somerset House, and thin, elegant leading barristers who never seemed to have anything to carry, as they all offered themselves, their bags and their pockets for inspection.

After a struggle, Scott reached the noticeboard to confirm which court he was in: Court 7, Lord Justice Tocket, Bart, sitting with two other judges whose names he did not know. The other two had no doubt been promoted to the High Court after years of patient paperwork in expensive chambers. Now was their opportunity to take it out on Scott. It would be good revenge for all those dusty years of rebuttals, surrebuttals, Tomlin orders, Farthingale schedules, Mareva injunctions, Calderbank letters, Anton Pilar orders, *quia timet* injunctions; requests for further and better particulars, answers to the same, refusals to answer the same; mandatory cost orders, pleadings and pleadings offered hereinafter to be amended, Bullock orders, applications for specific discovery, special avoidances, gammon and spinach. Scott looked around, half expecting Charles Dickens's Inspector Bucket to step out from the shadows.

'Lord Justice Tocket, Bart, for heaven's sake! OK. Well, let's see what he's going to do to me,' he said half aloud. A tourist looked at him.

Scott was alone. Monty Bach had said that there was no one to spare from the office, and Hilda Forgan had not been brought from Holloway. Scott was grateful. It was better like that – he didn't have to devote part of his attention to looking after someone else.

'Hallo,' said Nicky.

She was standing behind him as he turned. He had forgotten about her.

'Hi,' he said. It was difficult to get exactly the right tone, just on the dividing line between brusqueness and friendly politeness. She was good news, but he had his mind on other things.

'What an incredible place,' she said.

'Yes.'

He walked past the statue of the architect, the man who had built the place and was supposed to have gone mad trying to count the rooms. If the puzzled look on the face of his statue was anything to go by it was probably true.

'I've never been here before.'

'I don't come here often myself. Thank God,' said Scott.

'Look at those windows.'

She followed him into the passage that led down to the robing room, past a collection of badly made papier-mâché dummies in glass cases, displaying the collection of historic judicial uniforms. She paused to look at them. 'Pretty odd-looking models,' she said. She was right. The one of the Lord Chief Justice looked like a psychopath.

Scott said, 'You haven't seen the real thing yet.'

They went down a passage which became darker and darker, ending at a small door at the bottom of some steps. 'You'll have to wait here,' he said, and he left her at the door marked 'Male advocates only'.

The robing room, with its load of wet overcoats and umbrellas, was even damper than the entrance. It was full. With difficulty, Scott found a space to put his bag down and, feeling out of place, a criminal hack rubbing shoulders with people who sued doctors for a living, he began to change.

'Hallo there.'

Scott looked up. It was an old acquaintance with whom he used to do minor criminal cases when they were both beginners.

'Don't see you much nowadays.'

Scott's old friend had moved on to better things. 'We miss you,' said Scott.

'Don't miss the fees.'

'No, I can understand that,' Scott said. He was keenly aware that he was earning about the same this morning as his friend charged for an hour's advice. He wished he hadn't got involved in this, or at least that Harry hadn't got him involved. Not only was there no money in it, but he was turning down other work in order to be here.

He looked at his friend. The man had got his stiffly starched collar stuck. He was unable to slip the stud out. 'Can you help me?' he said.

Scott put his hands to the man's throat and started wrestling with the tiny piece of metal. 'Do you know, I've been wearing these damn things since the age of nine?'

'Me too,' said Scott. 'The difference between you and me is that I think it's about time we stopped.'

'There you are.' Scott reappeared fully robed. Nicky was waiting outside. 'What do we do now?' she said.

'We go to court,' Scott said.

They took the curving staircase that led to the first floor. Some of his worst experiences had happened in this building. No matter how well prepared you were, you were never prepared enough. Or at least that's what barristers thought, and it engendered a continual pitch of anxiety.

The passage leading past the courts stretched into the distance. On the left there were mullioned windows, the tiny leaded lights allowing a baleful light to slant across the tiled floor towards the doors of the courts. Under each window there was an oak bench built into the bay, and sitting on each one was a forlorn group of people watching Scott and Nicky. Scott could feel their eyes on him.

He knew the look. It was a mixture of fear and hope that this might be the man who decided things in their favour. After all, this was the Criminal Appeal Court. These were people, the families of the appellants, who expected the worst and were not quite sure just how it was going to happen. For them anyone in uniform could suddenly turn out to be the bearer of very bad news indeed. You didn't come to the Court of Appeal on a criminal matter unless something had already gone badly wrong anyway. He thought, Perhaps that accounts for the judges' jaundiced attitudes; they only ever see a self-selecting group of difficult, sad cases.

He said to Nicky, 'There's not much joy here. Most of these judges do this on sufferance. They would much prefer to sit deciding whether insurance companies should pay money to people. That's what they trained for, that's what they made their money doing.'

Scott stopped opposite the door to Court 7 and looked out of the window. Below it lay a white-tiled courtyard, filthy with the grime of a century of London air. Over the yard was stretched a net. It looked like the nets used in prisons to prevent suicides. On the net, suspended in the middle, lay a discarded can of Lilt. The can had been there for as long as Scott could remember. It hung there with something of the permanence and the majesty of the law itself. There was no reason why it should not survive, suspended in the dirt and gloom, for as long as the common law itself.

'What now?' said Nicky.

Scott turned his attention back to her. He had lived in this envelope of desperate hopelessness for so long that he no longer tasted it in his mouth. It had become normality.

'We wait,' he said. 'We're last on. There are some appeals against sentence before us.'

'Appeals against sentence?' she said. Even the simplest concept in his job was not necessarily generally understood.

'People appealing against the sentence that was passed in the crown court, saying it was wrong or excessive.'

Opposite them, a woman, clearly the mother of a

defendant, started tugging ineffectively at the door of the court. She was weighed down by a package and a suit on a hanger, obviously brought for her son to wear in court. That wouldn't be allowed. She would have to take the whole lot home with her.

Scott stepped over to her. 'The court won't be opened for a moment yet. I should just wait a little,' he said.

The woman turned towards him, her eyes hoping to see someone she would recognise. Scott had seen the look before. It was abject.

'If you wait I'll make sure that the court knows you're here,' he said. 'Which case are you concerned with?'

'Evans,' she said. She spoke in a strong Welsh accent. Perhaps she had come up from Cardiff that morning. 'Michael Evans.'

'Let's see.' Scott looked at the list stuck on the board outside the court. 'Michael Evans. Yes, third case on, just before us. Don't you worry, I'll make sure that your counsel knows you're here.' The woman sank on to a bench and began to move her packages around.

Scott sat in court watching counsel for Michael Evans trying to persuade the three judges that his client's sentence should be shortened.

'You say he was unemployed,' said the judge on the left, 'yet he owned a car. How could this be?'

'A car is by no means an unusual possession for a young man nowadays,' said counsel, 'even if he is unemployed.' Scott looked at the lawyer appearing for Michael Evans. He didn't look much older than twenty-six himself, but he was talking as though he was pleased to have arrived in his forties at last.

'Well, I find that an extraordinary state of affairs,' said the judge.

Scott always found it intensely difficult to listen to argument in someone else's case – he always wanted to join in. Why shouldn't the man own a car? Possessions aren't a privilege, he wanted to say. But counsel for Michael Evans ploughed on as though nothing had been said. Indeed, in a way it had not. The judge's intervention had very little to do with the case.

'Mr Evans had lost his job, m'luds, through no fault of his own. He was made redundant.'

The word m'lud always sent a shiver through Scott's spine. It sounded so dreadful to someone not used to it, redolent of serfdom, privilege and abasement. He tried to avoid it when he could.

'At the same time, m'luds, his wife had left him for another man, denying him access to his three children. He had no contact with them. She defied the court's order, and when she was brought back before the court she invented a story, accusing Mr Evans of abusing the children. The police investigated. They took a statement from one of the children with the assistance of a social worker who for reasons best known to her was convinced of my client's guilt. He was imprisoned for four months awaiting trial. That's when he lost his job.

'The accusations collapsed when his elder boy made a statement denying that what his mother said was true, and describing how the social worker had tried to tell him what to say. Your Lordships have seen the bundle containing a transcript of the boy's statement . . .'

'We have seen it, Mr Lewis,' said the judge in the centre, dismissively.

'Ap Lewis, m'lud.' It was the young counsel's only moment of complete certainty.

Scott had not heard the judge speak before. So here was Lord Justice Tocket, Bart. He had a thin, reedy voice, which conveyed profound indifference to the little tragedy being rehearsed before him. 'We do not think it greatly relevant,' he said.

He paused, and there was absolute silence as everybody took that on board. The judge looked up at the ceiling and then at the bookshelves that lined the sides of the court. It was a look meant in every aspect to point out who and what was important.

'We do not think it greatly important. Your client damaged by fire a car belonging to another man. He did so reckless of any possibility of danger to other people. His emotional turmoil, as we have seen it colourfully described in the papers, does not nearly approach the danger he caused others.'

'M'luds, he is not a man who has ever been in any other sort of trouble.'

'So we have observed, Mr ap Lewis. But unfortunately this is a crime that we find often committed by those who have never otherwise faced the courts. We cannot therefore give it the mitigation we would otherwise think proper. Or at least I say so. I cannot bind my colleagues who sit with me.'

He turned to the other judges on either side of him, to find them already nodding their approval of his comments.

Scott could see the young barrister wilting. He would soon be sitting down. There was nothing to be said to a judge like this.

'I understand, m'lud, the gravity of the offence, but it was an offence committed entirely upon the spur of the moment.'

'How can you say that, Mr ap Lewis? Your client had purposely gone to the house where this man was staying.'

'It was my client's own house, m'lud. When he went there he had no intention of harming anyone. It was his own house, he had built a great part of it with his own hands. And now his wife had invited another man to live there with her and his children. The CSA had' – counsel tripped over his words for a moment – 'the Child Support Agency who decide these things were insisting that Mr Evans keep paying the full amount of maintenance to his wife. He was threatened with imprisonment for not paying for the house where his wife was living with another man.

'He couldn't pay since he had been falsely remanded in prison on the trumped-up allegations I referred to, but the CSA had decided that was no good reason for not paying. When he got to the house that evening he was turned away.'

The judges looked down on the young advocate. His voice wavered in the darkness of the court. An usher opened and closed a door. A police car made its way hysterically down Fleet Street. High up to the left, in the prisoner's dock, Scott could see the top of Michael Evans's head.

'Mr Evans stood outside and saw that the man who was living rent-free in his house had just bought a new car. He was able to afford it no doubt because Mr Evans was paying his rent. M'luds the whole situation boiled over inside him.'

'Mr ap Lewis, are you suggesting that your client was in some way justified in doing what he did? If I may say so, that is a very novel approach and one fraught with much danger.'

'M'luds, I would not dream of such a thing.'

'But you are, Mr ap Lewis. It was only by good luck that the car was not badly damaged. Had that car burned instead of being badly scorched it could well have injured others. His own children maybe.'

'M'luds there was no chance of that.'

'No chance? Why then did he plead guilty?'

Scott could see, even at this distance, what had happened

in the trial court. Michael Evans must originally have been charged with arson 'with intent to endanger life'. If he had been found guilty of that, he would have been put away almost for ever. So he offered a plea to arson, the lesser offence of being 'reckless of endangering life' – thinking that his mitigation would reduce the offence to almost nothing. But of course the judge had then treated acting 'recklessly' almost as severely as 'intending' to endanger someone.

'But M'lud, seven years' imprisonment . . .'

Seven years! By the time he came out his life would be totally changed. His wife and children would have moved on, he would be forgotten.

'Mr ap Lewis, I say it to emphasise the gravity of what was done here. This was an attack on another man's property. If this court were seen to condone such behaviour . . .'

Scott got up and walked out of the court. It was becoming a distraction.

'I appear on behalf of the applicant Hilda Forgan.' It was something like a pleasure to get the formula exactly right. Hilda was, until she was granted leave to appeal, only an applicant for leave. When it was granted she would become an appellant. Of course, it was just this impulse towards legal accuracy that sent people who were not lawyers mad.

Scott looked at the three judges. They had sent Michael Evans's mother packing, back to South Wales. Scott had last seen her as she went down the passage outside, being comforted – or was it the other way round? – by the young barrister. Now the judges turned their attention to him.

'Yes, Mr Scott?' Lord Justice Tocket looked at where Scott stood in the back row, right over by the door. The position Scott had chosen seemed to suit what he was doing, signalling over the vast gulf that separated him from these people.

'The application before the court today is for leave to appeal against conviction, and for leave to call further evidence.' He paused.

'Yes, Mr Scott?' The judge repeated himself in just the same tone, dried leaves rustling in the wind. Now that Scott was standing up he could see that the judge was writing with a pen which he dipped in an inkwell in front of him. The sight was so astonishing that at first Scott couldn't comprehend it. He watched in amazement. The judge shook the pen slightly to free it from its burden of ink. As he did so he turned a face of parchment towards Scott.

'Need we decide whether you should call this extra evidence now?'

'It is the sole ground of appeal.'

'We observed that.'

The judge to the right – Scott had not heard him speak before – barked out, 'If we give you leave to appeal, will you be adding to the grounds?'

For a moment Scott said nothing. This he had not expected. Then he understood what was being asked of him.

'On that matter I will have to take instructions.'

'You mean you have not decided yet?'

'Not all the evidence has been put in proper order yet.'

'You hope to call further medical evidence?'

'We hope so.'

'I ask you again, Mr Scott. Will these grounds remain your only grounds of appeal?'

Scott noticed that none of the judges was looking at him when this question was asked. Their attention was fixed on the other side of the court, up towards the back. For the moment Scott was not able to turn to see what was attracting them, but then he got the opportunity. The senior judge said, 'One moment, Mr Scott,' and signalled towards the judges on either side of him. They got up and formed a huddle around his chair.

Scott turned to look behind him. At the back of the court, in the highest tier of seats, sitting directly beneath a tall bookcase containing black-spined law books, was Galbraith. He was dressed in a tweed suit and an overcoat. Scott could feel his eyes boring into him.

'What is it?' Nicky pulled his gown. 'What is the question they are asking you?'

'They want to know.' Scott paused. If it wasn't being said out loud, why should he repeat it out loud? 'They want to know.'

'What?' said Nicky. The judges were still arguing vigorously between themselves.

'They want to know if I am going to be adding a ground of appeal blaming counsel who acted in the trial. They want to know if I am going to say that the lawyers at the first trial were incompetent.'

'Are you?'

'I don't know,' said Scott. 'I hope not. They probably weren't, after all.'

'Mr Scott.' Scott looked up to see the three judges sitting in their original seats, all looking at him. 'Mr Scott, you shall have your leave. We have read your advice and your grounds of appeal. We are satisfied there is a matter here that ought to be enquired into. We do not need to invite further argument.'

Scott contorted his features into an expression that simultaneously demonstrated attentiveness and an appreciation of the obvious intelligence and fairness of the court.

'But we do not give you leave to call your witnesses. That, it seems to us, is for the court which hears the case. Do you wish us to make any witness orders?'

'No, that is not necessary.'

'We do not intend to give a judgment in this case, save to say this. If, Mr Scott, you wish to add any further grounds of appeal, then you must do so in good time, so that the court can make the proper enquiries of the various people involved. We do not wish to encourage you to add further grounds, Mr Scott. We cannot, of course, prevent you from doing so, but we remind you of your professional duty.'

The court remained still for a moment. Scott turned round. Galbraith was gone.

'That will be all,' said the Lord Justice Tocket, drying his pen nib on a piece of blotting paper.

'What's happened, then?' Nicky said.

'We're being allowed to appeal. Hilda Forgan can at least have the case heard.'

'What was all that about professional duty?'

'They want to know how I am going to argue the case.'

'But why the comment about professional duty?'

'Because I have to think carefully about it.'

'Why especially?'

'Because before you suggest someone has screwed something up you think very carefully.'

'Who says someone has screwed up?'

'They assume I am going to say that.'

'Why?'

'Because everyone here always assumes someone is going to blame someone else.'

'Well, will you?'

'I'm going to try not to. Or at least I hope not.' Then he said, 'Will you come to a party with me?'

'When?'

'Friday.'

'All right,' she said. 'Do I have to dress up?'

'Not much, just a bit. I'll be wearing a dinner jacket. It's a dinner at the Middle Temple Hall to mark the retirement of my old clerk.' He felt deceitful. Catherine would have been coming to this. But then he thought, Why not?

'Are you sure it's not too short notice?'

'No,' she said. 'There's nothing I can't get out of. I'd love to come.' She put her arm around him.

'That's great.'

'Why did you say you hope not?'

'Hope not what?'

'Hope you don't have to say he has screwed up the case.'

'Oh, that. Because it's extremely unlikely that it was screwed up. Whatever they're telling me, Galbraith is far too good a lawyer. And even if he did there's no way I would be able to convince the court he did.'

'Who's Galbraith?'

Chapter Fifteen

'I didn't know who he was then. Galbraith. They kept telling me I was lucky and that I should be grateful. Yes, they wanted me to be grateful that he had agreed to do my case. That young man, the first barrister who came to the magistrates' court, I remember, he said, "Oh, Miss Forgan, Mr Galbraith has agreed to do your case." ' Hilda Forgan mimicked a mincing face. 'It was as though I had been accused of murder especially so I could have the privilege of Galbraith acting as my lawyer.

'And do you know what? I believed it. I did. When I first met him I actually thanked him for coming. I had got into the same state as all the others: the great panjandrum is here.'

She looked past Scott's shoulder at the notice telling visitors not to give anything to prisoners, but she was seeing other things.

'That's a bit of an old-fashioned word, isn't it? "Panjandrum." Like juggernaut. Jagannath; when he was in India my father supervised the Jagannath being pulled out. I remember him telling me how a house had to be pulled down to make way for it. Odd how these expressions come into the language. Now it just means a big lorry. Anyway, they all behaved as though the great panjandrum had suddenly decided to call.

'Even the prison staff came over all funny. One of them said, "He's a bit grand, isn't he?" Well, I had my mind on other things, I was interested in getting this all dealt with and finished, so I wasn't watching out for the . . . the crap that was being handed out. I'd notice it now, though. Now I would. The Great Galbraith. Phooey. He was a fraud.

'He humoured me. He *humoured* me. Me! I can see it now. What was happening. I wouldn't stand for it now.'

Scott, who once again had been waiting for the moment to interrupt this unceasing flow of words, said, 'You'd tell me now, Hilda, would you, if you thought I was bullying you?'

'You bet I would. I don't let anybody tell me what to do now. It's a funny thing. You know? I had to be locked up before I began to understand how to be free.'

This was a different tone. She seemed to be changing.

'I used to take whatever crazy stuff was handed out. In my old life there were things I was allowed to know about and things I wasn't. For instance, I was allowed to know about who was on the church altar flower rota. Not just me. I mean women like me.

'Women like me were allowed to know about telling young children to sit up straight. But about my own trial for murder I wasn't allowed to know a damn thing. I took no decisions. They were all taken for me. This man waltzed in and told me what to do.'

Scott said, 'Miss Forgan, stop a minute. This is what I want to talk about. You've got to give me instructions. I mean, you've got to tell me what you want done. That's why I've come here.'

She looked at him. Scott had got her attention for a moment. He took advantage of it. 'During your original trial no one argued about whether your aunt was able to move or whether she could get out of the wheelchair. You remember you told me that? It was accepted by everyone. Did you agree with that?'

'I agreed,' she said, 'but it was like all the other agreements I've ever made. I was taught to agree with other people. I was taught that to disagree was bad manners.'

Scott had lost her and she was looking back again. 'You know, in life, I could have done anything. I wasn't stupid, my parents had money. I was educated. I could have been a doctor, anything. But you know what I was taught? I was taught to do what I was told. All my life we were meant to do what we were told and not cause a fuss, so that the men could have their lives. What a waste.'

She stopped talking.

Scott said, 'Miss Forgan, listen to me. We've got statements from people who think your aunt could move. We've got a statement from a doctor. He says she could well have got out of the wheelchair on her own. We need to know why it was so easily accepted at the trial that she was unable to move.'

'Move on her own? That's a thing we were never meant to do. "Nor leave the soap still in the water, that's a thing you never oughta." ' Hilda Forgan laughed.

Scott wondered whether she was going to drift away entirely. Then she answered his question. 'He told me not to. Galbraith. He saw a doctor and the doctor told him there was nothing to be said.'

'He saw a doctor? He told you that?'

'Yes. He told me he saw a doctor he knew. I think it was in his club.'

'In his club? He saw a doctor in his club?'

Hilda Forgan leaned forward, looking at Scott, her face right up to his. She said, 'You're repeating every word I say, Mr Scott. Did you know that?'

Scott suddenly saw another person looking out at him from behind the torrent of uncontrolled words.

He laughed and said, 'I was, wasn't I. Thank you, Miss Forgan.'

'No trouble,' she said. 'It's important to remain calm in these situations.'

She smiled at Scott. 'He told me he saw a doctor in his club and he asked his opinion, and apparently the doctor agreed with the consultant who had given a statement for the prosecution. They knew each other, they'd been to school together or something, university. And this doctor, the friend of Galbraith, said there was no point in arguing the point.'

'And you accepted that?'

'Yes. Wouldn't you? What was I meant to do? Join a club and find my own doctor?' She laughed.

'Did Mr Galbraith produce a written opinion?'

'You must remember I was ill.'

'He never wrote an opinion for you to see and think about?'

'I don't remember seeing one.'

'He never got a proper opinion from a doctor for you to read?'

'He saw him in the club. I told you.'

'Talked to him in the club.' Scott repeated it and looked at Monty who stared back at him.

'When did he tell you this?' Scott said.

'Here. Once.'

'Do you remember?'

'Yes. I remember it well. It was at the time I was taking those pills they used to give me, the ones that nearly made me go off my head. I was jabbering. They had to take me out of the room eventually.'

Scott leaned back. Her instructions were becoming

horribly clear. She was telling him she had received no real advice at all on this central point. He looked at Monty. There was no need to say anything to him; he had obviously come to the same conclusion. He was shaking his head slowly.

'Hilda . . . Miss Forgan.' Scott stumbled over how to address her. To call her by her first name seemed demeaning. He said, 'I'm not much good at first names.'

'You should learn,' she said. 'Most people do. It's quite all right. Most people are quite happy being friendly with others. That's your real problem, you know.'

Scott was brought up short again. For a moment he had lost his thread.

'The trouble with you,' she said to Scott, 'is that you're too distant. You think that if you like someone and show it, you're going to get rejected, or hurt somehow. I see it often in here. This place is full of people who've been hurt.'

'I'm sorry, Hilda. But I have to get back to what I've come here for.'

'No problem,' she said. 'I only said it in passing. I can see what you're like very clearly. You're still a young man – well, youngish. You're nice, but you're still frightened of things. You should trust people more. What happened to you when you were young? What hurt you?'

While they were waiting in the double door lock to get out of the prison, Scott said to Monty Bach, 'Have you managed to get the papers from the solicitors who acted for her before?'

'No. They're hanging on to them until they get paid.'

'They can do that?'

'Yes. Happens all the time.'

'Not in legal aid work it doesn't.' Scott digested the information and said, 'But this isn't legal aid work, is it?'

He thought about the three hundred pounds he was earning for all this trouble. 'So we are not going to be able to find out whether Galbraith gave her an advice on getting a doctor.'

'No. At least, not until she's paid them.'

'Is she going to be able to do that?'

'No.'

'Who's paying for what we're doing now, then?'

'Benefactors.'

'Who?'

'Just well-wishers.'

Scott's car was in the car park round the side of the prison. He helped Monty in. The closed-circuit television cameras watched them.

'Are we going to have to attack Galbraith?' he said.

'Yes,' said Monty.

'You know the law. We'd have to show that he was flagrantly incompetent, not that he just made a mistake. What chance do we have of showing that Galbraith is flagrantly incompetent? Galbraith! The great panjandrum. I don't believe her anyway. If we start trying to say he gave her no advice on this the first thing that will happen is that a copy of it will appear. He's far too good a lawyer to muck her about. Everyone knows that. I didn't tell you . . .' He stopped talking for a moment. Cars and buses were backed up solid as far as the Holloway Road and Scott had to try to cut across four lanes of traffic to go back the other way. He leaned forward, trying to see a gap, but there was nothing. '. . . I didn't tell you, Galbraith was sitting at the back of the court when I made the first application. The judges were paying more attention to him than to me, even though all he was doing was sitting there.'

Eventually a huge lorry stopped for him, the air brakes

hissing and sighing. Scott edged out into the traffic. He said, 'Why didn't Galbraith become a judge?'

'He didn't want it.'

'Did you know him well, Monty?'

'Yes. I used to brief him a lot in the old days.'

'No more?'

'No. Don't go near him now.'

'Why's that?'

A bearded man driving an old red Volvo and reading a book in the traffic jam stopped, leaving a gap that Scott could push into. Scott looked at the book as he squeezed past. 'Look at that,' he said, 'he's reading Elmore Leonard in a traffic jam in North London. What does that do to the nervous system?'

'What's Elmore Leonard?' said Monty.

'An American writer, pretty good too. Why don't you go near him any more?'

'He let me down once.'

Scott reached the other side of the road in time to turn right and pull away from the traffic jam.

'What happened?'

'It's an old story.'

'That's OK. Tell me.'

'I briefed him in a case, but when he got to court he had another appointment, so he persuaded the client to plead guilty.'

'He didn't.'

'Yes. There was a good run in the case too. And he knew it. I watched him do it.'

'That doesn't sound like him.'

'It doesn't sound like the image he's created for himself. But that's him.'

'What happened?'

'I stopped briefing him. And then I discovered that

he'd gone to my senior partner and complained, and he in turn wouldn't back me, so I left the firm. It was a difficult time.'

'He's always thought of as the great symbol of the defence lawyer.'

'He's out for what he can get and he always has been. You just watch him. Here we are.'

Scott pulled up outside Caledonian Road Tube.

'Are you sure this is OK, Monty?'

'Very convenient, don't you worry. I prefer to manage on my own.'

As Scott pulled away, he looked back. Monty had stopped and put his briefcase down. He was rootling in his pocket – to get his snuff out no doubt. He looked a forlorn figure, but he wasn't, Scott knew that. He had been fighting lonely fights on behalf of his clients for years. He could manage on his own.

Scott drove away, Pentonville prison on his left, white as a dream.

Monty wasn't going to allow him to do this case without attacking Galbraith, that was certain. For Monty it presented no problem at all. It shouldn't for him either, yet it did, because if he attacked Galbraith he knew he couldn't possibly win. The court just wouldn't listen to him.

There would have to be another way.

'Galbraith will be there tonight,' Gatling said. 'Years ago he was in Bill's old chambers, and he's been invited along to help give him a proper send-off. He'll be making the main speech.'

Gatling's dinner jacket was magnificent. It had a curious green tinge to it, and down the right lapel a faint trace of cigar ash. Scott guessed it had been in the Gatling family for generations.

They were walking between the pillars outside the Temple church towards the dinner celebrating Scott's ex-clerk's retirement. If Catherine hadn't gone away, she would have been there.

Behind them were the faint sounds of a choir. A young clerk appeared at the door of the chambers at number two, bumping a trolley down the steps. The trolley was loaded so high with books and papers that he could hardly manage it.

'That's a tax set,' Gatling said distantly. Through the archway Scott could see a large car draw up and people in evening clothes get out. 'I've been asked to say a few words before Galbraith speaks,' said Gatling.

'About Bill?'

'Yes.'

'What's there to say?'

'I'll think of something.'

'Is Harry coming?'

'Yes. He'll be there.'

'He used to work with Bill, did he?'

'Well, Harry was junior clerk to Walter in Trevor Townsend's old chambers, before Trevor split with Charles Taylor, who set up with Simon Mauleverer, and Walter and Harry went along with them, until Harry went off to number six with Gary and the boys, setting up with Sam, who had come from Charlie Gray's where Walter eventually went with Bill, who was the senior clerk. He had Harry as his junior clerk. But that all went wrong, so that's why Harry's with us and why Bill went to number four. And now he's retiring.'

'Oh,' said Scott. 'How do you remember it all?'

'Stuff of life, old boy,' said Gatling.

The semicircular steps of the Middle Temple Hall were dotted with people in dinner jackets going into the building or standing, waiting for others to arrive. Gatling approached them with a series of hearty hallos, eliciting yips of pleasure from a group of women dressed in peach colours.

'Gats,' one of them called. 'Is Marjorie coming?'

'Hallo, girls,' Gatling said. 'The boss'll be here in a moment. Shall we go in?' He left Scott on the steps, heading for the dark interior of the building.

Scott stood on the steps. Sally Donne appeared looking particularly beautiful, thin as a child. She was walking with Tony Jay. These were the people Scott used to work with. 'Hallo, Jeremy,' she said. 'Who are you waiting for? Catherine?'

Scott felt a stab of remorse, it was funny how he couldn't control it. Perhaps he didn't want to. 'No. She's in Amsterdam. I'm waiting for a friend.'

'A new person?'

'Catherine's away.'

'On the loose, are you, Jeremy?' It was Tony Jay. 'Don't get into trouble.' He disappeared into the hall with Sally. Scott watched them go. So he and Sally were an item. It had taken long enough.

Scott stood at the door. The noticeboards inside the entrance advertised scholarships to America and a public lecture on the implications of the modern European law on employee contracts.

Beyond them, the hall, seventeenth-century oak, black with age and candle smoke but polished, flickered and danced in the light. A roaring noise of conversation filtered out through the screen doors. At the far end, the Stuart kings looked down on the gathering people, incuriously, from huge portraits.

Scott had eaten dinners here when he was a student, meeting other students, mainly from India, and drinking Chilean wine. Chilean wine wasn't fashionable then. It was said to have been given as a fee by a bankrupt government to one of the senior members, who had solved a border dispute. There were five hundred cases of it. It had to be got rid of.

Later he had sat in this hall listening to lectures on sentencing from a small, furious Welsh don.

'God, what a place!' said Nicky, appearing at his shoulder. 'No wonder you lot are so arrogant. It's stunning.' They stood and gazed up at the huge carved roof. The hall *was* astonishingly beautiful. He turned and said to her, 'Where did you get this ability to appear out of nowhere?'

'Journalism school,' she said. 'It's part of the course on doorstepping.'

She was even more attractive in her simple evening clothes.

'C'm'on,' he said. 'Let's introduce you.'

Gatling was easily distracted from talk of his children's teeth, and Scott was amused by how assuredly he managed to hit exactly the wrong note with Nicky. 'Well, it's really good to meet you, m'dear,' he said, inclining his huge bulk over her. 'And what a pleasure it is to meet a new face.'

Nicky bridled.

At the same time Scott could see Gatling's wife breasting the crowd towards them. 'Douglas!' she said, from a distance of fifteen feet. Hearing the voice, Gatling snapped smartly to attention, while looking around him to see where his wife was.

She arrived and said, 'Why, it's Nicky. Nicky Vesey.' Marjorie Gatling held her hands up in front of her. 'I haven't seen you since that party at the Willoughbys' in Lincolnshire.'

'Marjorie. Fancy seeing you here.' Nicky and Gatling's wife embraced each other, careful not to crease anything.

Marjorie Gatling turned to her husband. 'Nicky's mother's sister is Charley's Aunt Steph. Don't you remember?'

Gatling started searching his memory. 'The house where there was the pillow fight?'

'That's it!' said his wife.

'But what are you doing here?' Gatling said. Any connection with Scott had been driven entirely out of his mind by this family analysis.

'I'm here with Jeremy,' said Nicky.

Gatling and his wife swung round to where Jeremy was standing, obviously expecting one of their own group, only to be surprised by his awkward presence.

'But how did you meet Jeremy?' Gatling said.

'I just met him. Is that so surprising?' Nicky said.

'At court,' added Scott.

'At court. Fancy that,' said Marjorie, looking at Scott as though it were his fault.

In the background a handbell rang and a voice said, 'Ladies and gentlemen, dinner is served.'

'Dinner, Douglas. Dinner,' Marjorie Gatling said. 'Where are we sitting, Douglas, at the high table? See you later, Nicky.'

She swept off with her husband.

'You didn't tell me you knew Marje Gatling,' Nicky said.

'I don't,' said Scott. 'I know her husband.'

'Well, that's the same.'

'What am I meant to do? Give you a list of people I know?'

'Dinner is served, ladies and gentlemen.' The voice was more insistent.

'Where are we sitting?'

'He said he would try to get Galbraith to speak to me. Or

at least get me to have a word with Galbraith. He's already mentioned the case to him.'

'But if Galbraith screwed it up why are you crawling to him? What does it matter to you?'

'It's much more complicated. What happens is that the Court of Appeal writes to him about the case and asks for his comments. Or I'm meant to write to him. The law's not certain.'

'But you get to see the comments?'

'Yes. But you don't really get to answer them. What he writes goes pretty well unchallenged. If he says Hilda accepted all along that the aunt couldn't move an inch, there's no answer. We're stuck with it. And I bet he does, because I'm not going to believe there was no advice on that point until it's proved. Really it depends upon whether he says that. Look,' Scott said, pointing at the high table, 'can you imagine a middle-aged lady charged with murder standing up to him?'

At the end of the hall beneath the massive portraits, a long table was raised up on a platform above the other diners. In the middle, facing the hall, sat Bill, Scott's ex-clerk, slightly flushed. On either side of him sat the senior members of his chambers.

'That's Galbraith,' Scott said to Nicky. He indicated one of the men sitting near the end of the row.

Galbraith was a compactly built, smiling man. He wore half-glasses, over which he was watching the people sitting below him. His expression was one of detached amusement. The others about him were already eating, but he was not, and sat leaning back in his chair, his feet thrust out beneath the table. Scott could see that he had one hand inside his waistcoat, in the other he was holding a large glass of wine. His plate of food was pushed to one side. Perhaps he wasn't going to eat at all.

On either side of him sat the wives of other guests. But Galbraith was paying no attention to them. His eyes were roving over the people dining below. The Olympian detachment, with which he famously snubbed judges and terrified witnesses, radiated from him.

'Who are you looking at?' Scott's neighbour spoke to him.

'Galbraith,' Scott said. 'I didn't know he'd be here.'

'He used to be with Bill way back when.'

'That must have been years ago.'

'It was.'

'Did you ever work with Galbraith?'

'Yes, once. I did that kidnapping case with him. It was the one where he cross-examined the chief inspector for three days.'

'What?' Nicky was amazed.

'Yes. For three days. I remember. The point he had to get across was how the police had completely disregarded the rules. It was extraordinary how he did it. First he painted this picture of out-of-touch civil servants sitting in Whitehall clogging up the police with useless rules, and then he asked the witness if he agreed.

'Of course, the policeman denied it. He had at least to pretend that he agreed with the rules, but every time Galbraith described the effect of them, he did it so vividly that you knew that it was exactly what the chief inspector really thought. In fact you felt sympathy for the poor overworked police, plagued by little men in bowler hats carrying briefcases. But then Galbraith pulled the rug out from underneath him and described to the court what the rules were really for – to prevent browbeating and the invention of evidence – and again, he did that so effectively that you wondered how you could ever have felt otherwise. The whole atmosphere changed with a word.'

Scott watched the man sitting above them. Still he was not eating but watching the hall beneath him.

Scott's neighbour went on, 'One moment the witness was a friendly neighbourhood copper put upon by little men from Whitehall, and the next he was extremely sinister, like something out of a totalitarian state.'

'Was the man acquitted?' Nicky asked.

'No.'

They laughed.

'That's the thing about getting to where Galbraith's got. The people he gets to defend are generally so awful that they can't *be* got off. They have to be convicted. But it's the way he loses the cases that's so amazing.'

Nicky turned to Scott and laughed. 'Doesn't sound much of a recommendation to me.'

Scott said, 'I remember that trial. His guy didn't have a snowball's chance of an acquittal, but he fought like crazy for him. He's a tiger, totally committed. If he's guilty that's not something Galbraith can help.'

They turned to look at Galbraith again. It was just the wrong moment – his eyes were on them. He must have realised immediately that they were talking about him.

Scott turned back to the menu. 'Well, what are we eating, then?'

'*Panache* of something or other. Panache? Is that what panache means?'

They examined their plates. Tiny pieces of carrot and celery were arranged with small layers of fish and meat in a fan-like pattern.

'Oh well. Let's eat it. Oh, for the days of brown Windsor soup. At least then you could throw the bread roll at someone when you'd finished. There's still the wine, of course.'

Galbraith got up to speak. By then the whole hall had

reached a state of hazy, friendly willingness to greet anyone with pleasure as long as they were amusing.

'I have been asked to come to speak to you,' Galbraith said. He stopped for a moment, then went on, 'And you have been asked to listen to me. All I ask is this.' He paused, took off his glasses and looked around. The whole hall held its breath waiting to hear what it was that he was asking. 'If you finish before I do, then please talk quietly among yourselves.'

There was a roar of laughter. The effort of listening to a new speaker dissolved into the shared pleasure of a really good joke. Before they could regain their equilibrium, Galbraith carried on, 'I'm only here because Bill's going.' More laughter. The comment meant nothing but expressed exactly what the evening was about.

'Bill gone? How can that be? Bill can't go. If Bill goes, then we've nearly all gone as well.' He looked around. 'Haven't we? Because Bill is part of us.' Even the younger people in the audience who hadn't known Bill for years were suddenly caught by the throat.

Galbraith carried on. 'Starson over there' – he pointed at one of the men who had spoken before him – 'said we were here because we *wanted* to be here. What bunkum.' Everybody laughed. Galbraith and Starson didn't get on. It was obvious they were different kinds of people, and somehow Galbraith's acknowledging it openly wasn't nasty, but funny.

'No, we're all here, in this ancient hall, because we have to be. We don't want to be here. We *have* to be here. We don't owe it to Bill.' He waved his glasses at the perspiring man. 'We owe it to ourselves. Because if we forget the people who were with us when we were learning and who helped us when we knew nothing, then we've forgotten ourselves. And, be warned, forget yourself and what you owe yourself, and you're lost.'

The hall had fallen silent. The man's genial personality perfectly transferred itself into what he was saying. Scott looked at the people around him. The diners had turned away from the tables at which they sat, or were leaning forward on the table-top, quiet, listening.

Galbraith's voice was soft, moving slowly, with great pauses which intensified the effort of listening. He had started to tell a story about Bill. '. . . the early hours of the morning . . . and Bill came into the clerks' room, unexpectedly. He wasn't expecting anything either. On his desk was a senior member of chambers, now, I might add, a judge' – Galbraith prodded a finger towards the High Court – 'and underneath him was a young lady, let's call her Miss Young. She hadn't been in chambers long. She's not here any longer, to save your blushes.' He surveyed the room. The dining hall quivered with anticipation.

'And Bill said, "Excuse me, sir, I was just looking for some papers, because I have another set of instructions for Miss Young. Of course, when she's completed those, sir."'

The hall dissolved into laughter. Galbraith stopped it with his hand. 'As you may have observed, Bill was always a man for maintaining the proper courtesies.' The laughter exploded again, intensified.

Scott watched the speech in distress. Was he really going to have to attack this man? Scott had never heard him speak before, but what he had been told was right. He was certainly one of the best speakers he had ever heard. Even the catering staff were beginning to crowd in through the carved wooden screens at the end of the hall to hear him, and as the crowd grew so did Galbraith's management of it.

When the staff were pushing their way into the back of the hall, John Donald came with them. The arrangement for catering staff had been a little disjointed. A couple of people were ill, and they had had to take on a number of irregulars. John Donald did not look so very different from one of the temporary kitchen porters, so he wasn't noticed as he made his way into the hall through the kitchen entrance. He was bored with waiting outside. He stood next to the carved oak screens at the back, picked up a dishcloth lying on a trolley and started to wipe his hands. No one gave him a second glance.

He had never been in such a place before. His eyes followed the great vaulting beams which ribbed the roof all the way to the huge back wall. The wall was half in shadow and half lit by the soft candlelight. Three massive portraits of men dressed in old-fashioned clothes looked down on the silver and polished oak below. At the far table a man in a dinner jacket and half-moon spectacles stood talking, occasionally interrupted by roars of laughter. Donald could not understand what was funny.

To his right, halfway down the hall, he suddenly saw Scott. Scott was sitting half turned towards the speaker. Donald moved so he could see him more easily. He listened to what was going on, accustoming himself to the dim light and the atmosphere. The room was quiet, attentive. The man at the end was speaking about someone called Bill. That must be Bill in the middle. You could tell by the way people were turning to look at him.

John Donald didn't understand it all, but he could tell one thing. It was crap. These people were congratulating themselves on their fancy position in society, and their fancy clothes. He knew. He'd heard of it before. Look at them rubbing up against each other. They'd spent the day putting people away and now here they were being, oh so nice to each other.

John Donald looked at Scott again. He was just as bad as the rest. A bully. Clever with his voice and ideas. As if he, John Donald, weren't entitled to say what he thought as well. He watched him and saw that Scott wasn't really listening. Instead he was looking around him. That was odd. John Donald really noticed it now. Once you saw it, it stuck out. Everyone else in the hall was glued to what was being said, but Scott was watching the others. He was watching, just as he, John Donald, was watching. He's not part of it, he's a watcher, he thought. John Donald's interest in the man he was following suddenly became more intense.

The speech continued and the laughter became louder, until at the end the speaker stopped, leaned forward and lifted his glass. 'Well, then, that's what I have to say about Bill. He was my clerk at a time when it mattered to me and he never let me down. He was always able to walk in the door and say, "Well, sir, when you've finished there's some more work for you." Here's to you, Bill.' He raised his glass. There was an immediate movement and everybody rose to their feet, the chairs and benches groaning on the wooden floor as they were pushed aside. 'Here's to you Bill.'

'Bill.' Some voices echoed and there was a soft stamping noise which was taken up by the clatter of knives on the tables, and then glasses tapping against plates. 'Bill. Bill.'

The clerk got up and the standing audience subsided into their seats. 'Gentlemen. Ladies,' he said. He paused and then said, 'Be fair.' There was immediate laughter. He had obviously repeated a phrase he was known for. 'You are all professional speakers. You hire yourselves out for it. I'm not.'

He was a medium-sized man with a full face, and perspiration was glistening on it, but his eyes were alive. The light of the candles on either side of him lit him up so that his eyebrows twisted up into shadow, giving him a devilish appearance. He looked around.

'No,' he said, 'that's wrong. You don't hire yourselves out. I hire you out. You couldn't hire yourselves out for a bunfight in a bakery. All the trouble you gave me.'

The hall was rocking with laughter. 'I'll say nothing about the young lady barrister and her briefs, Mr Galbraith. Only I don't remember the man involved being elevated to the High Court. If I remember rightly that particular party is still doing what you're doing – flannelling them in the courts.'

'Oh. Oh.' There were jeers of protest.

'Some of you needed selling. Some did not. But you all needed looking after. All of you. Mungo, the Bishop. Tozer there – you more than most.' There was a shout of delight at the mention of the name. 'All of you. Well, I'm not going to do it any more. Someone else can. Thank you for coming. Mr Scott. Mr Bond. Miss Donne. You're all here, but it's difficult to see you in this light.' He put his hands up to shade his eyes. 'Thank you for coming.' He held his glass up and it was clear he was moved. There was a cheer.

'What a load of crap.' John Donald said it out loud, but his words were drowned in the applause.

'Now,' a voice behind him said, 'now's your chance. Clear the tables now.'

The staff were being urged forward. 'Everybody, quickly, doesn't matter how you're dressed.' John Donald felt a hand pushing him. 'You, take that table on the right.' The staff swarmed forward and began to clear the remaining plates and silver. Cups appeared, and coffee pots.

The diners' attention returned to their own groups. One or two people got up and wandered around. Gatling complained to those who sat around him that he had expected to speak. 'No matter, dear,' his wife said. 'There'll be another chance.' She said it as though speaking to a small boy who had missed his turn, and then she turned away to speak to the man on her left. Gatling subsided, comforted, but at the same time feeling a slight annoyance that his wife could speak to him like that in front of others.

John Donald collected a pile of plates and took them to the back, through the hall doors and up to a large steel trolley. He piled them on to it. Someone took them from him and emptied them, stacking them up. The trolley was wheeled to a door where the plates were taken downstairs.

'Go on, get the rest.' The man who had spoken before urged him on as he stood, uncertain what to do next. He returned to the hall and started working at the next long table on the right. It was the one where Scott was sitting.

'C'm'on, love, don't be backward.' A woman spoke to Donald, encouraging him to gather up the dishes. As he moved down the table, piling up the plates from place to place, reaching across the people who were still sitting down, Scott stood up.

'You get those, love.' The woman pointed across to the other side where there were still plates to be collected. 'I'll take what you've got, pile 'em on here.' She took the plates from him.

As Scott stood up, John Donald saw two men approach him, the man who had made the speech from the table at the end, and another wearing a dinner jacket that was almost green with age. John Donald moved down the table, reaching across to take plates that had been used for fruit. He stacked a few up, just next to where Scott was standing, and reached over to gather the others. He strained to hear what was being said. The taller man with the old dinner jacket was speaking, introducing Scott. What was he saying? Something about a difficult moment to raise the subject.

'Get a move on, slowcoach.' The woman who had been

clearing before was behind him again. 'I'll take those. You get down there. They're getting the port wine out. You do the bottom of the table.'

John Donald walked back to where the senior waiter was standing at a table where a series of glass decanters had been laid out. As he approached him he became aware of his clothes. Jeans, an old shirt. He flicked the dishcloth over his shoulder then pulled it off and started to fold it. 'I shouldn't be upstairs,' he said.

'Well, now you're up here, just do this and we'll have it over with in a jiff.' He was handed three decanters. 'Pass them out, one between six people. And take some ashtrays. If there are any crumbs, come back here and take one of the table brushes.'

John Donald went back to where Scott and the other two men were standing. As he got nearer the tall one with the greenish dinner jacket left, leaving Scott with the man who had made the speech. He heard only a few words, quietly spoken. 'I know exactly what you're trying to do. If you think I'm going to agree with some jumped-up, second-rater that I let that damn woman down, then think again.' The man looked around him to make sure they were alone, not noticing, of course, the waiter laying out the port, and then spoke directly into Scott's face. 'Who do you think you are? Who's ever heard of you? What have you ever done?'

The man walked away, leaving Scott standing.

John Donald pushed forward.

'Some port, sir?' he said.

Scott said nothing. He just stood.

John Donald put a decanter on the table where Scott stood. 'There you are, sir.'

I'm quite good at this, I could be a waiter, he thought.

Chapter Sixteen

Scott sat down.

Nicky said, 'You know that waiter?'

Scott didn't look up. 'Which one?'

'The one who gave you that decanter.'

'No. What do you mean, "Do you know that waiter"?'

'I meant, that waiter. I think I know him.'

'Where from?' Scott turned round.

'I don't know. That's what I mean. Do you know that waiter?'

'Which one?'

'That one.'

Nicky pointed to the group of people clustered around the hall entrance.

'Which one?'

'He's gone now.'

'Oh God.'

'What did Galbraith say?'

'What didn't he say.'

'Like that?'

'Yes.'

'He's not going to help?'

'No. I don't understand why not. Why should it affect him?'

He poured some port out. 'Do you want some port?' he said.

He sat, still staring, then he said, 'I remember defending someone once and he appealed. He said I hadn't defended him properly, I hadn't taken a point for him. It was a technical point, which wouldn't have made any difference to the original trial at all. He would still have been convicted. But this man briefed Paddy O'Donnell – Sniffer O'Donnell.

'Well, O'Donnell came up to me and he was almost apologetic, as far as he's capable of it. He thought I was going to get terribly upset, as though I was meant to feel threatened that someone else had taken over the case. Well, of course, I wasn't. Why should I be? But then I realised that O'Donnell was merely projecting what *he* would have felt if it had been the other way round.'

Nicky could see that Scott was worried.

'Have you got a cigarette?' he said.

'No.'

Scott swung round. Robert Prendergast was passing. 'Robert, could I bum one of your cigarettes?'

'Why, of course.' Robert pulled out a packet of Player's.

Scott remembered when his parents smoked them, untipped, full strength. He took one and lit it. The smoke immediately began to make his head swim.

'Galbraith is deeply offended,' he said.

'So he's not going to make it easy?'

'No, he's not going to make it easy. He's not even going to say there's room for another point of view.'

'You think he should?'

'Well, yes. Because there obviously is another point of view. In criminal courts you're always having to make decisions about how to run cases. You abandon one way and decide on another. Why shouldn't you get it wrong occasionally? And who's to say he was wrong? I don't need to say that. In fact, so far I've no reason to think he was.'

Nicky said, 'On the other hand you don't get where he's got by admitting mistakes.'

Scott tapped ash into a saucer.

'I don't see why not.'

'Only weak people apologise.'

'That's rubbish.'

'It's not. Don't believe all that stuff about being a good loser. It's not true. You can only be Galbraith by being a very bad loser. If people think you're a good loser, to them you're just a loser. Forget the good bit.'

Marje Gatling appeared next to them. 'Nicky! Where have you been hiding, then? What have you been doing?'

She and Nicky immediately became deeply involved. Scott marvelled at the ability of the English upper classes to exclude other people.

Douglas Gatling had come back too. 'What did he say?' he asked.

'Galbraith? He was bloody rude.'

'I thought he would be,' Gatling said gloomily. 'Can't you dump this case somehow?'

'How can I possibly do that?' Scott said, but he could see Gatling wasn't listening.

'It's going to be really inconvenient having this frightful business in chambers.' Gatling said it aloud, but he wasn't talking to Scott any more.

Scott drifted off. None of them noticed.

'Hallo, Sally.' Scott sat down, lifting his legs over the bench so he could slide in. 'How're you doing?'

'I'm waiting for Tony to help me so I can stand up.'

They looked at Tony Jay, who grinned. He had obviously drunk a lot.

'Isn't there a proper way of doing it?' Scott said with interest. 'Aren't you meant to keep your knees and ankles together and then swivel on your bum? Like the Queen getting out of a car.'

'Yes, except if you were wearing what I'm wearing it would tear down the side. You can only get out of here properly if you're dressed right. That's why you're wearing trousers.'

'How did you get in.'

'Tony had the grace to stand with his back to me so no one could see. But now he's refusing. So I'm stuck, unless you can persuade that lot to pull the bench out enough for me to walk down between it and the table.'

Scott looked. Sally was in the middle of a long bench. At either end there was a group deep in conversation. They were not about to move. She couldn't get out without swinging her legs up, or at least one leg at a time.

'Didn't they teach you how to do it at finishing school?' Scott said. 'It must be a problem that young ladies have to face from time to time.' He was trying not to laugh.

'Piss off, Scott. Kingsmead Comprehensive School didn't know that places like this existed. Now are you going to help me?'

Scott glanced at Tony Jay. He looked as though he was falling asleep.

'I tell you what, Sally. I'll lift you out. But on one condition.'

'What's that?' She looked angry, but, Scott noticed, interested.

'You dance with me.' Scott gestured towards the band settling down in the corner of the hall. A few tentative notes echoed in the space.

'OK,' she said. They both looked at Tony Jay, but he missed his cue, pouring himself more port and laughing with Wilkinson, sitting next to him.

Scott put his arms round Sally's shoulders and under her knees and lifted her. She couldn't have weighed much -- she came up like a feather. He didn't put her down but carried her over to the band as they struck up the first dance.

'I didn't say you could do that,' she said. Her face was not far from his.

'Some things you don't need permission for,' he said, and he put her down. 'As a full-time sex offence prosecutor you should know that. Come on, then, let's dance.'

The band, encouraged by the couple that had arrived so romantically, set off on a slow waltz. Scott's anger with Galbraith dissolved in the dance. He held Sally by the waist and started to move to the music. There was scattered applause and, looking over her shoulder, he saw that they were the centre of attention. The music changed rhythm and he lifted her by her waist. She put her feet on his and they began to spin. People joined them and soon they were part of a crowd.

Sally said, 'So you had a word with Galbraith?'

Scott was so surprised he almost stopped dancing. 'How do you know about that?'

'Oh, come on, Jeremy. Where have you been all your life? Everybody knows you're doing the Forgan case. And everybody knows you're being asked to accuse Galbraith of incompetence.'

This time Scott did stop dancing. 'How? How does everybody know? I've only had the papers for a week or two.'

'Because everybody knew it had to be done. All they've been waiting for is to find out who was going to do it.'

'And they got me?'

'Well, not the person most people would choose, but good enough.' She laughed at him. Sally was never a person to spare anyone.

'Thank you for that.'

'You're welcome.'

'How do they know I've got to accuse him of incompetence?'

'Someone was going to have to do it eventually.'

'Eventually? What do you mean, eventually?'

'It's Galbraith, isn't it?'

'Look, I don't understand. You obviously know something I don't.'

'Jeremy,' she said, standing back and looking him straight in the face, 'that wouldn't be difficult.'

They were in the middle of the dance-floor. 'This isn't the best place to talk about it. Come on.' She led Scott out of the hall and turned right into the benchers' corridor. Scott was surprised to notice that she was holding him quite tightly. She said, 'Come outside.'

They went down the passage towards the Jerusalem Chamber. On either side there were softly lit, ancient paintings. The sound of the music echoing in the hall followed them gently. 'I'll tell you something,' she said, stopping. 'Same as you said – on one condition.'

'What's that?'

'I'll tell you that later.'

They stopped before the picture of the five Law Lords who had all been Middle Temple benchers at the same time. This was the place that represented the whole business of being a barrister, the grandeur and the pomposity of it. Scott had never felt comfortable here.

'What is it?'

'This brief was hawked around the Temple for some time. No one would touch it.'

'I was told that,' Scott said, 'after my clerk accepted it.'

'Everybody avoided it since it might mean attacking Galbraith.'

'Yes,' Scott said. 'I understand that.'

'Lots of people say Galbraith has lost interest in the business. They say almost everybody has stopped briefing him. That his clerk keeps up appearances and every outing is a favour, but there aren't many outings.'

'My God. I certainly didn't know that. What's the matter? He didn't sound ga-ga to me when he spoke.'

'He's not ga-ga. They say he just doesn't read the briefs any more.'

'What?'

'That's what they say.'

'Is it true?'

'I don't think so. I think it's jealousy.'

'Is he no good any more?'

'It's not that he's no good, he can't help being good, but they say there's no urgency any more, that he can make more money from after-dinner speaking. He's "The Great Galbraith". He doesn't have to prepare for an after-dinner speech. He just has to be himself.'

Scott said nothing.

'So how far are you going to go?'

This was far worse.

'You're going to have to say it in public.'

'That he didn't do it properly?'

'Yes.'

'I don't think so.'

'They'll force you to.'

'Why?'

'Just you wait.'

* * *

221

Scott said, 'What was the condition? You said you'd talk to me about Galbraith on one condition.'

Sally looked at him.

'Where are you going afterwards?'

'Why?'

'Where?'

'Going home to bed probably.'

'I want to come with you.'

'Why me?' said Scott. He was astonished. Here was another woman throwing herself at him. 'I'm not even thin any more.'

She looked at him.

'You're only doing it to get back at Tony, because you're angry with him,' he said.

'Yes,' she said. 'Why not?'

'It's a bit sudden.'

'I thought that sort of thing didn't matter to you men.'

'Yes, but Tony Jay is a kind of friend of mine.'

'So am I, and that's what I thought friends were for.'

'You're just using me.'

'Yes.'

'I'm not here alone. I came with someone,' he said, using his last line of defence, although as he looked at her he wondered why he was bothering to defend anything.

'No you're not. You're alone now. They've gone,' she said. They had walked back to the main hall and were looking around. Nicky and the Gatlings were nowhere to be seen.

'They've taken Tony too, or at least he's gone,' she said. 'We've been left behind.'

She had her arm around him.

'Mr Scott. Mr Scott.' The hall porter approached them.

'Mr Gatling has left a message. He and Miss Vesey, they've all gone on to a club. They said they'd see you there.' He handed a note to Scott. 'It's in Suffolk Street.'

Sally made no move to leave him.

'We'll get a cab up on Fleet Street,' Scott said. 'Suffolk Street. Isn't that Elephant and Castle way? It doesn't sound like the kind of place Douglas would go to. The taxi driver will know.'

They set off up Middle Temple Lane. 'Watch out for rats,' Sally said.

'Rats?'

'If I see a rat you'll have to pick me up again.'

'Are there rats?'

'Yes. All the building work has disturbed the rats. The all-night secretaries in the solicitors' offices off Tudor Street get rat money.'

'No!'

'Yes they do.'

Scott thought he saw a dark shadow scurry down the gutter to his right, but he said nothing. In a moment they were going to have to go through the passage above the excavations in the Temple gateway. He glanced down at the cobbles. Certainly Sally's ankles looked very good. That was a bit Victorian, being impressed by trim ankles. He let his hand slide down her back, and could feel the muscles moving beneath her silk dress as she walked.

The door to the nightclub was besieged by a group of young people trying to get in.

A doorman was blocking the entrance. He was astonishing. He stood at least a head higher than the people around him, dressed in a tiger skin, his muscles shining with oil, and his body glistening black in the night. He protected the door, not speaking, his legs planted wide apart, wearing a fur hat and carrying a trident. Behind him a burning torch on the wall glowed and flickered at the people below.

'He's never going to let us in,' Scott said. He was conscious of his dinner jacket, standing out from the silver Lurex of all the other would-be dancers.

'No trouble,' said Sally and she slipped through the crowd towards the man. Scott could see her trying to whisper in his ear, but he was too tall. Eventually he bent down slightly and then, after a moment, straightened up.

'C'm'on,' said Sally, beckoning to Scott. The man moved aside and they went up the stairs.

'How did you manage that?'

'I just said we were with Douglas.'

'How did you know that would work?'

'Douglas wouldn't come here on the off-chance, would he? And I was right. Tiger Skin just said, "You mean de judge?" and let us in.'

The doorkeeper at the top of the stairs stamped her wrist with an ultraviolet mark.

'Men have to pay,' she said. 'We get in free. I'll find Douglas.' And she disappeared into the dark.

'Hello, Jeremy,' said Douglas. 'Get some wine.' Scott waved to a girl standing at the bar. He ordered two bottles of wine.

Douglas was saying, 'I was defending this chap and he told me he worked here.'

Scott could hardly hear over the music. They all had to lean forward, putting their heads close together to catch the words. 'He was the charming black fellow downstairs who let us in, the one with the hat and the stick. He said to come any time I want. So we have.'

'What did you defend him for?'

'Murder.'

'What?'

'Murder. He killed someone by kicking them in the neck. Something known as kung-fu, apparently. I hadn't heard of it myself. Our hero said he was being attacked at the time, so self-defence.' Douglas subsided slightly, then he added, 'Charming young man. Very well spoken.'

Marje Gatling leant forward and said conspiratorially, 'He was at Uppingham, you know. Or was it Repton?' She turned to her husband to find out, but he was engrossed in gazing at the two girls in cowboy clothes who were dancing on the balustrades. 'Douglas!' she said in a warning voice before returning her attention to the group. 'He was somewhere, some jolly good school. But when he works here he talks in this funny voice – "De man, de judge" – you heard him. He says it's camouflage.'

The wine arrived. She leaned back while it was put down and then carried on. 'Of course, he doesn't just work here. He's a part-owner. Otherwise he couldn't have afforded Douglas.'

She looked pleased at the thought of her husband being so expensive. 'Douglas got him acquitted and two cases of claret arrived in chambers.'

Douglas heard that. He said, 'Bouchray Gevres Spoliak '85. Pretty good stuff. I say, Jeremy, pay for the wine, there's a dear boy.'

Scott looked up. No one else responded, so he pulled out a credit card. 'How much is it?' The waitress picked up the wine list and put her finger under the price. It immediately doubled the cost of the evening.

'Was he guilty?' Nicky asked.

'Dear child, how should I know?' Douglas took a gulp of the wine and made a face. 'Whether or not he was guilty wasn't up to me. That's the jury's job. The doctors said that he happened to hit the one point in the neck that killed, and

Wethers – you know, Wethersedge, for the prosecution – was saying that was what kung-fu was. Well, the jury didn't agree. They thought he had just kicked out in self-defence. Nuff said. Total acquittal.'

By this time the waitress had returned, responding to Douglas's upraised arm. He was at his most magnanimous. He said, 'I'm afraid, young lady, this wine isn't awfully good. I think we'd better have something a trice nicer.'

The waitress looked at him desperately, trying to place him in time and space.

'What I suggest,' Douglas said confidentially, leaning forward, making the waitress lean forward too, 'is that you speak to young Yeats-Brown on the door. The chap with the trident. Tell him that the judge wants something rather better to drink. A Chablis perhaps.'

Surprisingly the waitress seemed entirely willing to accept this, gathered up the glasses with the full bottles and disappeared.

'Now, how about a jig?' said Marje. They all got to their feet, unhooked the velvet rope that separated them from the dance-floor and trooped out.

Inside the circle of loudspeakers, it now became impossible to say or hear anything at all, save the grinding beat of the music. As they reached the floor, strobe lights came on, creating the flickering effect of an old black-and-white film.

Douglas had produced a large cigar and clenched it firmly between his teeth, where it stuck out, unlit. He started to weave his hands around like a tick-tack man and, with unexpected agility, began to run on the spot in time to the pounding music. His wife began to circle him. She had pulled her skirt up at the hips to allow some freedom for her knees. She specialised in a mincing movement, while at the same time prodding her index fingers upwards, one after the other, as though balancing a set of scales. This extraordinary sight created a widening space for them in the centre of the dance-floor, until they were dancing alone in a clear semicircle in front of the drummer.

At that moment, Yeats-Brown, Douglas's acquitted murderer, stalked down the steps and planted himself next to the drummer. He was even bigger than Scott had thought. In his Cossack hat, to which he had now added a pair of horns, he stood closer to seven foot six than seven foot. The trident was planted firmly on the ground as he stood guard. 'This is my man,' he was saying, 'and his woman.'

Douglas and Marje Gatling bopped away, blithely unaware of their satanic protector.

They returned to their seats to find different wine and glasses. It was champagne.

'Come on, Jeremy. Do the honours.'

Scott squeezed the cork off one of the bottles, aiming it in the least dangerous direction, where it dislodged a small plate from the wall. There was a cheer from his table. He poured out the wine, uncomfortably aware that he had not yet got his credit card back. The cost of this would surely melt it.

Everybody was hot with the exertion of dancing and the strain of coping with the sound levels.

'It was Wethers who prosecuted your case, Jeremy, wasn't it?' Scott was surprised to hear Douglas returning to a subject that obviously distressed him. 'Have you talked to him yet?'

Scott said, 'No.'

'You should, you know.'

Both Sally and Nicky were looking at him.

'Will it help?' Scott said.

'I shouldn't think so,' said Sally.

'Why not?'

'Haven't you ever met him?' she answered. 'He's the nastiest man at the Bar. Look, when I last went down to Winchester, I was with Tom Spring who, as you know, is lovely, a real huggy-muffin bear.'

Scott looked at Sally, the tough prosecutor, with astonishment. 'A huggy-muffin bear?' He glanced at Douglas, who seemed to think this way of speaking was quite normal. Perhaps she had drunk too much.

'Anyway, Tom Spring said something, and Wethersedge said, "That's not the way we do things in the West Country." Plain insulting.'

'What did the judge say?'

'Nothing. It was The Youngster. He just sat there like a Buddha. In fact he said nothing for six weeks. Then he summed up the whole shebang in an hour. Astonishing.'

'You don't think he'd help, then?' Scott said to Sally.

'I doubt if he'd even speak to you.'

Nicky said, 'You don't need help, do you?'

They all looked at her, lawyers looking at an outsider straying into their territory.

Nicky was not put off. 'Well, from what I saw, you don't need help. I was in court with Jeremy.'

'Is that where you saw him, in court?' said Marje. 'How nice. I went to court with Douglas once, but I didn't understand a word.'

Nicky took the opportunity this interruption offered to subside back into being a bystander. Almost immediately they forgot her presence.

Sally said, 'If you don't know Wethersedge, you don't know what's coming. He would take any advantage he could. If Galbraith weren't completely prepared, for instance, he wouldn't help him.'

Douglas tried to protest. 'Galbraith not prepared

properly? You're not going to say that?' He turned to Scott.

Scott shrugged.

'Are you going to say that?'

'How can I?' said Scott. 'I've got no reason to think it. All I have is rumours. That's no way to fight a case.'

'You've got to say something, though,' said Gatling. 'The court will force you to.'

'I know,' said Scott. 'And no one is going to help me say it, are they?'

Sally and Douglas looked at him.

'What happened?' said Nicky.

'I don't think I want anything more to drink,' said Nicky.

Scott continued wrestling with the bottle.

He was surprised to find himself at home with Nicky. It hadn't been his decision. She had taken over as they left the nightclub, leaving Sally Donne standing, staring after them. The two of them had gone into the women's cloakroom together, but had come out not speaking to each other. Clearly Nicky was an extremely tough operator if she could deal with Sally Donne. Scott wasn't used to being fought over.

'Oh, bugger,' he said. The cork began to break up.

'I really don't want another drink, you know,' Nicky said.

The words penetrated Scott's head. 'You don't?' He looked at the bottle with the little bits of cork spilling out of it and said, 'Now you mention it, nor do I much.'

'Why don't you stop then? Sit down.'

He sat down.

'I like your flat.'

He looked around him. 'I'm used to it,' he said.

'Did a girlfriend make those curtains for you? Or am I being a bit personal?'

Scott said nothing. The red ochre of the curtains reflected the lights on to the walls, filling the room with a warm glow. Catherine had made them.

'No,' he said.

'I like your pictures.'

The canvas above the fire looked back at Scott. It looked the same as always, it never changed. Only he changed.

'Why are you not married?'

'I was.'

'That's obvious. What I meant was why are you not married now?'

'How is it obvious?'

'It's fairly clear, I should say. You're not in your original wrapping.'

She sat next to him on the sofa, her legs pulled up. It should have been inappropriate, the gesture of a much younger woman, but it was not.

'Why are you a barrister?'

'What a lot of questions you ask.'

'I'm a journalist. Why are you a barrister? I can understand why that Sally is a barrister and why Gats is a barrister, but I can't understand why you should be one. Did you always want to be one?'

'People always ask that. Do they ask journalists why they are journalists?'

'No,' she said, 'I don't think they do. That's because a journalist is a reasonable thing to be. Being a barrister is so odd that people want to know how it happened.' She stared at him. 'So they can avoid making the same mistake. Did you always want to be a barrister?'

'No. It happened quite by accident. I don't know how.

One moment I was at Cambridge reading English and the next I was here, doing this.'

'Do you like it?'

'No, not much.'

'Why?'

'I've been trying to work that out for years. It's the people. They're so intelligent – but at the same time they haven't got a clue.'

He tried to work out what he meant. He was saying something that he had never formulated properly before.

'Sometimes, if you talk to the really clever ones, you think you're visiting a kindergarten. The kindergarten at All Souls, that is. You probably think the whole system is built on favouritism and class, but that's not true. The brightest really do get to the top. I mean, these people are very smart. And yet at the same time there's something missing. Like clever, awkward children, there's something missing, and you can't tell them what it is. Of course, if they could understand it then they wouldn't be good lawyers.'

'Why do you go on doing it?'

'Because when it works it's fun.'

'Not because you want to stand up for Miss Forgan?'

'Not really. Is that very disappointing? Am I meant to be more heroic about it?'

'You could be.'

'Not really. The whole job is too badly compromised for that. I use the same tricks that the prosecution use to convict people, only I use them to get people acquitted.'

'I think you should be more generous.'

'More generous?'

'Yes, with people. People don't want to be disillusioned all the time, they want to believe in you.' She smiled at him. 'For that you have to believe in yourself first. Why did you leave me alone at the dinner?'

'Did I?'

'Of course you did. You went off with that Sally girl, and left me with the Gats.'

Scott wondered. It hadn't felt like that to him.

'And all because she wanted to take you home with her.'

'That was her idea, not mine.'

'And it surprised you?'

'It did a bit.'

'Why should it surprise you? After all, I wanted you to take me home with you. Am I so odd?'

Scott looked at her and then put his hand on her cheek.

She said, 'Believing in yourself involves respecting other people as well. Maybe they like you. How can they like you if you don't like yourself?'

'How do you know all this?'

'All women know this.'

Chapter Seventeen

'We were all together last night and they talked about the case. It's clear that there are stories being circulated about it. The argument is not that Galbraith was no good but that he's bored.'

'Are you certain?'

Nicky said, 'Yes. They were talking as though I wasn't there, you know, repeating what people were saying in the job. Not trying to impress anyone.'

Toby Beyt thought about it.

She went on. 'I don't think Scott knew about the Galbraith stories, though. Obviously they're the kind of thing that don't get out easily and only to those in the know.'

'Like the Lord Chief Justice being ill,' said Toby.

'What was that?'

'One of the Lord Chief Justices, quite some time ago now. He was ill, ill so that he wasn't fit to go on, but instead of his going, it was hushed up.'

He thought for a moment, 'Scott didn't know?'

'No.'

'He's a bit naïve that one,' Toby said.

He put the car in gear and they set off towards the park. Toby Beyt's production company offices were in Bayswater. 'It's a bit louche round there isn't it?' someone had said about his street. 'The loucher the better,' he had said. 'Who wants to be in Wardour Street?'

They were driving to Sussex. Going down Park Lane Toby said, 'We do need to know when this case is going to be heard. You are thinking about that, aren't you?'

'I spoke to Monty Bach about it,' said Nicky, 'and he said it's going to be sooner rather than later.' She put her feet up on the dashboard in front of her. 'I asked him what that meant and he said he didn't know. But he said he'd be consulted. I got the impression he could arrange it pretty much for any time we wanted.'

'Good.'

'He knows someone in the right office, apparently.'

They drove in silence until Toby said, 'Do you think Scott is tough enough for this case?'

Nicky didn't reply for a moment. The odd thing about working with men was that you couldn't always tell them how you really felt.

'I don't know,' she said.

'What time did you get in last night? I called you.'

'I didn't get in,' she said. He looked at her. She laughed at him and then ran her hand through his hair. 'Now don't get jealous. It's all for the good of business.'

Toby Beyt grunted, and then he said, 'He may not be tough enough, but he's making a lot of money out of it.'

'Is he? He told me he was being paid peanuts.'

'That's rubbish. He would say that, wouldn't he? We gave Monty Bach five thousand as a starter, and for that he didn't have to do much, only send the papers to Scott. So he must have given him at least half. That's two and a half grand for reading the papers and then five minutes in court.'

Nicky said, 'Yes, that's a lot of money.'

'And now they're asking for more.'

Toby pulled up in Battersea and parked outside the Pot Shop. Nicky got out, crossed the road to the side door of the café and rang a bell for one of the flats above. Then they sat and waited for the cameraman, who always had trouble getting up in the morning.

Toby Beyt's first visit that day was to the St George's nursing home just outside Haywards Heath.

It was a pleasantly decorated, low, early nineteenth-century country house and, standing looking out over the lawn from the large drawing room's French windows, it was still possible to sense something of the old family home it had been. Now the drawing room was full of elderly ladies sitting, staring, as the last part of their life drifted away.

Sunesh Patel had spotted the opportunity when the old house had come up for sale. He had left his corner shop to his brother and had taken the risk. He had been successful, and now he owned four similar houses spread across Sussex and into Kent.

He was no doctor; he did not pretend to know anything about medicine, 'But,' he said, 'at each of our houses – I prefer to call them houses, not homes – of course we have fully qualified nursing staff, at least one on duty all the time. And I have arranged that we can get straight through to the local medical practice any time, day or night. It is a worthwhile expense. We cannot possibly afford any scandal.'

Mr Patel's own mother, very elderly now, lived at home with him. He wouldn't have dreamed of any different arrangement.

They were shown the terrace, and the view of the house from the second lawn. Then he and Nicky were taken down past the roses to the summerhouse where Mr Patel did the accounts.

'One day,' said Mr Patel, 'when I am older, I shall return

this property to its original condition, a family house. And I shall live here.

The wind lifted the leaves of the wisteria fanning across the back of the house and it fluttered like a ribbon. Generations of gardeners had been needed to tame this plant, and without Mr Patel's gardener it would, by now, be forcing itself up through the eaves, into the roof, and lifting the slates. One hundred and fifty years old now, it was still waiting its chance.

'I'll ask Nurse to step down here,' said Mr Patel, and he spoke into an intercom. Toby, Nicky and he sat in silence in the hot dry cedar room. Around the front of the house the cameraman slept in Toby's jeep, parked on the gravel drive next to Mr Patel's dark blue Volvo.

Nurse Donoghue breathed confidence. It was immediately clear that she knew what she was talking about. Hers was the triumph of practical knowledge over theory. She had been nursing old folk for longer than she could remember and did not regret one moment of it. 'All of us will come to it. We all come to that long end. Though they can be difficult, truly these old folks can be difficult.'

'She'll be perfect,' Toby said with his eyes on Nicky. He knew Nicky thought the same.

No television audience would believe that three Appeal Court judges knew more about the care of the elderly than this nurse. For a moment he considered the possibilities. Might it even be possible to hint in the film that the judges themselves were in need of Nurse Donoghue's good strong common sense?

Toby Beyt knew what the outcome of the appeal would be. He had seen too much of the law. When it came to it, the Court of Appeal always protected the system. After all, it was only grudgingly that the court let the Birmingham

Six go – when the truth had been apparent to any sensible person for years.

They would refuse this appeal. They would say that the system had worked properly. And the more certain their refusal the better his programme would look – common sense against obtuse legal stupidity.

'Wander off?' said Nurse Donoghue. 'To be sure they do. Sometimes they want to go home. Why, Mr Porteous, the other day. We found him at Haywards Heath station in his carpet slippers. But of course he was mobile, he gets around, so he is not an illustration of what you need. But I have known cases that would make you blink. Old people who've not moved a mite for years and suddenly you find them in the garden. For no reason. Just standing there. Why, when I came here, one of the first things I had Mr Patel do was drain and cover the swimming pool.'

Mr Patel nodded. 'I did that,' he said. 'Although we fill it again for three weeks every summer and we encourage the families to come here. I like the sound of children in the garden.'

Toby made a sign to Nicky.

She went to fetch the cameraman. She had difficulty in waking him, and as she tapped on the glass of the car door fifteen old women watched her from the front room.

'That was great.'

Nicky and Toby had piled all the equipment back in the car and had said goodbye to Nurse Donoghue, Mr Patel and the nursing home. 'She was terrific.'

Toby started to drive across country to the Brighton Road. 'We'll cut her into the doctor's piece. We need to draft that carefully to bring out the main point: no one knows why or how, but experience shows that people who are apparently bedridden do get up and walk. The whole point is that it's something doctors can't explain. And they don't try to.'

'Will you send Donoghue's statement to the lawyers?'

'Yes. I don't see why not. That court is so bone-headed that if I served Albert Schweitzer's sworn statement on them it would make no difference.'

'Who's Albert Schweitzer?' said Nicky. Toby kept driving.

'Here we are,' he said, 'the nerve centre of the Sussex branch of the Euthanasia Society.' Toby double-parked in the great crescent formed by two huge curving terraces of Georgian houses running down to the sea. 'Imagine what this looked like when it was built. It must have been open country then, and yet they plonked down these great metropolitan houses here. What nerve they had.'

They left the cameraman sleeping in the back. 'Have we got his phone number?' Toby checked. 'We don't want to come down all those stairs just to wake him up.' They crossed the broad road to the house and rang the bell. There was a crackling noise from the intercom and, in amongst the crackle, a voice saying, 'Who is it?'

'Toby Beyt from Foregone Conclusion Productions, Mrs Williams.'

A buzzer sounded and they were able to push open the huge front door. 'Third floor.' The faint voice spoke after the buzzer stopped.

When they were shown into the flat, the first thing Nicky noticed was the light. It shone down through the great white clouds that rolled out over the sea, reflected off the water and the white houses opposite, through the windows into the long, low room. The whole place seemed to float in light.

*   *   *

'Yes, we had a letter from her.' Mrs Williams went to her files. 'I could see that it had been dictated.' She produced a lavender-blue sheet of writing paper. 'Yes, here it is. I sent her our introductory package. That's made up of a little booklet, a photocopy of one of Ludovic Kennedy's articles – I do think he's marvellous, don't you? – and a note about our meeting times. I can tell I did that by the tick I've put at the bottom, and the little "three" here inside the circle, and here's the date I did it. Two days after I received her letter.'

She paused over her filing cabinet and looked up. 'That was slow for me, two days, and the reason would be' – she spoke slowly, thinking back – 'that this letter was the result of an article I had published. After an article we always get a flood – no, not a flood, a good heap – of letters. There are a lot of sad people out there, but people who are very brave.'

She closed the cabinet. 'Would you like some tea?' She led them into the kitchen. 'Yes, people think we are a bit odd. And there are lots of jokes, you know. If we arrange a meeting of our little group, then someone always comments that the aim of the society must be that no one should turn up.

'And then there are those who are frightened of what we are saying, though they don't know it. Now here is something I've noticed. If you have feelings you can't deal with, you transform them into something else. The policemen who came about Mrs Beatty were like that.' She laughed. 'And they were so young.' She glanced at Nicky apologetically. 'Being young and being clumsy do sometimes seem to go together rather, and if you're nervous or feel out of your depth it can show a bit. It's unfortunate, but it's true.'

She walked around the table, leaning on it for a moment. She was tired today.

'One of them said something about life being holy. Did

he actually use the word holy? I think he did. I advised him not to talk that way until he had seen a bit of life. You see, I have delivered hundreds of babies, and seen babies die. I grew up when household diseases – nobody uses that phrase any more, do they? – were killing people all the time, when pneumonia was known as the old man's friend. If you see that, you don't go around with any ideas of the holiness of things. What's holy is doing what you can to help others. All this guff about the sanctity of life is demeaning, it demeans people's bravery.

'Biscuits? I have some biscuits, if you like. No? I've been in control of my life all the time, even more so now. And I want to remain in control. Until the end. Is that so bad? Anyway, the letter. You can see. Read it. It's like lots we receive. She says that she is no longer in control. She actually uses that expression. It's very common that writers use it, obviously partly because it is a phrase I use in my articles, but it's a phrase that strikes a chord.

'I have many friends now. There was a time when that was not so. I have been happy. I have been unhappy. I was married to a marvellous man – generous and kind, even though he was a bit stubborn about some things. But now I'm on my own. I'm not frightened of looking clearly at what's before me. Our generation were always like that, we looked things in the face and saw many evil and horrible things.

'My father's generation, they were almost gone, wiped out. And then the next war came. These were terrible things. What we learned was not to be frightened. Now I look about me and find that people aren't learning not to be frightened, because they have no practice in confronting frightening things. Then suddenly it happens, and there is no resilience. You know, people really can be very foolish when they are frightened.'

She looked steadily at Toby Beyt and Nicky, and then said, 'And I'm also interested in Thomas Hardy. He kept his first wife in the attic, you know – she was quite mad.'

There was a moment when the sheer force of her personality made what Toby and Nicky were doing seem utterly trivial.

Then Toby said, 'Didn't the policeman take the letter?'

'No. He only wanted to see the handwriting. As for what it said, well, he wasn't a great listener. He would only listen to what he already knew. Or what he thought he knew. Perhaps that's what policemen are like? I felt sorry for him. He will not have an easy time.'

'What do you mean?'

'Well, if you have an explanation for life which makes everything obvious, then when you find one day, which you will, that it isn't adequate, then on that day you suffer. Cold winds sweep in. No. It is better from the start to let the cold wind in. Accept that things must be more complicated than you cater for.'

They drank tea, looking at each other. 'I've become a great lecturer in my old age,' she said. Then, 'No, he did not take the letter. They were rather brusque, actually. But that's by the by.'

'In what way?'

'I told you earlier. The whole subject threatened them. They weren't used to their own inadequacy. What policeman ever is?'

'Why didn't we film her?' said Nicky.

'We can't,' said Toby.

'Why not?'

'Because she doesn't fit. People don't like to see that sort of freedom. They like grannies to behave like grannies. The most they want in that department is a battling granny. They don't want to sit on their sofas being challenged.'

Their car passed a windmill on the way down the hill towards the London Road. On the left the slopes towards the Devil's Dyke rolled upwards. A vast blue sky hung over the South Downs. A vivid field of yellow rape gleamed in the distance.

'We're dealing with simple images here. A wrongfully convicted woman. Bone-headed judges. Lawyers out to make money. Policemen who care only about getting a conviction. It's all simple stuff. Independent old ladies who look at you and see right through you don't fit.'

Chapter Eighteen

'Well, I've drafted it. It's gone. The court's got it and they're arranging a date for the hearing.'

Ronnie Knox said, 'What did you say in it?'

'I said they should hear the new evidence of the doctor and the neighbours.'

'Of course, but did you mention Galbraith?'

'In the end, I had to. But I've only tacked it on. I haven't made it the main point of the appeal.' He felt he had to justify himself, even to Ronnie. 'Look, any appeal suggesting that Galbraith was incompetent just will not succeed. I am arguing that the case should have been run differently and as far as I am concerned that doesn't necessarily involve attacking him. On what he knew at the time his decisions were probably perfectly reasonable.'

'What about his general competence?'

'You know I can't introduce that. How can I? How would I prove it – call some of his previous clients? I've advised on that too, I set out the ways in which we can complain about Galbraith and the ways we can't. And I've said' – he repeated his justification, as though hoping to convince himself – 'I won't even attack him unless I'm forced to. This is a law case, not some sort of crusade against the Establishment.'

Scott looked at Ronnie.

Ronnie said, 'You're not going to be able to avoid it. Either the court or your opponent is going to force you to attack him. They won't let you get away with saying the case ran the wrong defence without forcing you to say exactly how and whose fault it was.'

Scott knew he was right. He said, 'Well, it's done now. Perhaps I can think about something else instead for a while.'

'Perhaps.'

Ronnie's gas fire puttered gently. Scott watched it. It was the kind of fire people had in Doris Lessing novels, set in the fifties in Notting Hill. It was so unsafe that it was probably illegal. The long sticks of ceramic glowed recklessly.

'Ronnie?' he said.

'Yes?'

'How's the line dancing going?'

For the first time Ronnie showed some signs of life. 'Pretty good,' he said. 'We've branched out a bit now. We go to Edmonton a lot. Fat Ljubo's.'

'Who's Fat Ljubo?'

'He's the cook. He's Serbian, or Croatian – I don't think he knows himself. One moment he's Ekavski, the next he's Jekavski. There's a band and a good dance-floor.'

Scott reflected on the idea of a Serbian country-and-western restaurant.

'I asked you because you've been spotted.'

'Spotted?'

'Yes. Douglas told me. Someone saw you dancing with the delicious Miss Farson in Romford.'

'Who can that have been? One of the clerks probably.'

'No, Douglas said it was "a Member of chambers" – capital M.'

'Who can that be?'

'That means there are two members of chambers who go line dancing. Three if you count Miss Farson who's a pupil.'

'Why don't they declare themselves?'

'Perhaps they see it as a secret vice.'

Neither of them said anything for a while. Then Scott said, 'I'm going home.'

He looked out of the window at the Inner Temple gardens. It was still light outside, just beginning to fade. 'I'm going to walk,' he said. He gathered his things together and set off into the deepening gloom.

Near where Scott lived there was a strange little pub, the whole place no bigger than an ordinary room, with the entrance from the street set into the angle of the corner of the house. Originally it must have been an ordinary front parlour, and had been turned into a place where the servants and coachmen of the big houses could drink beer. But long ago it had been swept up in the gentrification of the surrounding streets. That was probably why it had survived. Now it was a smart little pub serving the people who lived in the flats that had been converted out of the big houses.

He would walk as far as that and stop for a drink. Forty-five minutes' walk, along the Embankment, up under the Savoy, out past the Charing Cross arches and through Whitehall.

Lots of things were jumbled up in his mind. This damn Forgan case, Ronnie Knox's line dancing, Catherine going to Holland – his own strange behaviour which had caused it, come to that. Harry the clerk being difficult. Monty Bach. Were they really going to pay him almost nothing to do this? At least he had got a cheque for the Ellie Johnson case, and pretty quickly. Would he go out to eat? There was no food in the flat.

He passed Victoria. It was getting dark. On his right was the statue of Marshal Foch, covered with roosting pigeons. French students seemed to gather there. Was there something French near by? Or was it just that they naturally arrived at Victoria as the Welsh used to at Paddington? Perhaps it was Marshal Foch they liked.

He walked down Ebury Street. It was quite dark now and getting cold. He could feel the sweat from the exertion of walking beginning to cool beneath his jacket.

There were not many people about. Why had he noticed that? He concentrated and then realised it was because he was being followed. There was someone walking behind him. He did not look round, but crossed the road. The footsteps crossed after him. He had just passed Elizabeth Street. There was a long stretch before he would reach a shop or a pub. This must be the man on the telephone. He had not heard from him for some time and had almost forgotten about him.

He arrived at the corner where the Metropolitan Police Commissioner used to keep a flat, before he fell off a horse and had to retire. There always used to be a policeman stationed there. Not any more.

'He took my briefcase.'

'But he didn't get your wallet, sir. Nor your money?'

Scott was making a statement, trying to give a description of the man who had attacked him. It was difficult. He had only seen him for an instant, but he'd swear he had recognised the voice. 'OK, let's see what you have in the bag.' The man had said that just before he received the blow that knocked him down.

'I have to tell you, I've been having some trouble with a man who has been following me. I have reported it.'

'To the police?'

'Yes. To Inspector Hilton.'

'Should I contact him?'

'Yes, I think you'd better.'

The inspector came while Scott was sitting in St Thomas' casualty department. He had not wanted to go to the hospital but he had been knocked out and the young constable had insisted.

Hilton said, 'How do you know it was the same man?'

'I recognised the voice.'

'Nothing else?'

'No.'

'What did he say again?'

Already Scott was beginning to experience what he had seen happen in his work. As he told the story again and again, he began to confuse the event itself with his repeated description of it. This was the third or fourth time he'd gone over it – once at the scene, then twice at the hospital and now again to Hilton.

'You've got the exact words written down.'

'You can't remember them?'

'Yes, I can. But I wouldn't swear I remember them exactly now. Something about seeing what was in the bag. Let's see – or something.'

'And you assumed it was the same man?'

'I didn't assume. I recognised the voice.'

'But you thought it was him because he didn't take your wallet?'

'No, that was the constable's idea. I don't own a wallet.'

'But your statement says, "He made no effort to get my wallet or my money." '

'Those were the policeman's words. I didn't feel like arguing with him. They represent the truth, but I don't own a wallet.'

'How can they represent the truth if you don't own a wallet?'

Scott said nothing.

'You think you're being followed?'

'I am being followed.'

'By someone to do with the Forgan case.'

'It fits.'

'We're being a bit dramatic, sir, aren't we?'

'I was just attacked.'

'Lots of people get attacked.'

'OK, Mr Hilton. Forget it, then.'

'How can I forget it if you ask me to come to see you?'

'Given what I think is happening, I'd be a fool not to report it to you, wouldn't I?'

'Absolutely. You must act on what you believe. But I have to decide whether what you believe is enough for me to act on. What is it you want me to do?'

'I don't know. What do you normally do?'

'Your case is quite unusual. You said you had your briefcase taken? What was in it?'

'Only papers. And a book.'

'Important papers?'

'A set of appeal papers for Hilda Forgan.'

'And you think he was going for those?'

'No. No, I don't. He couldn't have known I was carrying them.'

'But of course, if he was following you because of Hilda Forgan's case, then it would fit?'

'It would. But it could merely be a coincidence.'

'So that at least is coincidence, but nothing else?'

'I recognised the voice.'

'Let me ask you this. Before you were attacked, did you realise you were about to be?'

'Yes, I think I did.'

'And did you immediately think it was this person who has been following you?'

Scott realised what his answer would mean. 'Yes. I did.'

'So even without recognising the voice . . .'

'No. I recognised his voice.'

'But that's what you expected. You were prepared to recognise it.'

Hilton looked at him. Scott's head ached. This was going nowhere.

'OK,' said Scott. 'Let's just leave it.'

Now the policeman had him. 'We can't just start things like this and then stop them, sir. You've made an official complaint.'

Silence.

'Can I ask you, sir, were you or Mr Bach involved in organising the public meeting protesting about Hilda Forgan's conviction?'

'What meeting?' said Scott.

'I believe you, sir,' said Hilton.

John Donald did not read much. But that did not mean he could not read. When he was in prison he read a lot, and once when he had been in hospital he had read all day. He opened Scott's briefcase.

He had found a room in an area where no one knew him. He was totally anonymous and was going to be able to do what he wanted without anyone knowing his movements.

He spread the papers out on the table. They were mainly legal documents. One lot was clipped together and wound round with pink ribbon. He had seen exactly the same thing in the hands of his own solicitor.

'R v. Forgan' was written on the face of the bigger bundle, and underneath it 'On the appeal of Hilda Forgan with the leave of the full court'. All gob-rubbish. Just language to put people off.

Inside the bundle one of the documents was headed 'Advice on Evidence'. He began to read it. It was about a man called Galbraith. 'We cannot base the argument upon Mr Galbraith's reputation for complete indifference to his professional obligations, even if it were true, and I have seen no evidence to suggest that it is. The only argument we can pursue might be that his handling of the trial was such that Miss Forgan was denied a proper opportunity of a defence, and that therefore the conviction was not safe.'

John Donald went back to the beginning to read it again. The ideas were very dense.

'But I advise that this question need not even be raised. There is no need to attribute fault to anyone. Mr Galbraith and those representing Miss Forgan no doubt thought that the line they were taking on her behalf was proper. We may differ now with the advantage of hindsight, but that does not imply any criticism of Mr Galbraith. Our position is simply this, that the new evidence is enough to show the conviction is unsafe. Why should irrelevant and unprovable questions of reputation be allowed to get in the way?'

All guff. John Donald looked at the other documents. They were signed Jeremy Scott. It was odd how, just by holding them and reading them, John Donald felt he was getting nearer to the end. This tone of voice, this – he searched for the word that conveyed what the documents were – this superiority – there, he'd got it – this superiority was what he had always been fighting against. Once it was gone he would be able to start over again.

He looked in the briefcase. There was a book, *Six Easy Pieces*, about physics – it didn't look interesting and a postcard from Holland. It was signed Catherine. She must be the woman he had gone to Holland with. She said – he tried to figure out the writing – she was going sailing, was it? Sailing at the See. Spelt wrong. And then this word, 'Stravinhagen'. Was that a place? Something about yawning. Yawning. He remembered how he had yawned at Scott on the bus. So it had had an effect. Even this girl was talking about it.

He had learned to do that in court. A barrister had looked at him once when he was in the witness box and yawned. Skinner – that was the man's name. He remembered it. He stopped to think. He would never forget it. Never. It was at the hands of these people that he had been degraded.

More papers. He found some money. Twenty pounds shoved into the side pocket. And a letter. Foregone Conclusion Productions, inviting Scott to appear on television: 'We shall be talking about the role of the defence advocate, followed by an examination of a specific case', giving the date and the place. The programme was well known. It was the one where the main person sat in a leather armchair and was questioned by the panel. *Inquisition,* that was it.

John Donald decided that he'd be there.

When Scott discovered that Hilda's appeal was fixed to start the day after he was due to appear on the television programme, he lost his temper with Harry.

Harry had heard the date from Monty and hadn't bothered to tell Scott until the week before the actual day. By then it was too late for Scott to get out of the television programme. He was going to have to do both.

'Harry, why didn't you tell me?'

Harry merely looked at him. 'Why, sir?'

'So I can organise myself.'

'What is there to organise? You're working, sir, aren't you? I can do the organisation.'

Scott marvelled at it. What other profession would allow itself to be dominated in this way by its staff?

'Harry, I want a little consideration. This is a complicated case. I need to know when it is coming on so that I can prepare for it properly.'

Harry didn't react at all and said nothing.

Foolishly, Scott changed the subject. 'It's not even as if I'm being paid properly. What have you got me for it now? Are you really suggesting it's fair to do the whole thing for a thousand pounds?'

'That's good money for a day's work.'

'Good money, Harry? It's not for a day's work, anyway. It'll take at least three days to prepare it and that's without the conferences.' Scott had not lost his temper in front of the clerks before and there was a hush in the room. 'Harry, you're just using me as a loss-leader to get Monty's work.'

Harry didn't bother to deny it. 'It's for the good of chambers, sir.'

'For the good of chambers?' He was repeating what Harry was saying, just as he had with Hilda. 'It's for the good of chambers for me to be paid properly for work properly done, and not treated with complete indifference.'

'What? Me treat you with indifference, sir? It was I who got you the work in the first place, sir.'

That was a bit much.

'What crap, Harry. The client asked for me. It was nothing to do with you.'

'Ah, but how did she hear of you, sir?'

Scott looked at him, astonished.

'What?'

'Ellie Johnson. You were recommended by Ellie Johnson, apparently, and who got you that work, sir?'

There was no arguing with the man. Scott tried nevertheless. 'Look, Harry, I defend these people. I go to court. I cross-examine for them. I do the work, not you. If Ellie

Johnson recommended me, then it was because of what I did, not because of you.'

'That may be so, sir. But the criminal Bar is a marketplace, and where would you be without the stall-holders?'

Scott was sent the outline of the programme and the way it worked. After an introduction by Moira McRae, he would be questioned by their two personality panellists and then a short film and commentary would follow. Scott looked at the letter again. It really used the word personality, as though being a personality was a distinct category of humanity.

One of them was the regular, Sparky Skuse, the Oxford historian. The other had not yet been finalised.

After the introduction, Scott would sit in the famous chair and be interrogated, both by the panel and the audience – the whole thing going out live. Going out live – that was what had made Scott hesitate before accepting. That, and of course Dr Skuse. Scott had heard him question people on the programme before. He was overbearing, clever and perfectly willing to be extremely offensive.

Nicky reassured him. 'You'll manage, no problem. After all, you know your job, you live it every day. These people are just arguing about what you do for the sake of it. They actually know nothing about it at all.'

Scott was still unsure.

Nicky said, 'There'll be nothing about any particular case. It's all general stuff.'

'Oh, I'll manage the argument,' he said, 'the real trouble is that my mind won't be completely on the job. I've got the Forgan case coming up the next day.'

It was only later that he realised she had not asked about that at all.

Chapter Nineteen

In the end John Donald didn't find it difficult to get a ticket for *Inquisition*. He pestered the TV channel, who eventually produced one to get rid of him.

Wanting something gives you an aim in life. John Donald thought about that.

It was amazing the changes he had gone through. The new room he had found was pleasant. He was beginning to lead an ordered life, putting things away, controlling the tide of objects that normally swirled around him. Moving away from where he had lived had made a difference. He left in order to drop out of sight, but the absence of his friends had an unexpected effect. He used to meet them in the pub and then drink until he could hardly get himself home. Now there was no one to go out with, he found he didn't go out. He had stopped drinking. No, he hadn't stopped drinking – drink had stopped happening to him.

Bored in a bookshop, he had read in a self-help book how it was having an aim that counted. It turned out to be right. For the first time in many years he found work, and kept it, because when he felt like walking away, which he did every morning and most of the day, he reminded himself of why he was here. He had found the way that would give him freedom. For the first time in his life he felt focused. It would not be long now. Soon he would be completely free.

Most nights when he returned from work he read the papers he had found in Scott's case. After a while they became clear to him. It was a case about some old woman who had been convicted of murder, and Scott was saying the conviction was all wrong. But at the same time he was not going to blame the other lawyers for the conviction. He was saying what they had done wasn't relevant.

That was typical, just doing what they always did, looking after their own.

He bought a television, second-hand but working, and he watched *Inquisition*. It was on every Monday evening. Every week someone had to sit in what they called the hot seat, justifying himself under questioning. John Donald saw the programme and he especially noticed Dr Skuse.

Skuse behaved like Scott had at the Old Bailey – unfair, not giving the man in the seat time to answer, ridiculing him, pouring out so many words that the man being questioned sometimes did not know where to turn. Every time John Donald watched it he was reminded of how Scott had managed to deny the truth. Bullying and pushing, twisting and turning, and none of the people in the hot seat knew how to hit back. They sat there like he had with Scott and let Skuse humiliate them.

Going on his knees up to the screen, he watched him closely. The man's mouth seemed to move independently of the rest of him, and Donald noticed the growing look of pleasure on the man's face as he attacked the victim. He reminded John Donald of someone, and it wasn't always Scott – there was someone else there in the background, in his memory, someone who also made John Donald's mouth dry and the back of his neck itch with anger. Who was it? He watched the programme greedily.

When real Monday, as he called it, came, he made certain he arrived home early. He washed and changed. He had bought himself a suit, dark blue linen, and a shirt to go with it. It felt good. His shoes were not new but as he surveyed himself he decided he looked fine. It was a long time since he had dressed up to go out.

He remembered those times at home, but then his memories went the whole way and he remembered the girls, and the laughter, Johnny Donald, McClaister's pet, and the anger and the fights. He remembered the sheriff, and as always the memory ended in reliving the humiliation as the investigating sheriff spoke to him as though he were dirt.

He snapped back to the image looking angrily back at him in the mirror. He worried that the knife would show, especially in the pocket of a suit of such light material, but it didn't. He folded a handkerchief in after it to make sure. Anyway, he did not look like himself any more. He saw a different person in the mirror. Now he wasn't the kind of person that the police stopped and searched.

He checked his room, leaving the television on – it wouldn't do any harm if people in the other rooms in the house thought he had been in all evening – and he walked down the steep hill to the train station. In half an hour he was in central London, making his way to the studio.

He had put his ticket in a small plastic wallet, not touching it once with his bare hands. Fingerprints could be lifted from paper. Nobody would know he had been there. Nobody who knew him would recognise him, even if they saw him. At last the time had come.

The studio seats were filling up. The audience was being

divided up into sections, and John Donald found himself-with a group who were obviously students. The man who was telling them where to sit handed out sheets of paper. 'You were asked to think of questions. Could you write them on these? If you want, someone will help you get the wording right.' He looked over his shoulder at the area where the interviewers were going to sit, and then said, 'What we're looking for is more unusual ones. Dr Skuse will be asking most of the obvious ones, in his own special way' – there was laughter – 'so perhaps you can ask about the lawyers' closed shop, especially barristers, and their privileges.'

He was encouraging. 'Nice and aggressive, now,' he said, grinning.

The buzz of the waiting audience began to grow.

Nicky showed Scott the studio. He saw a mass of faces, but here and there he was able to focus on one or two, all looking at him curiously, as though he were an exhibit.

'You'll sit there,' said Nicky unnecessarily, pointing at the famous chair. It was set directly under two spotlights. Scott was reminded of pictures of police interrogations on the covers of old pulp crime novels. Suddenly he wondered what he had let himself in for.

'You'd better get to make-up,' she said.

'Do I get to meet the others?'

'Not till afterwards,' she said. 'We like to keep this as real as possible. After all, you wouldn't normally meet interrogators in advance.'

His made his way to the make-up room. 'Have you had this done before?' the girl with the make-up asked.

'No.'

'Then you don't know what's best for you?'

'No.' It was an extraordinary idea that someone might know such a thing.

'Well, let's make you look thinner, and a little more angry, then.' She started working on Scott's face.

'Remember the rules,' said Nicky. 'If Moira thinks you are avoiding the question, she'll ask for it to be repeated. If you think they are being unfair, then you can appeal to Moira, but I wouldn't do that if I were you. It looks a bit wimpish. Otherwise are you happy you know the format?'

Scott said 'Yes,' now sitting in the studio chair, everybody looking at him. It was like public dentistry.

On a monitor to his left, Scott saw the titles of the programme coming up. There was no sound and the lack of the familiar pounding beat that accompanied the introduction when watched on television made everything seem rather detached. A man with a clipboard, the floor manager – was that what he was called? – started counting, opening his fingers in dramatic gestures, and Scott saw Moira McRae's rather puffy face fill the screen. He looked to his right and saw her from a different angle. The contrast between her and the television image was odd. It was as though on the television a layer had been wiped off and replaced by an artificial shine such as you might see on a puppet.

'Tonight we examine the role of the advocate. The man – nowadays, of course, we are pleased to say, more and more often the woman – who speaks on behalf of those who, for whatever reason, find themselves in court.' It was a desperately complicated sentence, but Scott was interested to see that on television it came out only as a series of separate remarks. The screen seemed to suck complexity out of things. She went on, 'We ask, "Why do they do this? How well do they do it?" And, most of all, the question that *Inquisition* always asks – how does the man in the hot seat explain himself to our sceptical panel?' As she said that she grinned in anticipation and swung round to face the panel.

'Now, our interrogation team.' The television picture opened up to include the two people who were sitting opposite Scott. 'Dr Skuse, who of course needs no introduction' – there was a sigh from the audience as though in anticipation – 'and with him a formidable wit, a great intelligence and, most important for us, a professional sceptic, Dr Geraldine Parr.'

There was applause. Scott could see it was being encouraged by the man with the clipboard.

'Geraldine . . .' Moira McRae's slight Scottish accent came out. 'Lawyers. Have you had any experience?'

'Yes, I have.' She said nothing more. There was only the trace of an Australian accent and a look. For that she got a laugh, the floor manager miming for the audience to follow.

'I'm not going to ask our Dr Skuse the same question. I think we can already guess what he has to say. So I'll turn directly to our guest, Jeremy Scott. Now, you're a lawyer, but a lawyer of a particular sort. An advocate, a criminal advocate.'

Scott tried to look bright, but succeeded only in looking slightly dazed.

'Oh, look at him!' said Catherine, watching British television in Amsterdam. 'What on earth does he think he's doing?'

Moira McRae went on. 'Jeremy Scott, I think we should know a little bit about you. You work in the courts. Sometimes you prosecute criminal cases but mainly you defend, and once you went into the witness box on behalf of a client.'

The photograph of Ellie Johnson kissing Scott in the street flashed on to the screen. 'Now this lady wasn't that client, but the people you defend are not above publicly

demonstrating their affection. Presumably she was satisfied
with the result of her case.'

The clipboard man orchestrated laughter.

'You live alone now, though you were once married. Some
people say you are a bit of a loner, and some say that a good
advocate has to be that. Your latest case involves an appeal
on behalf of a woman convicted of murder.' Scott saw a
picture flash on to the monitor opposite him. Was that
Hilda Forgan? He was astonished but had to pay attention
to what was being said to him.

'You will say, on her behalf, that had she been properly
defended she would not have been convicted.'

The smile dropped from Scott's face. What were they
doing? They couldn't expect him to talk about that, could
they? It would be incredibly tactless just the day before the
appeal, and it would certainly get him into trouble.

'So, he says he's living alone, does he?' said Catherine.

Moira McRae went on, 'You have worked in the courts
for some years. My question is this: are you satisfied that
you do your job properly?'

Scott was prepared for this. He had seen how she normally
began the questioning.

'No,' he said.

There was silence at the unexpected reply, and, as he had
calculated, he had all the time in the world to qualify what
he had said. 'When you look back on anything you do, you
can always see ways it could have been done better.'

'That's a cop-out,' said Geraldine Parr.

'If it is, then I'm sorry, but I don't think it is.'

'What is your job?'

'Presenting an argument to a court on behalf of someone
who pays me to do it.'

'You're not going to include anything about justice, or getting the answer right, in that?'

'No. I don't think so.'

'Why not?'

'Because the whole format of a trial in this country is arranged on the basis that if the opposing arguments are presented properly, then the correct decision will be reached by the people there listening to each side. And those people are the jury.'

'Do you believe that's true?'

'Not always.'

'So you don't believe in the system?'

'It's what we've got.'

Geraldine Parr was relatively easy to deal with. She at least allowed the logic of the answer to lead to the next question.

'Where does it most often go wrong?'

'Sometimes the drama of the event can get in the way of the logic. For instance, if an advocate provokes a witness into anger or incoherence, it can affect the jury's judgment of the truth of what the witness is saying. I remember one case where a witness almost jumped . . . No, why minimise it? He did jump out of the witness box in anger. I felt very sorry for him.'

'If you saw someone provoke a witness intentionally, would you approve?'

'No, I don't think I would.'

'Would you say so publicly?'

'I don't think so, no. Mainly because I would have no occasion to.'

'You mean you wouldn't attack the behaviour of an opponent?'

'It would depend.'

'Depend on what?'

'On what had been done.'

'Are you sure you wouldn't because he's a colleague?'

Moira McRae interrupted. 'A question from the audience. I think this is relevant.' She took a question from the bundle. It had been marked with a star.

The researcher who had worked the audience for questions had not, at first, understood what it was Donald wanted to ask. She had not believed it, but when she saw Scott's address, and the photocopy of the advice, she was convinced. She took his question and rewrote it.

Moira McRae read it out. 'You have said, and I quote, "It is not possible to attack an advocate for his general conduct, for example whether he is interested in, or particularly efficient at, what he is doing." '

Scott was flabbergasted. This was a direct quotation from his advice, the one in the stolen papers. His head whirled. Did this mean that it was these people who had taken his briefcase? His first reaction was to protest, but then he realised he could not do that. People listening did not want to know where the quotation was coming from, they wanted to know if it was true. This is what politicians had to deal with all the time.

Luckily Moira McRae did not know how to ask a question, even though she worked in the courts. She preferred to repeat the point rather than let the quotation speak for itself. 'You're saying there just what Dr Parr suggested was true, that the solidarity of the Bar, membership of the club, is more important than defending the client properly?'

Scott waited a moment before replying, then said, 'No, not at all. What I said there is a simple proposition of law. In a particular case the reputation or commitment of the advocate has nothing to do with the facts of the case. You can't add it to the argument.'

'That, if I may say so, is complete rubbish,' Dr Skuse interrupted. There was a stir in the audience as his angry voice cut through the proceedings. 'The reputation of an advocate is something a jury has always taken into account.'

Scott took his time again, concentrating on the event and not on the implications of what was being done to him. Despite his anger, he felt surprisingly relaxed. If they wanted to be tough, then he would be too. He'd been in the chair for about ten minutes and was beginning to feel in control.

'I'm afraid you've got yourself a little confused, Dr Skuse, although I'm sure your confusion extends only to this.' Scott was encouraged to hear a small laugh from the audience. 'What I said is just a proposition of law. It's about whether or not, in an appeal, one can argue about the reputation of a man's lawyer rather than the events of the case. Obviously you cannot. If you wish to provide me with authority . . .' He stopped. You couldn't talk like that on television. People would think you were a pompous berk.

'So you would never attack another lawyer?'

'I do, all the time.' Skuse was stopped in his tracks and Scott was able to continue. 'Of course, it has to be done carefully in case the jury think you're going too far. But now I'm talking about a jury.'

It was pleasing to watch Skuse discovering what other people often discover, that professional arguments are a little more complicated than the mere repetition of opinion.

Skuse found another complaint. 'That's all it is, though, isn't it? Playing games?'

'Yes, it's playing games. But some games are very serious.'

'You know quite well what I mean.' Skuse modulated his

voice, demonstrating exasperated restraint at such stupidity. He was getting into his stride now. 'And you're avoiding the question.'

'Well, you'll have to ask it again.'

'You're more interested in the rules than what the trial's about.'

'Yes, that's true. Interest is not the correct word, though.'

'What is?'

'Controlled by the rules.'

'Again, you're avoiding the question.'

'Which is what?'

'You'd put rules before an obvious injustice.'

'That's wrong.'

Skuse continued with his next remark, but Scott cut through it. 'You disregarded my reply. I'll tell you why I said what I did if you want me to.'

Skuse had to say, 'Go ahead.'

'Most rules in court procedure are designed to prevent people deciding things on insufficient or unreliable evidence. They're not unfair, though sometimes they feel restrictive.'

'What about your funny uniforms?'

'There you have me. Old-style hats and coats.'

'They're another attempt to confuse people and intimidate them,' Skuse said.

John Donald watched Scott as Skuse attacked him. It was interesting what Scott had said about the witness – that must have been a reference to him. Perhaps Scott did realise what he was doing. They continued talking. Now Skuse was beginning to lose his temper.

'But you're just bullies dressed up to make what you do seem dignified.'

'There's some truth in what you say.'

Donald could see that Scott was being very polite but was not afraid to admit things. This was becoming interesting, more interesting than he thought. Who was it Skuse reminded him of? Seeing him in the flesh and not just on the screen made the memory even stronger, and there was the trace of an accent as well. A Glasgow voice.

'You think that by agreeing with me you'll destroy the effect of what I'm saying,' Skuse said.

'No, I'm agreeing because what you say has some truth in it.'

'So you say.'

'Why do you get angry when someone agrees with you? I thought it was meant to be the other way round.'

There was laughter. This time it did not need the man with the clipboard. Skuse became more angry.

'Be serious, Mr Scott. What we are talking about is important.'

Donald realised who it was. McClaister. The schoolteacher. It was McClaister who had forced him out of that school. McClaister who had never given him a chance.

'I'm going to ask you once again,' said Skuse. Donald could not believe it. That was the exact phrase McClaister had used to him. He remembered sitting at the back of the class. McClaister had said that. He remembered how the heads of the other children turned, intruding their smiling faces into his corner. So many faces. He could not deal with so many. One or two he could have dealt with. But so many. He felt the old, old anger. McClaister had won then. He was not going to win again.

Scott spoke again. 'Repeating the question doesn't mean you'll get a different answer, Dr Skuse.' Donald wished he had said that all those years ago.

It was very hot, wasn't it?

John Donald found himself sweating, his heart was racing. McClaister's face seemed to settle on Skuse. His mouth moving independently of his eyes, mocking him, mocking everything, and McClaister had touched him, had put his hand on his at the back of the class, asking how was it such a sweet face could be so slow, and the girls had laughed at him and called him McClaister's pet. He had left the school. He wouldn't go in. He had spent his days up by the concrete overpass, just waiting until the schools came out and he wouldn't be on his own. But even then he was on his own and the girls would laugh. McClaister's pet. And in Borstal, where that sheriff had sent him, after he had used the knife for the first time, the name had followed him.

'He's not doing too badly,' said Catherine. 'He's standing up for himself.' Jeroem could not see the point of it all. 'You English,' he said, 'always being nasty to each other.'

'That's all we have time for,' said Moira McRae. 'We have to thank Mr Scott. Now a different matter, but connected with our discussion.'

Picking up some papers, she turned to face a different camera. 'Tomorrow in the Court of Appeal Hilda Forgan's case will be heard. Perhaps viewers will remember this extremely disturbing case. Ms Forgan is presently serving a life sentence. Jeremy Scott is her lawyer. He will present the appeal.'

The screen flashed to Scott's face, which was blank with astonishment. He had not been told about this. Everything he had just said would now be seen as an introduction to the case. It would look as though he were trying to run the appeal in public to influence the court.

Moira McRae continued, 'The question at the centre of

the appeal will be, "Was Hilda Forgan properly served by her lawyers? Was she properly served by the system?" '

The man with the clipboard had been counting down – three fingers, two, one – and the screen switched to a picture of Hilda Forgan as a voice started to tell the story of the case.

The studio stopped broadcasting live. Scott erupted out of his chair, tearing at the wires attached to his jacket. 'You didn't tell me. You didn't tell me that you were going to deal with the Forgan case.'

Moira McRae looked up at him, puzzled. She clearly hadn't a clue what he was complaining about. She put her hand to her ear. She wasn't even listening to him, but to what was being said from the control room. Scott turned to find someone to complain to, to shout at. There was no one. He could see some figures in the control room through the dimming lights above the audience's heads. Toby Beyt was there. He had done this. But Scott did not know how to get at him.

He watched as the story unfolded, seeing the pictures of the close where he had visited Mrs Beatty's house, Hilton standing on the steps saying how he believed in Hilda's guilt. That must have been the day he was there. Toby Beyt. Of course – he was the man Scott had seen get out of the Jeep. Why had he not realised it?

The screen showed Mrs Dalrymple sitting in her drawing room, and then it cut to a large hall where the group of people Scott had seen from Sussex and many others were gathered to speak about the case. He recognised faces here and there. This must be the public meeting that Hilton had asked him about. Scott had not been told about any of this. Over the pictures a voice was repeating the argument that Miss Forgan had not been defended properly. Scott was furious. They made it seem so simple. It was all the lawyers' fault, they were saying, fat, fee-earning lawyers. Scott knew the other side of it.

The film clip finished.

Moira McRae said, 'Well, it remains to be seen what the Court of Appeal makes of this most distressing case. Of course, I can't be too specific but those watching may now be asking this question. "Will the court look again at what happened to Ms Forgan?" or will they, as so often happens, as Dr Skuse says always happens' – the screen flashed to his nodding head – '"Will they protect their own? Will they close ranks?" We shall see. We will return to this case in the future.'

In the confusion of the programme breaking up, Donald could see that Scott had not returned to his chair. He had seen him jump up and shout something at Moira McRae. She had not replied. Then Donald had seen Scott disentangle himself from the wires that must have been connected to the microphone and move off to the right to watch the screen. When he looked again Scott had gone.

Skuse got up and went out the same way. If John Donald wanted to follow he had to go now. It was always best to carry something. Donald took the legal papers that he had shown the researcher and picked up a clipboard lying at the bottom of the steps. He walked towards the stage set and gathered up the microphone lead that Scott had dropped. He examined it, walking down towards the door by which they had left.

Someone approached him with a question in her eyes. 'I'm with Dr Skuse,' Donald said, putting the microphone in his pocket next to the knife. He had waited all these years. Now he was absolutely sure what he had to do.

The girl was used to seeing Dr Skuse accompanied by young men and pointed Donald towards the hospitality suite. It was so inconsequential that later she could not even remember doing it.

Scott walked from the studio down a long passage into the dark night. He didn't want any hospitality, nor did he bother waiting on the offer of a taxi. He needed to get out into the open air. The very worst had happened. He had known all along that journalists were not to be trusted. He went back over what had been said during the programme. He himself had said nothing about the Hilda Forgan case. Thank God for that. Then he remembered the passage they had lifted from his advice. It would look as though he had provided confidential material for the programme. This was awful. At least if he was challenged he could show he had reported the theft.

But the worst thing about these sorts of situations was that there never was a direct accusation, only an atmosphere of suspicion, and you couldn't shake such an atmosphere, you couldn't deny it while it remained unspoken.

He went over the events again. It was unbelievable. Not only had they been willing to set him up, promising not to talk about the case, but they had also stolen from him. It was inconceivable. Toby Beyt had got the documents. Scott thought about it as he turned the corner and set off along the long road. Did that mean that Nicky was involved? Of course it did. She had made the running all along. All that stuff about his being good at his job, all the flattery, the idea that she was envious of what he did, that she would have liked to do his job. All lies merely to entrap him.

In the dark his anger seemed to spread out and diminish. The street was empty and the quietness began to relax him. There was no one about. He slowed his pace and tried to think about how he should deal with this.

*   *   *

John Donald had never killed anybody before, but he had met people who had. Each had said much the same thing about it. It was a kind of barrier. Once you'd gone through it you were different somehow.

He remembered becoming friendly with a lifer in prison once, who had told him that after he killed 'his man' he felt freer living his own life. It was the reverse of saving a man's life.

John Donald was looking forward to that freedom. Only a death could give him life. Any death.

Chapter Twenty

'No, Mr Scott's not here. He's not come in yet. No, I don't know where he is.'

Harry did not like being disturbed. He had his work to do. He looked around the clerks' room. The staff avoided his eye. They had a different explanation for his bad temper. Harry did not like his guvners – he still called them guvners – but nevertheless thought he owned them, did not approve of them striking out on their own. Scott appearing on television was striking out on his own.

'He's due at the Court of Appeal at eleven thirty this morning. Until he doesn't turn up there I'm not concerned.'

Another phone rang.

The first junior picked it up. He said, 'I'll see,' waited until Harry put his phone down and said, 'It's the BBC.'

'Sod the BBC,' Harry said.

'He says "Not today, thank you." ' The first junior spoke sweetly, as if fending off a double-glazing salesman. There was a stifled laugh from the most junior clerk of all. Harry looked at him, but by then the boy was picking something up from the floor.

The door opened and Douglas Gatling stood in the entrance.

'Is Mr Scott in?'

The first junior answered him. 'Not been in this morning, Mr Gatling. He's over the road at the Court of Appeal today.'

'I know he is,' said Gatling. 'May we have a word, Harry?'

'I'll be with you immediately, sir,' said Harry, not moving an inch. It was not until Gatling left the room that he got up. In such a fashion were the proprieties maintained.

'Did you see it?' said the first junior after Harry left.

'Yes. I thought he was good. He saw off that Skuse bloke, didn't he?'

'But that's not what all the fuss is about.'

'What is it about?'

'They practically ran Scott's appeal on television, the night before going to the Court of Appeal. All the witnesses he wants to call were interviewed. Remember the doctor? He came here to a conference. And all those people in the church hall talking about how unfair it was? Scott wants to call a selection of them, and first he parades them all over the television. The Court of Appeal won't like that.'

'Why should it matter to them? They're grown men, aren't they?' said the second junior. In the first junior's opinion, the second junior did not really understand these things. He was about to say so when the phone rang. He picked it up and listened. Then he pressed internal phone buttons.

'It's the Appeal Court office for Mr Gatling.' He put his hand over the phone while he waited. 'Surprise, surprise.' Then, 'I'm putting you through now, sir,' he said, all politeness.

On the pavement outside the High Court, Toby Beyt was waiting with his sleepy cameraman. 'We need pictures of prosecuting counsel and of Scott, if you can. I've told the doctor to contact you here. Then there'll be Dalrymple. You remember him? We went to his house, the one with the silver pheasants on the window sill. Can I leave you to do that? Also a few shots of the crowd. Leave out the banners, though.'

The crowd consisted mainly of other journalists and some young women who were protesting on behalf of a wife who had been convicted of gouging out the eyes of her drunken husband. 'What is the sight of a wife-beater worth anyway?' one of the banners read.

Toby Beyt went in through the high doors, looking for Monty. He found him at the phone where the old post office used to be. He was with Nicky.

'We can't find Scott,' she said.

Monty interrupted, 'Last night, on your programme last night, where did you get that information about what Scott wrote in his advice? You shouldn't have had that.' There were some things even Monty drew the line at.

'Scott's not at his chambers. They haven't seen him and the phone at his flat is not being answered.'

'When does the appeal begin?'

'In about an hour,' said Monty. Then he insisted, 'Where did you get that document? The one that was quoted from.'

'Somebody showed it to the staff at the studio.'

'Who?'

'I don't know. It didn't seem important. The girl thought these documents were available.'

'I'll go over to his chambers to see if I can find Scott,' said Nicky.

Douglas Gatling had a difficult time on the phone.

'Well, certainly I'll speak to him. But it's a problematic area. I can't tell him what to do, you know.'

He listened, then said, 'Of course there are proprieties. Of course I understand that.' More listening. 'You've got a what?' He did not believe it. 'A transcript? And he said what?'

Douglas grabbed a pen. 'Look, can I make a note?' He wrote quickly. 'He quoted a private opinion. He said he wouldn't attack Galbraith for not being up to the job any more because the court would not allow it. He was saying it in public so at least everyone knew what the truth was? Not the last bit? That was your conclusion, that's what you think he was doing? Look, let me get this down.'

Gatling listened quietly for a while, then he said, 'Well, I must say that wasn't my impression, but if you say you have a transcript . . .' He looked for support towards Harry, who was standing opposite his desk, looking out of the window affecting not to listen to his guvner being told off.

Hilda Forgan had been woken in prison at five thirty. By eleven o'clock she had been sitting by herself on one bench or another, alone, for about four hours. She had spent an hour in a prison van. That was her morning. She had nothing to read and, save for eating a sparse breakfast, she had done nothing except sit and stare at the wall. That was all there was to do.

'I don't know why they bother,' she said. She stared straight ahead of her. 'I've read about how they behave. They exercise scrupulous care about points of law and proper proof and things, I suppose that's their business, but then, out of the blue they suddenly launch into extraordinary propositions about the way people behave. That's what the Court of Appeal is like.

'I've been reading about the Guildford case. I couldn't believe it. Those judges were desperate to get all the details exactly right, and yet, at the end of the appeal, they suddenly started making judgments about witnesses that people in real life would never make.

'Anyone, especially the policemen, who had anything to say that threw doubt on the convictions was apparently "motivated by malice" or "disturbed" in some way. It's almost as if they need to keep the thing going to justify their existence. They were frightened. They were frightened of admitting anything had gone wrong.'

She sat back and stared at Scott.

He was not going to get anything sensible out of her this morning. He put his hand on hers and said, 'I'll see you upstairs, Hilda.'

Chapter Twenty-One

CRIMINAL APPEAL ACT 1968

Section 23 2. The Court of Appeal shall, in considering whether to receive any new evidence, have regard in particular to –

   a) whether the new evidence appears to the court to be capable of belief

   b) whether there is a reasonable explanation for the failure to adduce the evidence at the original trial.

'I appear in this matter for the appellant,' said Scott. He was standing at the back of the lawyers' benches, facing Lord Justice Tocket, a good fifty feet from him.

The court, except where Scott was standing, was crowded. The press benches were full, the public gallery was overflowing, but on his side of counsel's benches he was alone. Above him the court rose into blackness where old windows allowed a moss-green light to filter through. His voice rose upward into the space as he spoke.

The judge said, 'I remember, Mr Scott.'

'My learned friend, Mr Wethersedge, appears for the crown assisted by Mr Steel.

'Miss Forgan appeals from a verdict of a jury directed by . . .' Scott recited the name of the judge and the dates of the trial. 'Convicted of the murder of Anna Beatty on the . . .' He gave the date.

Scott remembered how he used to have to write out the dates and names of this preliminary recitation, and how he used to hear nervousness cracking in his voice as he read it out. That was a difference – now at least he felt at ease in this court. As he spoke, he looked around at the people watching him. He was, after all, making a public announcement.

'The grounds of appeal are set out in the amended document dated . . .' Scott picked it up. 'Our principal ground invites the court to say that after hearing new witnesses for the defence, the conviction is not safe.'

'If we hear them, Mr Scott.'

Scott had expected the remark. 'And of course the first matter that falls to be considered is whether the court should hear the witnesses at all. The test to be applied in deciding whether to hear them is set out in section twenty-three . . .'

'Do you oppose this, Mr Wethersedge?' Lord Justice Tocket interrupted. For Scott this intervention set the atmosphere of the appeal immediately.

'I do, m'luds.' Wethersedge got to his feet and Scott was surprised to see exactly what Hilda had described, the man leaned forward on his podium, waggling his arse. Scott looked at Hilda, sitting in the dock at the side of the court. She was staring up at the dark ceiling.

Wethersedge said, 'This is evidence which, if it was even worthy of consideration, would have been called at the trial.'

He turned and looked at Scott. 'Counsel who appeared at the original trial is not unknown to these courts. The real basis of Mr Scott's appeal must be that Mr Galbraith was completely wrong in his presentation of the case.'

Wethersedge was intent on emphasising that this case was Galbraith's, the great Galbraith's, and would clearly do so throughout the hearing.

He had treated Galbraith with complete contempt during the original trial, Scott had seen it in the transcript, but now it was clear he would say anything to maintain this conviction.

'Mr Scott?'

Scott disregarded Wethersedge. 'For the moment I wish to argue that the new evidence is capable of belief as set out in the act. Before I go any further, I should outline the central events that affect, or are affected by, the new medical evidence I wish to call.'

Scott described the evidence that had been called to prove that Mrs Beatty couldn't move. 'The evidence wasn't of course certain. First the diagnosis was speculative . . .'

'All diagnoses are speculative.' He was interrupted.

'More than most in this case. For the reasons set out on page eighty-four of statements.'

The court turned to the papers. Scott read the doctor's warning on his diagnosis.

'And the second point. No evidence was called from any-one who knew her to say Mrs Beatty could not move.'

'But the defendant herself said she knew her aunt could not move.'

Scott waited before replying. If he was able to contradict an intervention it was far better to do it slowly and effectively. He opened his second notebook. As he did so he looked to his right. Behind him, two rows back, sat Galbraith, his eyes boring into Scott's back.

He found the place in the notebook immediately and was pleased to feel things working smoothly. Some days you put your hand on the book and it wouldn't open to the correct page, however carefully you prepared your argument.

The judge on Scott's left, Mr Justice Barker, stirred and interrupted him. He spoke dismissively. 'The summary of the evidence says that the defendant admitted that Mrs Beatty could not move from her bed unaided. Is that not right?'

This was typical of the criminal courts. If a defendant admitted something then it was a short cut to proof. It saved everyone the trouble of doing their job properly.

'That is so,' said Scott, 'but Miss Forgan wasn't necessarily correct. There is evidence of other people who believed for a while that Mrs Beatty could not move. But they discovered they were wrong. Miss Forgan did believe that Mrs Beatty could not move, and she might have been wrong. Look at what she said in the interview. If you look at the series of questions . . .'

Then came the first helpful intervention, from the judge on Scott's right, Mr Justice Colover. 'In bundle three at page forty Miss Forgan says, "One day she stopped, just stopped and lay in bed. Almost as though she had decided to." '

Scott let the judge's remark sink in, then he added, 'If you turn to page . . .' He had to pause to find it, but again his notes did not let him down. 'If you turn to another of the statements, the statement of one of the temporary nurses, Nurse Hoskins . . . Perhaps I should read it out. "Miss Forgan told me her aunt was a difficult woman and that sometimes she thought she was pretending to be more helpless than she really was." '

Scott had the feeling he was making progress, but then Lord Justice Tocket spoke. Until now he had restricted himself to making meticulous notes with his pen, dipping it regularly in the inkwell. He wiped it carefully with a piece of blotting paper and said, 'This is all very well and good, Mr Scott, but . . .' It was as though someone had opened a door and a draught of cold air had swept into the room. 'What you are suggesting is this, is it not?' He steepled his fingers. 'You are asking us to say that a defendant can present one case at the trial and then, if that case fails, come to this court and ask to be allowed to present a different explanation.'

Of course, that was exactly what Scott was asking. The only way of answering it was to repeat himself. 'No. I am asking this court to say that in this particular case a mistake was made and that therefore the conviction is unsafe.'

'A mistake. You are saying a mistake was made. You criticise counsel who appeared in the trial.'

'If saying that a mistake was made is criticism, yes. But it may not be. Mistakes are as much the essence of good decision-making as a correct answer is.' It was the phrase Scott had settled on in his mind beforehand. It meant, as far as he could make out, nothing at all.

The judge said, 'But if it was a mistake, it was no ordinary mistake. The defence must have considered the point very carefully. Indeed, you enquired about it in your letter to Mr Galbraith. We have his reply. He has written that he did discuss the matter with his client during his second conference, on the fifteenth of July.'

Scott said, 'I make this clear. I am not asking the court to enquire into the correctness or competence of Miss Forgan's representation. I wish only to call evidence before you that will demonstrate that her conviction, based on an assumption that was wrong, is unsafe.'

He had let the wolves in by using the wrong word.

'An assumption,' said Lord Justice Tocket. His voice was slightly more edgy, perhaps the nearest he could get to anger in his bloodless state. 'It was not an assumption. Whether Mrs Beatty could move must have been a piece of evidence carefully considered in conference, the subject no doubt of advice by leading counsel. And you call it an assumption. Well!' He threw his pen down.

Scott said, 'I meant that once the point was not argued, and it was never argued, then the medical evidence was assumed to be correct.'

'It was more than that. Any advocate, let alone one of Mr Galbraith's eminence, would have realised that there were two ways of approaching this case. Upon the basis either that Mrs Beatty somehow secured her own death' – again Scott noticed the curious unwillingness to say suicide – 'or that there was an outside agent, the hand of a murderer. Miss Forgan gave instructions on that matter and received advice.'

Scott said, 'Then I must say this. As to advice, there was never any advice. On this central point Miss Forgan recalls no advice at all. We are not aware that any doctor was consulted on this vital point, and on the day when we are told Miss Forgan confirmed her instructions to Mr Galbraith she was admitted to Holloway prison hospital. Mr Galbraith refers to that himself. She needed sedation and spoke not a word to anyone for three weeks. You'll remember she was not even brought to one of the preliminary hearings of the case because of her illness, and it was at that hearing that the defence indicated that the medical evidence was not contested.'

'That sounds like an attack upon the nature of your client's representation,' said Barker, the judge on Scott's left.

'I think you had better make your mind up how you approach your case,' said Lord Justice Tocket. 'Perhaps you should do so during the luncheon adjournment.'

Scott stood in counsel's row organising his papers as the public in the gallery left the court. Was his use of the word 'assumption' enough to justify Tocket's outburst, or had the judge been looking for an occasion to attack him?

He looked up at the the judges' empty seats and thought, Why after all the years that it has taken for them to become judges, are they still not in control of their feelings? It was as if Tocket were taking it personally. Perhaps Hilda was right.

Nicky was waiting for him in the passage outside. Scott nearly turned away from her. At first she did not notice his reluctance. She said, 'We didn't know where you had got to this morning.'

Scott paused a moment before replying. The way this woman had behaved was incredible.

'I don't see why it should matter where I was. I was in the cells seeing the client.' He nearly added 'doing my job', but managed to stop himself before he began to sound pompous.

'But,' her surprise made her say, 'of course it matters. We're in this together, aren't we?'

'No, we are not,' said Scott. He looked at her. 'All I am doing is presenting an appeal. I'm not doing this as an exercise to provide you with a television programme.'

Still she stood, surprised.

'Don't you realise what you did last night? You compromised this case. You made it look as though I was arguing the case on television the night before the appeal. This isn't America. I can't do that to this court and expect to be taken seriously.'

'But you didn't say anything about the case. I promised you that you wouldn't.'

'That's not the point. I was being interviewed moments before it was discussed. And you read a passage out from an advice which I had written about the case. Where did you get that, anyway?'

She hadn't a clue what he was talking about now.

'Where did you get it from? Did you get it from the thief, or did you arrange for it to be stolen?'

Nicky Vesey was entirely on Hilda Forgan's side, and she had assumed that Scott was on Hilda Forgan's side in the same way. Her position was simple. The conviction was absurd. The judges were absurd – they were clearly out to destroy Hilda. Everything Nicky had done she had done because she was helping an innocent woman, and here was her counsel accusing her of not helping. This was Scott, whom she had urged on when he had an answer to every objection the judges had raised. This was the man whom she had really begun to admire.

If this was what he was like. Now she remembered small things. The picture became clearer. She remembered how he had not really wanted to take the case originally. He had said that he did not want to attack Galbraith. And moments ago it became clear again. Every time the court, or anyone, had approached the subject of Galbraith, he had avoided the issue. He wasn't interested in the justice of it at all. 'All this grief for a thousand pounds,' he had said. And she knew Toby Beyt had paid five thousand to start with. There was another bill for ten thousand on his desk now. Scott had lied to her about the money. He was like the rest of them. He was a lawyer.

'I would have thought you appreciated the help.'

'Help!' said Scott contemptuously.

This was the woman who had tricked him into the radio interview, who, it was clear now, had got friendly with him solely to find out about the case. She had inveigled him on to television to make it seem he was a party to that damn film. He had been tricked all along the line. And she, or at least someone she worked with, had stolen the documents from him. 'How you can say we're in it together when you steal my documents and then produce them on television to embarrass me' – he was really angry, and as so often happens in anger, he finished lamely – 'is beyond my understanding.'

She stood rooted to the spot.

'Stole your documents?' The accusation was so extraordinary that she could say nothing.

He looked at her, dressed in her smart clothes, dressed-to-the-hilt clothes, so sophisticated, so pleased with herself, so dishonest.

He walked away.

In the robing room he took a cup of water from the cooler. There was a container for money and he put ten pence into it. Amazing. They would be charging for providing a peg for his coat next. He sat down in one of the uncomfortable chairs. This was not going well.

'Mr Scott, sir.'

He looked up. It was Monty. He nearly said, 'Monty, you shouldn't be here,' then did not.

'If I may say, Mr Scott, you're doing it very well, but there's just one thing.'

Scott got back into character. 'Sorry, Monty. Yes?'

'You're going to have to say Galbraith didn't do it properly.'

'Look, Monty, I don't want to, you know that. And it's not because I'm frightened of doing it.' He knew in his bones that if he were forced into attacking Galbraith it would be the end of the case. He said, 'If I do attack him, I'm giving them a reason to find against me. We've got the vital point. The new evidence. Come on, Monty, we've been through it before.'

'But they'll always say that if you don't blame Galbraith you're accepting the trial was done properly. And if it was done properly that means the evidence was correctly abandoned. You have to attack Galbraith. You've got no choice any more. They're forcing the issue.'

'You really think that?'

'Mr Scott, sir, you know I don't like Galbraith. I told you that, didn't I?'

'Yes.'

'But do you think I would let that get in the way of a client? Do you really? I've been doing this job for forty years now. It's the grubby end of the law. I know what people think of me. I do things barristers don't do. I handle money, for God's sake – how demeaning! But I've never run a case in a particular way just to satisfy my likes and dislikes. Here the system demands it. If you don't attack him then they will use that as a reason for finding against you. They won't allow a middle way.'

He looked at Scott with his head on one side and said, 'Why do you think I let Hilda brief you? Do you think the whole thing was a mistake, and that the old girl got your name in her head and that nothing could get it out? Do you think I would have allowed that to happen? I wouldn't have briefed you if I didn't think you were up to it, Mr Scott.'

Scott was silent. No one had said that to him before. Monty had hit the mark. He had always thought that the work he got was pure fluke.

Monty was right about the case too. It didn't matter if the court turned against him. That was their problem. 'Turned against him.' Even the phrase itself showed the mistake he was making. Courts either accepted arguments or they did not. There was no room for worrying about whether the court might 'turn against him'. If it was right to say that Galbraith had made a mistake, then he would say it.

Monty went on, 'But I'm not going to go on about that. I'm going to ask you one thing. Could you have defended the Hilda Forgan trial without getting a medical report? No. You'd have got two of them at least. And yet Galbraith has the gall to say that she was a difficult woman, but . . .' He stumbled, and then said, 'Here it is.' He pulled a document from his case. 'Here's the letter.' He read it out. ' "My client was an extremely difficult woman, but I am certain that the decision was correct" – do you hear that? That's a subtle way of undermining her.' He read on. ' "Of one thing I am certain and that is that Mrs Beatty could not move unaided." And he didn't get a report. Mr Scott, forget for a moment who he is. Forget it's Geoffrey G. Galbraith, QC. Would you have done that, sir? Would you?'

'No, Monty,' said Scott. 'I don't think I would.'

'The question of whether or not Miss Forgan asked the jury to decide the matter of her aunt's immobility was never properly decided. There was no proper medical evidence considered by the jury. There should have been. The doctors who gave statements for the court should have been cross-examined. In the light of Hilda Forgan's mental state for a large part of her stay in Holloway prison before the trial, the defence had no real instructions that her aunt was immobile. In view of the ambiguous nature of Miss Forgan's answers to the police, it is by no means obvious that the Crown could rely upon her answers to prove that point. The jury should have been left to decide it.

'The new evidence I propose to call before you is certainly credible. The doctor's evidence is supported by an academic colleague. The evidence of the experienced nurse, Miss Donoghue, who has worked in geriatric care for twenty-five years, the statement of Miss Forgan's neighbours who regularly saw Mrs Beatty, and the statements of two of them who say independently that they concluded that Mrs Beatty sometimes did move . . . All this evidence fits together.'

Scott summed up the arguments. He had taken Lord Justice Tocket and his two colleagues through the statements, attempting to show that the new evidence was credible.

He thought it was blindingly obvious that it was so, but during the argument he had been constantly interrupted, mainly by Lord Justice Tocket, occasionally by Barker. He noticed, however, that Colover had gone quiet.

'Your doctors never saw Mrs Beatty,' said Tocket.

'Neither did the Crown expert,' replied Scott.

'But he spoke to Mrs Beatty's general practitioner.'

'Our doctor has seen the practitioner's notes. Had the general practitioner been available he would have been seen also.'

'Your nurse does not qualify as an expert.'

'She does by dint of experience. She has, as you see, worked with elderly people for more than twenty-five years.'

'She did not know Mrs Beatty either.'

'Her evidence is not intended to be given on that basis. It is general evidence showing how difficult it is to be certain of a person's immobility.'

'You say she is an expert, then?'

'I certainly do.'

'Your evidence from the defendant's friends who called on Mrs Beatty is not expert evidence?'

By now it was clear that Tocket was interrupting Scott with any objection that came into his head. Scott was struggling to stay calm.

'If they were in possession of this information, why did they keep it to themselves?' said the judge.

'It was not the kind of thing one would discuss.'

'But, Mr Scott, they had ample opportunity to pass it to the authorities.'

Scott was puzzled. Why should the neighbours go to the

police because they thought an old lady was exaggerating her illness?

'Most people would think it was not a matter for the police.'

'Not a matter for the police?' Lord Justice Tocket looked at him triumphantly, as though he had cornered him in some nice argument about the law of trusts.

'Not a matter for the police? Here we have the police investigating a murder, the whole basis of which was that the old lady was immobile.'

Scott realised that they had been at cross-purposes. The judge meant that they should have gone to the police after the arrest.

'Stop, please,' he said. 'I misunderstood you. I thought you meant why did they not, when they first suspected Mrs Beatty could move, go to the police. Before all this happened.'

'Mr Scott, are you really suggesting I might have meant that?'

Scott was stuck. That is what he had thought. The other objections Tocket had made were equally absurd, so why not this one? But he could hardly say that.

'Sometimes even a simple question and answer can be misleading,' he said. 'In answer to your question, the neighbours did not realise the importance of what they suspected until after the event.'

'Do they not read newspapers?'

'Not in this case. And for very good reasons which are shortly set out in Mrs Dalrymple's extra statement.'

Scott had foreseen the argument and obtained an extra statement about the journalists' behaviour, the reason why people in Briar Close had just shut their minds to the publicity.

'But these matters which Your Lordship raises are

questions that ought to be asked of the witnesses,' Scott said, 'when they are called. They cannot be reasons for not calling them.'

Scott had to keep reminding himself that at this stage he was only applying to have the witnesses heard. The court seemed to be dealing with his argument as though they had already heard the evidence. To put it brutally, they were rehearsing reasons for disbelieving it in advance.

'Mrs Williams.' Lord Justice Tocket spoke even more sharply. 'In her you seek to call a witness who is the secretary of a society in Sussex devoted to self-immolation. I would remind you, Mr Scott, that not so long ago that in itself was an offence.'

Toby Beyt watched from the back of the court. He thought this would happen. He had sat through the second appeal of the Birmingham Six and had been amazed by what he had seen. So he wasn't surprised now – it was exactly what he expected. What astonished him was how these men were behaving like a parody of themselves. They were clever men getting it wrong.

Lord Justice Tocket talking about 'self-immolation', a nib being dipped into an inkwell, the dismissal of Nurse Donoghue, a woman with more experience of the world than these three men put together . . . He would have liked to have seen Mrs Williams offer Lord Justice Tocket a few home truths.

Scott was winding down now. He had not done badly. No, that was unfair – every neutral observer in the court must be convinced that this verdict was unsafe, except the people who counted, the three judges. Scott had done well, better than Toby Beyt thought he would.

But the result was a foregone conclusion. He was going to be able to make something out of this one.

'Are you really saying, Mr Scott, that an advocate of Mr Galbraith's experience would so mishandle the case?'

'No. It is not as simple as that. What I suggest is that there was a wrong turning at the start of the journey. Decisions in trials made at an early stage often have a dramatic effect later on, dramatic ill effects sometimes, and yet at the time the decision may have seemed right, in fact may have been right. I have no doubt that the evidence facing the defence of Mrs Beatty's immobility seemed overwhelming at that stage. This court knows the premium criminal courts put on clear, early decisions. What Mr Galbraith did was perfectly understandable, though it turned out to be wrong.'

'Mr Scott, we have had placed before us a document in which you discussed this case last night. There you said, "The reputation of an advocate is something a jury has always taken into account." For the moment we are not concerned with the propriety of your indulging in public discussion of this case. That is for others to consider. But do you abide by that?'

They had a transcript. He was staggered. Scott forced himself to think not of the implications of what the court had said, but of the question itself. Had he really come out with that? He thought back. He hadn't said that, had he? Hadn't he stated just the opposite?

He replied, 'It may be a jury takes it into account, but this court ought not. It is of no relevance at all . . .'

'Do you really mean to say . . .?' Lord Justice Tocket began to speak. He was almost shouting when Scott saw something that for long afterwards remained in his mind's eye. The judge on Tocket's left, Colover, had edged slightly closer to him, and as Tocket began to interrupt he laid his hand on his arm. It was a gesture no one but Scott could see.

Tocket stopped speaking, and there was a look of pale sadness in his eyes. Colover looked at Scott. His glance lingered for a moment. He was trying to tell Scott something.

The court silent before him, Tocket was being prevented from speaking. Scott said, 'The relevance of the advocate's reputation is of no importance whatsoever, even if it is of the highest – as is Mr Galbraith's. Only the facts of the case matter. In this case a wrong turning was taken at the beginning. I invite you to hear the evidence that will put that right.'

There was silence.

For a moment Scott thought perhaps he had got his argument on its feet, but he had not.

Lord Justice Tocket said, 'We need not bother you, Mr Wethersedge,' and he stood up.

Scott stood, aghast. Tocket was dismissing his argument without even asking the prosecution to reply. They weren't even going to listen to the new evidence. Tocket had decided the point without even referring to the other judges. Scott caught Colover's eye as he turned to leave the court.

The court sat hushed as the judges left.

The case had been argued through the whole day and it was approaching four o'clock. The Lord Justice's clerk came back through the curtain covering the judge's door, leaned over the bench and spoke to the court clerk beneath him.

The clerk stood up and said, 'Judgment in the preliminary application will be given tomorrow at ten thirty in the forenoon.'

One of the journalists detached himself from the press

bench and came to Scott's elbow. 'Why preliminary application?' he asked.

'Because they're about to refuse my application to call new evidence. They are not even going to listen to the evidence. Without that the appeal is dead,' Scott said, hardly even looking at him.

'I don't understand.'

'Today was the real appeal. We wanted to call new evidence. We have to get preliminary permission for that. There is no other appeal. That's it. We're finished.'

'How do you know?'

'Because the court didn't ask Wethersedge, the prosecutor, to reply. That means they thought my argument didn't merit a reply.'

'What, even after your argument today?'

'It failed.'

'Even after your programme last night?'

'My programme – it wasn't my programme.' Scott laughed. 'That didn't help at all.'

'But you were dynamite. The way you were so polite about Galbraith. You could have destroyed him.'

'Why should I?' Scott said.

'Much better that way,' said the journalist. 'And Skuse last night. You slaughtered him. Except that's a bit close to the bone.' He laughed, and when he got no reaction from Scott he said, 'Did you hear what happened?'

Scott could not follow what he was saying. 'I don't want to be rude,' he said. 'I'm very sorry, but I have to get downstairs to see Miss Forgan.'

But the prison staff had been too quick for him. Hilda Forgan had gone, had been taken back to prison. Scott thought of asking the man at the door whether out of simple humanity they might not have waited for him, but that would have been like asking chickens about the accountancy side of laying eggs. The staff would have thought he was taking the piss, their heavy faces shutting down with resentment.

The small door in the corner of the huge hall closed on him, and Scott turned and looked at the Gothic arches and the long main hall stretching away into the distance. Queen Victoria watched him from her plinth.

'Mr Gatling has been looking for you, Mr Scott, sir.' Thus was Scott welcomed to the clerks' room.

As usual at this time, the place was a flurry of activity as tomorrow's work was found for forty barristers.

'Any messages for me, Harry?' Scott said.

'Sian rang. Could you contact her? And there was a call from Amsterdam.' Scott was surprised to feel a twinge of excitement in his stomach.

'Any number?'

'No, sir, no number,' Harry said gloomily. 'Mr Gatling was looking for you. Were we on time at court this morning, sir?'

This annoyed Scott. It wasn't Harry's place to ask him that.

'I was on time, Harry. You mustn't excite yourself so.'

Harry's eyes flashed at him and there was a slight grin. Scott couldn't tell if it was of pain or pleasure. Harry turned to the junior clerk to criticise him for something. It must have been pain.

Gatling was sitting behind his desk, bolt upright. He *was* in pain. 'Jeremy, the court actually phoned me.'

By now Scott did not care very much. 'Why you, Douglas?'

'I am your head of chambers.'

'Do they still think like that?'

Gatling digested this. Then he said, 'They objected to you running your appeal on television.'

'I didn't run any appeal on any programme. I was interviewed. I didn't know what they were going to show on the programme and the fact that the whole event happened the night before the appeal was nothing to do with me. It must have been fixed for transmission weeks ago.'

'Well, they were a bit upset.'

'I'm the only person with a right to be upset. That court behaved like a bunch of dishonest politicians. At times I think they even astonish themselves with their own behaviour. If they ever do, then they did so today.'

'Who was it?'

'Tocket and a couple of thugs whom he'd found skulking in the Chancery division.'

'Tocket? Was he all right?'

'All right? He was rabid with prejudice. Eventually they provoked me into saying Galbraith had got it wrong and having done so considered my conduct a plain impertinence. At one point Tocket had to be restrained.'

'Restrained?' Gatling looked worried. 'They say he's been ill.'

Scott said, 'Ill? In what way?'

'It just makes it worse,' Gatling said.

'What's the matter, Douglas? What are you worried about?'

Gatling said, 'Well, coming so soon after the Ronnie Knox matter, it's all very worrying for chambers.'

'Douglas, what Ronnie Knox matter is that? Are you talking about his dancing in Romford?'

Gatling sighed.

'On that I can reassure you. He's moved his area of operation to Edmonton.'

Scott was nearly laughing it was so absurd. 'Douglas,

grown men are allowed to go dancing. You sound like a divorce lawyer from the fifties. Soon you'll complain that he's been found in places of ill repute – Chinese restaurants, for instance.'

Scott turned and looked at the picture of Marje regarding them sternly from the table. 'I once saw a High Court judge in a Chinese restaurant in the King's Road. I had a drink with him. He was celebrating the death of his mother.'

Marje's photo didn't react.

'Life has moved on, Douglas.'

Gatling sat morosely at his desk.

'And the next time the Court of Appeal rings up, tell them collectively to fuck off.'

Chapter Twenty-Two

The next morning Scott did not even pretend to be hopeful when he saw Hilda Forgan, and he told the doctor outright that they had lost.

It was more difficult with Mrs Beatty's neighbours from Sussex. They gathered round him when he approached the court. Mr Dalrymple, who had sat through the previous day's hearing, had been outraged.

'I don't understand it, Mr Scott. I thought they were meant to be impartial. I thought they were just meant to listen to the arguments and then make a decision. They're not doing that. They've been hostile to you from the start. Was I wrong, Mr Scott? That's what it seemed like to me.'

Scott searched for the words. How could one describe the very special sort of bias that was inherent in the Court of Appeal? He tried, 'Well, we start on the back foot, Mr Dalrymple.' But the euphemism wasn't good enough.

'On the back foot? What you're saying is they are against us from the start.' Mr Dalrymple swung round triumphantly to the group gathered near him. 'You see, I told you.' They looked back at him, saying nothing. It was clear they were shocked. Scott had seen this reaction before when people came into contact with courts for the first time, their illusions crumbling.

'How?' Mr Dalrymple paused, then he said, 'Why?' He couldn't find the right question. 'The one thing a judge should be is impartial. Is that too much to ask? After all, they're not stupid, are they?'

Scott remembered his attempts to explain how he felt about these men the night he was with Nicky. He was right then and Mr Dalrymple was right now. It was not explicable. All you asked of a judge was that he be impartial, and that included not taking things for granted, however strongly he felt. No, not too much to ask.

Mr Dalrymple was waiting for a reply.

'I can't explain it, Mr Dalrymple. I can't.'

'I've read about it, and I'll be honest, Mr Scott. I didn't believe it. I've seen it on television and in films and I didn't believe it. Can't you do anything?'

'Mr Dalrymple, that's what is meant by power. They have us, they have Hilda, in their power.'

'It's a disgrace.' A large, florid woman joined in. Scott thought this might be Mrs Pottock. 'If they treat us like this' – she emphasised the 'us' – 'how do you think they treat other people?' Scott didn't feel scornful of her for emphasising the 'us'. It was natural enough. These were people who felt part of society, used to having their opinions considered.

'Well, they needn't think we are going to take it lying down.'

'I'm afraid there's not much we can do, Mrs Pottock.' Scott had never heard himself sound so weak.

The court settled down. The ushers, who had been returning books to the shelves that lined the sides of the court stood by the curtains waiting for the judge's knock. Scott also waited, tense. Perhaps he was wrong. Maybe the court's failure to ask Wethersedge to answer his argument was because there was nothing he could say in answer and they had decided to hear Scott's witnesses. He looked up. Only two judges filed into the court. Lord Justice Tocket's seat was left empty.

Mr Justice Barker said, 'Lord Justice Tocket is not able to be here this morning. We shall read the judgment, then the court will rise and return after a short time. Lord Justice Tocket will be with us then. Of course, for this first short period, the court will not be properly constituted. We ask your agreement to this course of action.'

'Of course,' said Scott.

The judge turned to prosecuting counsel. Scott looked over towards the end of the bench and noticed for the first time that Wethersedge was not there. Steel had taken over.

'Do you object, Mr Steel?'

'No, m'luds.' Steel's smile and eyebrows started working overtime. 'M'luds, I should mention that my leader, Mr Wethersedge, has an engagement elsewhere. He hopes his absence will not discommode the court.'

'Discommode us?' The judge repeated the word 'us' with care. 'No, it will not discommode us.'

Did Scott catch an edge in his voice? Perhaps he was imagining it. He was certain this court had found against him. Wethersedge had not even bothered to turn up – he must have thought the same thing. And yet there was a change of atmosphere. Perhaps it was because Tocket wasn't there.

The moment the judge started reading the judgment, Scott knew he had been right all along. As they said in prison, Hilda was going to get a knock-back.

The judge said, 'In this appeal a preliminary point is raised. Mr Scott, on the appellant's behalf, asks this court to hear evidence that was, Mr Scott says, unaccountably not called in the trial. In making our decision we have to take account of two things. Is the evidence that is sought to be called credible, and at the same time is there a reasonable explanation for the failure to call it? These two questions are in this case, in our opinion, intertwined.

'Miss Forgan had the advantage of representation by Mr Galbraith in the court below, which was, we judge, a very considerable advantage.' The judge looked up slowly.

Oh yes, thought Scott, they're angry about that too. The judge continued, 'Why did Mr Galbraith not call this evidence on Ms Forgan's behalf? Why, unaccountably, if I may use Mr Scott's word again, did he not call it?'

Scott stopped listening. He still heard what was being said, but it took its place along with everything else happening at the same time.

He looked over his shoulder. The benches behind him were full now, the group from Sussex bunched together on one side. They were listening carefully and Scott could see from the occasional angry face that they had already grasped the drift of the judgment.

He concentrated on the judgment, listening to the cadence of the language. These were not the judge's own words he was reading, they were Tocket's. Scott could hear Tocket's voice: 'Mr Scott asked us to rely upon Nurse Donoghue's lengthy experience in order to set aside Mr Galbraith's judgment. Of course we note that his judgment is the result of an even longer time in his profession than that claimed by Miss Donoghue.'

Did Tocket sit in his room at the Royal Courts scratching out this stuff with a brass pen-nib or did he, when he got back to his room, fire up a word processor?

'Mrs Williams, the secretary of an organisation concerned with, as she describes it, "taking control of one's life", by which she means hastening death, says in her statement that Mrs Beatty wrote to her.'

He droned on. 'A group of neighbours were put forward as witnesses. They were in our opinion no more than an organised cabal.' Scott heard a sharp intake of breath behind him. 'They seek to persuade us that Mrs Beatty could, despite the expert medical evidence, move freely on her own and that it is therefore possible that she encompassed her own death – a dreadful matter to contemplate.'

This was exactly what the trial judge had said. Scott remembered thinking what an absurd remark it was when he read it. Dr Wilson had said the same thing.

At the exact moment he recalled this, a cultivated voice behind him repeated exactly what Dr Wilson had said. 'No more dreadful than murder. In fact, rather less so. If you are willing to accept that Miss Forgan committed murder, why is the possibility of Mrs Beatty killing herself so unlikely?'

The remark was quite conversational, expressed in a resigned tone of voice. It was hardly loud enough to be an interruption, more like a remark overheard, passing between bystanders. If it was an interruption of the court then it was a perfectly civilised one. Later Scott realised this was why it wasn't immediately stopped.

The judge looked up. He would have seen a perfectly calm group of middle-aged people looking at him, the kind of people whom he must often have entertained to lunch. The clerk of the court flickered, and then took his cue from the judge. Neither of them said anything. The judge carried on.

'We remarked to Mr Scott during argument that it is unlikely that friends of the deceased lady would have known of her ability to move and yet for that knowledge not to come to light earlier.'

In the silence a voice replied. 'That's because the police didn't want to know.'

The interruption was in the same conversational tone, again not threatening, quite relaxed. Scott had not looked around the first time, and didn't do so now. But he thought he recognised the voice – Mrs Dalrymple.

The judge was about to carry on when he was interrupted again. 'And if the defence solicitors had been more efficient they would have made sure everybody knew.' This time it was Bessie Pottock speaking.

Someone else added, 'The whole thing was messed up from the start, and now it's quite clear that there is no intention of putting it right. It's a disgrace.'

The last remark was the only interruption that was anything more than conversational. Otherwise the drawing-room atmosphere, which Scott remembered from Mrs Dalrymple's house, was precisely maintained. Scott sat looking resolutely in front of him, forcing himself not to smile.

The judge had to take notice now.

He turned to Scott. 'Mr Scott, perhaps you would remind those witnesses sitting behind you that they should not interrupt. Otherwise I may be forced to have the court cleared.'

'Witnesses?' Another voice behind him spoke. 'But it's quite clear we're not going to be allowed to be witnesses. If I hadn't seen this with my own eyes I would never have believed that the country would allow such a thing.'

'Mr Scott?' The judge spoke to him again.

Scott got to his feet. 'M'luds, I shall of course speak to my solicitor.' He turned and saw the impassive faces of Miss Forgan's friends sitting behind him. None of them looked at him; each was staring at the judges.

'That's not the point.' Again one of them spoke. 'We're not here to be pushed around by one side or the other. We're here because we know the truth of what happened. It's not for Mr Scott to tell us not to speak.'

The judge looked at them and did nothing. Colover on

the other side of the court did not react at all. It was almost as though these people were saying something he agreed with. Was there a split between him and the other judges? Scott was surprised.

Barker was losing control of the court. That did happen occasionally, but it was about as rare as mutiny in the army. He had seen it only once, down on the South Coast, when a taxi driver who illegally worked Gatwick Airport started flirting with a tempestuous lady judge, who, instead of stopping it instantly, had responded for a second. Then it was too late, just as it was here.

A voice behind him said, 'It's a complete denial of responsibility. The court's responsibility to decide fairly on all the evidence.'

Again Barker did not react. His problem, of course, was that the interruptions were so pertinent. Far from not listening to them, they were affecting him. It would have been so much easier for him if the gallery had stood up and started shouting, rather than taking him on so conversationally.

There was a silence and the judge continued. He turned to the statements of the doctors. He described Scott's professor of geriatric medicine as an 'academic'.

'That's ridiculous,' a voice remarked. 'Doctors in teaching hospitals aren't academics. The whole point of the job is to mix practice and teaching.'

'We are unable to accept that the professor's speculations . . .'

'Speculation! How can they possibly say that? You can't just brush aside years of experience with a word.'

'We turn to Dr Wilson. His proposed evidence is nothing more than a farrago of anecdotes . . .' Scott had been right – they were totally unimpressed by Dr Wilson.

Hilda's friends were not standing for this. There was a

hiss of displeasure that for a moment made Barker's voice waver, then someone said, 'The whole point is that these doctors are independent. Will no one listen?'

Scott stared at Barker. The unfairness of the judgment had been summed up in a sentence. When the judgment reached Scott's criticism of Galbraith, it became even nastier. It assumed that Scott had attacked him.

'This was an attack after the event. An assault on the conduct of counsel made with hindsight, no longer in the heat of battle. It was an assault on counsel's judgment which had been foreshadowed, and we may say not assisted, as it was plainly intended to be, by most regrettable publicity. We may remark at this point that Mr Galbraith is counsel of the highest standing in the profession and he retains the complete confidence of this court.'

Again the response of the gallery was to the point and accurate. 'This is Hilda's trial, not Galbraith's.'

This stopped Barker in his tracks. The interruptions had finally got to him. He seemed to falter and cut short the rest of his judgment. He said, 'The application to call this new evidence is refused. We find the proposed evidence wholly incredible.'

The two judges stood up. They were the only ones to do so. Everybody else remained resolutely seated. At the back of the court Galbraith rose and slipped towards the door. The judges left the court in the midst of the deathly hush, as though they had broken something and the onlookers were holding their breath at the waste of it all.

Hilda Forgan had been absolutely right in her forecast.

'Vascular senility, Darroch's syndrome, that's my guess,' said Dr Wilson, 'Tocket may not think I'm much of a doctor. That judgment was written by him, wasn't it? But I know enough to spot his problems. It's irreversible, a particularly choice form of Alzheimer's, marked at its onset by increasingly erratic behaviour. It's an odd illness because at first the only sign is an intensified form of the patient's ordinary behaviour.

'One can imagine his colleagues saying over breakfast, "Tocket is out-Tocketing himself today, what?", and they've got exactly the right diagnosis. He's a candidate for your Mrs Williams's self-immolation society down in Sussex, if ever I saw one.'

Scott listened to Dr Wilson. He didn't seem in the least put out by the court's remarks about him. Of course, doctors had a different point of view. For Dr Wilson these were three elderly men, and he dealt daily with the oddities of elderly men.

'I wouldn't be surprised if he's quite bright when he arrives, on the rebound, unaware of the way he behaved yesterday. They're coming back in at twelve, aren't they, and he'll be there?'

Scott said, 'Yes.'

'I think I'll stay. Purely out of professional interest. If that's all right?'

'That's OK.'

Scott looked round. Everyone else had gone. The anger had been palpable. He could still hear raised voices in the passage outside. He was numb. He hadn't expected to win easily, indeed he had thought there wasn't much chance, but to have the evidence dismissed out of hand like this was inexplicable. Unless you agreed with Dr Wilson and thought Tocket was unbalanced. What was it Gatling had said? 'They say he's been ill.'

Scott went outside. The crowd was disappearing down the passage and he followed them slowly. He had an hour – time to have a cup of coffee and phone Amsterdam again. He had been trying regularly but had got no reply.

The telephone boxes outside were empty. He dialled the Swiftcall number, entered his PIN code, then the Amsterdam number. It took about a minute of concentration to get it right, listening to the indifferent machine generate voices on the way. 'You have eight pounds fifty pence credit left,' the machine told him.

There was a whirring noise and the Amsterdam phone rang, or rather whistled. After two rings another machine answered, this time in Jeroem's voice. No one was there, or at least no one was answering the phone. He listened to the end of the message and was about to say something after the bleep, but in the end he did not. He did not want to start leaving anxious messages everywhere. He wished Catherine was with him now.

Scott looked at the court clock. He had plenty of time. Outside on the pavement there was a scrum of cameras and journalists. He walked over with the cup of coffee he had collected and watched.

Mrs Dalrymple was in the centre. She was very angry. 'An organised cabal, they called us. Frankly, I don't believe it. Who are these people? Where do they come from? What is it they know which enables them to be so sure?' The last question stuck in her throat and she repeated the idea. 'How can they be so sure?' She stopped and stared to her left. Everybody turned to follow her gaze.

In the midst of another small group stood the police officer, Hilton. Scott noticed how the journalists stood around him differently to the way they had approached Mrs Dalrymple. The cameras were slightly lower, looking up at him. His was a similar pose to the one he had taken on the steps of Mrs Beatty's cottage. Perhaps this was being taught to police officers now – the way to project their opinions.

Hilton's certainty about life made the judges look mere

beginners. Scott heard similar words to those he had heard on the television when Hilton had been interviewed on Mrs Beatty's steps. 'Evil, calculating evil. She tricked us, perhaps because we did not imagine that anyone could behave like that. And now she has tried to organise a group of people to lie on her behalf . . .'

This was too much for Mrs Dalrymple. She lost her temper completely. Scott was amused to see that the more angry she became, the further up the class ladder she climbed. 'You frightful little squirt!' she shouted.

She moved over to the group. Hilton was startled out of his self-assurance and looked round to see what the noise was. The cameramen from both groups backed off slightly, busily adjusting their lenses. This was too good to miss.

'You stand reeking there like a bucket of stale piss and mouth off about evil and you haven't got a clue. I saw you on television mouthing off. And yet what is so strange' – by now she had gone right up to Hilton, who had gone rigid, a fixed grin on his face – 'is that you are so bloody incompetent.'

She paused. Her torrent of language had for a moment completely silenced Hilton. She gathered her breath again. Hilton recovered himself. 'Now, now, madam,' he said.

Scott had heard the tone of voice before – the standard response of an offended official trying to exert his authority. Mrs Dalrymple was having nothing of it.

'Don't you madam me, you erk. If you think you can push me around, you've got another think coming. I've had enough of you and your kind.' She advanced on him. Hilton couldn't believe his eyes. He shot his cuffs in distress. He tugged at his collar. Mrs Dalrymple hadn't finished. 'If I hear another word out of you . . .' She stepped forward and grabbed him by the balls. A great laugh went up as Hilton stood on his toes, his head thrown back.

'Joan, Joan.' It was Mr Dalrymple. 'Let the poor man alone. He isn't worth it.' He pulled his wife away, leaving Hilton standing, clasping his groin, his knees bent together.

'Hilda is worth more than the lot of them put together,' he said, and he led her away. Scott saw, as they left, that Mrs Dalrymple was beginning to cry.

The crowd surged around the police officer. Scott began to turn away, then he realised he was standing next to Toby and Nicky. He heard Toby say, 'What perfect timing. She'll be on the one o'clock, six o'clock and nine o'clock news, and then we'll be on at half past nine. It couldn't have been better arranged if Monty had fixed it.'

Scott's coffee burnt his mouth.

He understood now. They hadn't wanted him to win at all. Perhaps that was why he had been chosen – to lose the case. He turned on them. 'Well, at least *Blind Justice* are pleased at the result,' he said. 'If it had gone the other way you wouldn't have had a programme, would you?'

The case was over as far as the public and press were concerned. There was nothing Scott could point to, no mistakes that might make the verdict unsafe, nothing more he could say to the court.

He arrived back in the courtroom and gathered up his robes from the shelf. The rows of seats behind him were now completely empty; even Monty hadn't returned. The only member of the public, sitting at the back in the middle, directly opposite where Tocket would sit, was Dr Wilson, professionally preoccupied, waiting for the patient.

At the other end of Scott's bench was Steel. He had no one behind him. His solicitor had disappeared too.

The judges came in. Hilda was escorted in. She looked

even more defeated than when Scott had seen her that morning. Tocket, on the other hand, looked quite bright.

'The court extends its thanks to you, Mr Scott, for allowing proceedings to continue this morning. It allowed me to attend an appointment that would have been very difficult to miss.' He turned to the prosecutor. 'Thank you, Mr Steel.'

As Scott turned to look at Steel he caught Dr Wilson's eye. The doctor nodded, I told you so.

'Now, where are we?' said Tocket. 'Mr Scott, you are now going to press your appeal, are you not? Ground one, application for new evidence, not really a ground, Mr Scott, an application, but I understand why you phrased it that way. Well, that's gone now, hasn't it?' He spoke as though the complete destruction of Scott's case were just one of those things, which of course, for him, it was.

'Where do we go now?'

Scott had to be intellectually honest at least. He said, 'The other grounds fall, I think. They all depended on the new evidence.' There was a movement to his right. Scott knew Galbraith had come in.

Tocket said, 'Unless you wish to press the appeal on another basis, Mr Scott, which of course you may choose to do.'

He sounded almost hopeful. The change was amazing.

'No. No, there is nothing further to say there.'

Scott was about to say that it left them, even if this didn't include Hilda, free to go off for lunch, when he was interrupted.

It was Mr Justice Colover. 'What puzzles me is the question.'

As a remark it seemed unfinished somehow. The judge looked at Scott, who did not reply. It sounded like something Hilda might have said. Come to think of it, she had said it, at one of their first meetings.

'The jury's question, Mr Scott. I'm puzzled by it.' The judge was obviously trying to help, but Scott was completely baffled.

'Of course,' the judge said, 'you can't have seen it, can you? It's at page three hundred and twenty-one of the transcript, fifteenth day.'

Scott looked. 'My bundle stops at the verdict, page number . . .' He turned to it. 'No, there's no number.'

'You haven't got the complete transcript, then. That sometimes happens. Are you privately instructed?'

'Yes.'

'That would be it,' said Colover. 'Privately represented clients often only obtain the narrative part of the judge's summing-up. The passage with which I am concerned occurred when the jury returned with a question. Here, take mine.'

He tore a page from his bundle and handed it to the usher. As it was carried round the court, Colover said to Steel, 'Does the crown have this?'

'Yes, m'lud,' said Steel.

The piece of paper came on its long journey round to Scott. By now his brain was racing. What was this about? The passage was marked by two heavy strokes of the judge's pen, with a question mark against it.

Scott read the paper. Colover interrupted him. 'You'll see, Mr Scott, that the jury returned at twenty past four. They had been considering their verdict for some time and then they sent in a question. The judge remarked that he did not intend to show the question to counsel since it contained information normally kept confidential.'

'Yes, m'lud.'

'You'll also see that Mr Galbraith wasn't there. Where was he, Mr Steel?'

Again Scott caught a changed tone in the court's questioning.

Steel was taken by surprise. 'He had left. I remember now, we all expected the case to be adjourned to the next day.'

'He'd returned to London?'

'Yes. We had been told that the judge would send the jury to an hotel at four thirty. It seemed certain nothing would happen in the remaining few minutes of the day, so Mr Galbraith with everyone's agreement had left to catch the four twenty train. Then this question occurred.'

'Did you see the note, Mr Steel?'

'No, I did not. I understood it contained jury voting figures. Such notes are not usually disclosed.'

'No, that's right. I think the prosecution did not see it either?'

'No, Mr Wethersedge would not have seen it, no.'

'But Mr Wethersedge was in the judge's room when the note was brought in to him?'

'That is right, m'lud.'

'We do not know, therefore, whether he saw it?'

'No, m'lud.'

'The exchange in the transcript is ambiguous? It doesn't tell us that?'

Steel looked at it again. 'So it is, m'lud.'

While this was happening Scott was scanning the rest of the page. It continued: '*Jury* returns: 4.20.'

The jury would have been brought into the court to receive an answer to their question.

Judge:
Ladies and gentlemen. I have received a note from you. You say what a number of you think. In answer I say this: Please do not speculate. Certain evidence is agreed, other evidence is the subject of argument in the

*case. For example, the medical evidence is agreed, other
evidence, such as who might have had access to Mrs
Beatty's bathroom, is the subject of argument. May I
advise you to concentrate on what matters.*
<u>*Jury leaves*</u>

4.30 Verdict: . . .

The judge let Scott finish reading, then he said, 'Have you
read the rest of the page, Mr Scott?' Scott looked at the
court and nodded.

'Mr Scott, you are a criminal advocate of considerable
experience. I do not presume to tell you how odd what
you've just read is. You already know.'

'Certainly I do,' said Scott.

'Mr Scott, I reflected on this last night. I realised you
could not have seen this or I am certain you would have
included it in your very capable advice and grounds of
appeal.'

Scott was amazed. They were beginning to flatter him.
What was happening?

'This morning I sent for the original note and a search is
being made for it now.' He and Scott were thinking exactly
in step.

Lord Justice Tocket said, 'We shall rise until it is found.
When it is found, please copy it and hand the copy to
Mr Scott.'

Scott turned. The only person behind him was the doctor.
Where had Galbraith gone?

'What's this about?' Dr Wilson said.

'The original jury sent a note in to the judge while they
were considering their verdict. Unless it was only concerned
with numbers – say, nine agree guilty, three not guilty or
something – then it has to be shown to counsel. This note

obviously contained more than numbers, because of the direction the judge gave. Something funny happened.'

'Like what?'

'I don't know. All I can say is that if I had known that question had been asked I would have insisted on seeing the note. But now we discover that we have never had the full transcript of the trial.'

'Perhaps your Toby Beyt has it.'

'What? Toby Beyt? Why should he?'

'He had it when he interviewed me.'

'When he interviewed you?'

'He told me that he had obtained a transcript.'

'Who from?'

'He bought it from the court transcription service.'

'My God!' Scott said.

'He told me his company was paying for the whole appeal so he has a right to it, I suppose.'

Scott didn't want to hear this.

The waiting was painful. Every minute he looked at the clock. He wanted to go and see Hilda, but just when he was about to leave the clerk said, 'It will be here any second now.' There was no point in going to see Hilda until he had something to say.

Two tourists stuck their heads through the door. Nothing was happening, only Scott standing by the court clerk's desk and Steel leafing through some papers. Scott spoke to him. 'I didn't know you were in this case, Steel.'

'You didn't ask.'

'I didn't know you were in it, so I couldn't ask you whether you were in it.'

'What's Colover doing causing this trouble? It was only a note,' Steel said. He seemed worried. Did he know something?

'Do you know what's in the note?' Scott said.

'No, of course not.' Steel was protesting too much. Scott moved away.

Just then the papers arrived. 'Here it is.' Scott spoke out loud to no one in particular. He took the photocopy of the jury's note outside and, wanting complete silence, walked down to the end of the corridor. There was a man standing at the end. Scott turned his back on him.

The note was in neat handwriting, on a plain sheet of paper. At the top was the date and the judge's initials. Scott read it.

We are concerned about the evidence of Mrs Beatty's illness. Perhaps the old lady could move. I and four others have nursed elderly people, and we have decided she might have been able to move.

But if she could move wouldn't the defendant be equally guilty – leaving her in the bathroom with a dangerous hairdryer, just near the bath?

Scott stood looking at the handwritten piece of paper. Fitting it properly into the precise timing of the transcript took his whole attention. He worked it out. Ten minutes later this jury, after they had been sent back to continue their discussion, had found Hilda guilty of murder, and five minutes after that she had been sentenced to life imprisonment.

And they believed that leaving someone in the bathroom with an electric hairdryer might amount to murder. No one had corrected them.

Scott imagined the scene. At about the time Hilda was being sentenced, Galbraith would have been sitting on his train just outside Winchester, unaware of what was going on. Unable to help. There was nothing anyone could do to help her.

Scott turned and looked at the man standing in the passage behind him.

Chapter Twenty-Three

Dr Wilson was sitting at the back of the court, waiting for Scott to come back, when a man edged his way along the bench in front of him and said, 'Are you a doctor, sir?' Normally Dr Wilson tried to avoid such calls, but he was cornered now.

'We have a problem, sir. Could you help?' Dr Wilson followed the man, who was clearly an official of some sort, wondering what he was going to have to deal with. A heart attack? A broken limb? He wasn't a first-aid man. An ambulance would probably be of more use than he was.

Eventually they reached a barred door. The official knocked. It was opened almost immediately and he was taken along a passage and shown into another small room.

Hilda Forgan was standing looking directly at him.

'Ah, good,' she said, as though a tradesman had arrived at her back door. 'A doctor.' She paused and then said, 'You know, I think I'm going mad.'

'Tell me about it,' said Dr Wilson, reverting easily to his bedside manner.

'Have you now had a chance to read the jury note?'

'I have,' said Scott.

'We have the original here. It is the first time this court

has seen it. It has the judge's initials on it with the time, presumably, when the judge received it.'

'On my copy the time has been obscured,' said Scott.

'No matter, Mr Scott. No doubt you will take it from us. It is marked four ten p.m.'

Scott felt the onset of the symptoms of shock. When something went wrong in court proceedings the first thing to be done was to make a list of dates and times. It was the legal equivalent of battening down the hatches. Of course, in this metaphor Scott was going to be the storm.

'Miss Forgan is not here.' Suddenly Mr Justice Colover noticed her absence from the court.

The judges and the advocates looked at each other and then at the empty dock. There was silence, then slowly the door leading from the dock to the cells opened. To everyone's surprise, Dr Wilson stepped through it.

'Gentlemen,' he said, 'Miss Forgan is in no condition to come upstairs.'

The judges digested this.

'She is behaving,' said Dr Wilson, 'in a very disturbed manner and, in my opinion, would not follow what is happening here.' He then said something he had always wanted to say in a criminal court. 'She is displaying a marked guilt complex.'

'Are we able to proceed without her? Perhaps not,' said Lord Justice Tocket. Scott saw him brighten up for a moment. Perhaps he thought he could get shot of the case.

'Yes,' said Scott, 'we are.' He had to make them continue. This was too good to let go. 'Miss Forgan wants this finished. She told me so this morning. She need take no further part in the proceedings. She has nothing to say or do.'

There was a moment's consultation, during which Scott's heart was in his mouth then Lord Justice Tocket said, 'We shall continue.' He returned to his notes and took up exactly where he left off. Scott would have loved to have seen his notebook. What did it look like?

'The note is timed four ten p.m. The judge's initials are on it, as are some other initials. These may be the initials of the court clerk. For the moment we do not feel it is necessary to establish whose they are.'

Scott said, 'Yes. Then I have the same note.' This crablike movement towards the important bit was hard to bear.

'Eh? Yes,' said Lord Justice Tocket. For the first time Scott saw the old man beneath the starched manner.

'Well, what do you say, Mr Scott?'

'I suggest there has been a material irregularity. This note ought to have been shown to both counsel. For it to have been kept back was wrong.'

'Your authority?' Tocket continued making his list in the notebook.

'Gorman, in 1987, reported in *Weekly Law Reports*, number one of that year, at page five hundred and forty-five. The exception that the trial judge here relied upon not to show the note to counsel was not a proper exception for this situation.'

The judges gathered around each other. Scott stood looking at them. That was clear law. It was not only the authority but it was common sense as well. There was no arguing with it. After a while the other judges returned to their seats on either side of Lord Justice Tocket.

'If we find that what the judge did amounted to a material irregularity, which it seems we are likely to do, we shall still have to consider whether it makes the conviction unsafe.'

Tocket was not looking at Scott now. It was like a viva examination. If Scott did not make a slip, then he was going to win this. He had to get it exactly right, each step of the argument, and force them to follow his line. Any sort of mistake and they would skitter away from him and order a retrial. He didn't want that, he wanted Hilda freed, now.

Tocket said, 'But Mr Galbraith could call no further evidence, could he? Even had he wished to do so. After all, no further evidence could be allowed at that stage. This jury had retired to consider their verdict.'

'No,' said Scott. 'Mr Galbraith could do nothing. He could not have called any further evidence. By then the matter was out of his hands.'

Steel looked at him, surprised. Was Scott giving in?

'So I must ask you again to explain what difference it made.' Tocket still didn't look up. Mr Justice Colover was looking steadily at Scott. The room was quite silent. Nothing stirred.

Scott said, 'The jury had clearly come to a decision on the facts. It was a decision to which they were entitled to come. They had decided it had not been proved that Mrs Beatty could not move. If Mrs Beatty could not move then the jury could not be certain that another hand, Miss Forgan's hand, had caused her death. In those circumstances their verdict could only be one of not guilty.

'Dealing with their second point, leaving a helpless person to remain in dangerous circumstances is not murder. The jury seemed to think it might be. To allow them to continue their discussions uncorrected was certainly a material irregularity.'

'So again I ask, must there be a retrial?' Lord Justice Tocket said. This was the weak point. The idea of another trial made Scott feel very tired.

'No. Hilda Forgan was denied the chance of an acquittal which was fairly open to her. The test is set out in the case of Cohen. This conviction must be quashed.'

Lord Justice Tocket dipped his pen in the inkwell, wrote for a long time, wiped his pen, put it down and, for the first time in two days, turned his basilisk stare on the prosecution.

'Mr Scott is right, isn't he, Mr Steel?'

For a long time Steel did not get up. Scott felt a huge weight lifting from his shoulders. He had won the case.

'I knew she was on the edge of doing something awful. I haven't told anyone, but I can't keep it bottled up any longer, I have to tell someone. She had got in touch with those people in Brighton. I read the letter from Mrs Williams. I know it had appealed to her since the letter was so sensible, so honest and brave.'

Hilda Forgan began to weep gently. Dr Wilson sat and watched her.

'And there was something in the letter that reminded her of the old times. I know when she read it, she was hearing a tone of voice she had known in her youth. She had been a nurse, you know, at UCH, University College Hospital, and they were remarkable people, the standards which they set themselves and by which they lived. She even said she thought she had known Mrs Williams then. After all those years, she could still hear the voice. It was the voice of the training they had been given. Gone now, of course. It's every man for himself now.'

She sat up straight and looked directly at Dr Wilson.

'I knew my aunt might try to harm herself. And I forgot. Or at least I made myself forget. There was a part of me that knew quite well what I was doing. I left her in the bathroom on her own with that electrical thing.

'I wasn't surprised when I saw what had happened. But how could I admit to that? It would have been a dreadful thing to accept. So when I was asked I said she couldn't move and I stuck to it. I didn't know where it would lead to. I never imagined people might say I murdered her. How ridiculous.

'That Mr Galbraith guessed, you know. He was a clever man, for all that grand manner. He knew. He asked me directly. He told me what I was doing, but it was too late then. I told him not to get a doctor to speak for me. In fact, if you think about it, he has been very brave, because he didn't say what he knew. He protected me. He could have told the court what I said, but he didn't. He's allowed himself to be attacked. That's real bravery, isn't it? To allow yourself to be criticised and say nothing.

'And what was I meant to do? Tell that nice young Mr Scott that the way the trial went was all my fault? Then I certainly wouldn't have had any grounds for an appeal, would I?

'I've been trapped inside a lie told in support of the truth. And the truth would have seemed like a lie.'

Hilda Forgan appeared at the doors of the High Court leaning heavily on Dr Wilson's arm. Scott held the door for her, looking nervously around for the press. 'Everyone's gone,' he said, 'they obviously thought it was all over.' The pavement outside was empty.

'I'll take her to Victoria,' said Dr Wilson. 'We can phone someone in the village from there.'

'They'll be surprised to see you, Hilda,' Scott said.

'The whole thing was a bit of a surprise to them from the start,' she said. 'And to me.'

A cab pulled up. As the door shut she said, 'Thank you, Mr Scott.'

'That's OK, Miss Forgan,' he said.

The cab swung in a circle under Samuel Johnson's statue and joined the traffic going west down the Strand. Scott watched the retreating back window for a moment and then realised that cars were stopping for him at the pedestrian crossing. He raised his hand to thank them and set off across the wide street. His arm began to ache from the weight of the files he was holding.

It began to rain as he threaded his way through the passages to his chambers. As he emerged in the courtyard outside the Temple Church itself, a gust of wind carried a fresh shower towards him across the courtyard.

There was a wedding. 'Sad day for it,' he thought.

He glimpsed the bride in the porch and momentarily a dispirited flutter of confetti floated from the open door towards him.

He pushed on, and as he reached the door of his chambers the rain began to come down in earnest. He was hot from the restriction of his suit and the papers he was carrying. He struggled up the tight stairs and stood at the glass door of the clerks' room. They were all in there. He pushed the door open.

'Mr Scott!' said the junior. 'You look wet.'

Scott put the papers down and brushed some of the rain from his face.

Harry looked up at him but said nothing. Scott went over to check the little square on the noticeboard which carried messages for him. There was a piece of paper. 'Ring Amsterdam,' it said.

He pulled the yellow note down, feeling better. Maybe Catherine had decided to come back. It wasn't dated. 'When did this come?' he said.

No one answered.

'Harry, when did this come?' he repeated. 'It's your writing.' He put it down in front of him.

'Oh, that's an old message, sir,' Harry said. 'You've already had that.' He took the message, screwed it up and threw it, along with Scott's hopes, into the wastepaper basket. Catherine hadn't rung.

'Anything else?' Scott asked.

'Yes, there was a call from a Miss Vesey. Here you are, sir, Nicky Vesey. She said the meeting was off. They've cancelled it.'

'What meeting?' Scott didn't know of any meeting, but the message was fairly clear.

'The BBC,' said the junior. 'She was from the BBC or some television company or something.'

Scott digested this information.

'Speaking of the BBC,' the junior said, 'what about what happened to that Skuse man?'

'I won the case,' Scott said to Harry.

Harry looked up. Scott knew what he was about to say. He said it. 'I wouldn't have expected anything less of you, sir.'

'He was stabbed,' said the junior clerk. 'Didn't you read about it? In a cupboard at the BBC after your programme, sir.'

Scott looked at him blankly. 'What?'

'Among the mops.'

The second clerk got up and as he did so said, 'Homosexual murder. He was gay, wasn't he? Some young man Skuse had picked up stabbed him.'

The clerk walked past Scott. 'You've got something on your shoulder, sir. Cherry blossom or something.'

He brushed Scott's jacket and a piece of confetti fluttered to the ground.

'Gay? Skuse was gay?' said Scott.

'Of course he was. That's the trouble with you, sir, you're too cut off. You don't know the facts of life.'

Scott looked at the confetti on the ground and said, 'It's not cherry blossom. It's the wrong time of year for cherry blossom.'

JONATHAN DAVIES

GIVEN IN EVIDENCE

If you have ever believed a lie or doubted the truth, then you'll know how the truth can breed its own doubt. The truth won't always set you free.

Emily Clarke is determined to get a start as a trial lawyer, but she faces discrimination wherever she turns. Jeremy Scott looks like a successful barrister, but his life has a raw ebbing emptiness at its centre.

Which makes it all worse when they are thrust together.

It's an ordinary case, no surprises. Until, gradually, the usual presumption of guilt gives way to the nagging doubt that the man at the centre of the trial might well be innocent.

And Emily is no longer as innocent as she once wanted to be. Will she be swept away? Will she eventually be
GIVEN IN EVIDENCE?

HODDER AND STOUGHTON PAPERBACKS

JONATHAN DAVIES

UNDISCLOSED MATERIAL

A legal thriller that tackles the topical and controversial issue of police informers and the concealment of material from the defence in criminal trials.

A worrying pattern of deception is emerging. Yet defence lawyer Jeremy Scott's belief in the system has so far prevented him from seeing it. Catherine, an American working for him, has rather less respect for the majesty of the law. And she is intent on opening his eyes – in more ways than one.

Scott's last two cases have been apparently unrelated. But he has been up against the same prosecution team, with the same Detective Inspector as their main witness, and the same judge presiding.

Both times the prosecution have asked the judge to withhold information from Scott and the defence. Legal term:
UNDISCLOSED MATERIAL.

And when Scott finds himself clinging to a ledge halfway up a Welsh mountain, being chased by a deadly assailant, it strikes him that someone will stop at nothing to ensure that that material remains undisclosed. Permanently.

HODDER AND STOUGHTON PAPERBACKS

A SELECTION OF BESTSELLERS
FROM HODDER & STOUGHTON

❑   0340 63231 3   GIVEN IN EVIDENCE   £5.99
❑   0340 65397 3   UNDISCLOSED MATERIAL   £5.99

All Hodder & Stoughton books are available at your local bookshop or newsagent, or can be ordered direct from the publisher. Just tick the titles you want and fill in the form below. Prices and availability subject to change without notice.

Hodder & Stoughton Books, Cash Sales Department, Bookpoint, 39 Milton Park, Abingdon, OXON, OX14 4TD, UK. E-mail address: orders @bookprint.co.uk. If you have a credit card, our call centre team would be delighted to take your order by telephone. Our direct line is 01235 400414 (lines open 9.00 am–6.00 pm Monday to Saturday, 24 hour message answering service). Alternatively you can send a fax on 01235 400454.

Or please enclose a cheque or postal order made payable to Bookpoint Ltd to the value of the cover price and allow the following for postage and packing:
UK & BFPO – £1.00 for the first book, 50p for the second book, and 30p for each additional book ordered up to a maximum charge of £3.00.
OVERSEAS & EIRE – £2.00 for the first book, £1.00 for the second book, and 50p for each additional book.

Name..

Address...

....

....

If you would prefer to pay by credit card, please complete:
Please debit my Visa/Access/Diner's Card/American Express (delete as applicable) card no:

Signature...

Expiry Date...

If you would NOT like to receive further information on our products please tick the box.❑